High Tea with Ophelia

Edith Walsh

2700 N. Portofino Road
St. Augustine, FL 32092

Scotoma Books Publishing

Scotoma Books Publishing—Hamilton, OH
ISBN: 978-1-7323245-3-4
Library of Congress Control Number: 2020921197
Title: *High Tea with Ophelia*
Author: Eleanor Tremayne
Digital distribution | 2020
Paperback | 2020

This is a work of fiction. The characters, names, incidents, places, and dialogue are products of the author's imagination, and are not to be construed as real.

High Tea with Ophelia
Eleanor Tremayne

Dedication

High Tea with Ophelia is dedicated to Dr. Malone, for believing that a shy, eighteen year old girl could reach for the stars before she ever saw them. And, Dr. Mary Sisney, my Graduate Advisor, at California State Polytechnic University, Pomona, who taught me to appreciate all forms of literature.

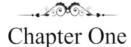

Chapter One

I've died a thousand deaths, each time reinventing myself brighter, stronger, and purer than before. From the midst of destruction, I became the creator myself. From the midst of darkness, I became my own source of light.

—Christen Rodgers

SABRIEL

A muted light casts a shadow that reflects twisted faces, virtuous pagans, solemn sinners, all tossed around a tempestuous storm. I am now one of the untouchables, surrounded by lustful transgressors who have betrayed intelligence to fulfill their empty souls with ravage uncontrollable desires.

There is malefaction dripping from the brow of a feline monster with razor teeth. Cruel, uncouth, he prepares to usher us across the muddy waters to the abysmal inferno.

I now realize that it is the river Acheron. A place of "sorrow without torment", where a seven walled castle offers rolling meadows that illuminate reason. We are all philosophers, authors, non baptized children, on the brink of grief. Here there is no punishment, only sadness and remorse. I am in Dante's limbo.

This has been where I have spent most of my life. Like my name, Sabriel suggests, I have no real direction. Even my name is non gender, deriving from the Hebrew word "sabi" meaning stop and rest; and, "el" meaning God.

If this is not enough, there is also a prickly pear known as a Sabral plant. If you put all of these strange connotations together, Sabriel is a "cactus of God." None of these allusions make me feel any better.

Escaping into the pages of literature it does offer me a temporary seclusion from the outside world.

It was first *The Doctor Doolittle* books, by Hugh Lofting that I enjoyed the most. The very idea that a doctor would shun human patients to communicate with animals that speak to him in a different language, fascinated me. The variety of stories to select from, kept me well entertained as a child.

Doctor Doolittle's Zoo, became one of my favorites. Perhaps because in that story Lofting includes a collection of crossbred dogs, and a club for rodents. These were all misfits that I could relate to.

In 1986, after my grandmother passed, social services sent me to the Atlanta Children's Center, in Georgia . I was ten years old and had no idea what was happening.

A friendly young lady at the institute, whose name I can no longer recall, explained to me that this Center was to be my new home. Although I do remember everyone was welcoming , there was no intimacy. No hugs. No cuddling, and absolutely no kissing was ever tolerated.

During my eight years at the Center I can never recall any physical contact. For years I just accepted that any touching was considered intrusive.

My consolation was reading. It may have been a coincidence, but in every story that I selected there was a young child in search of herself, or a heroine who was learning how to become independent.

Mary Poppins, Pipi Longstocking, and Nancy Drew were my role models. They were all strong, young women that overcame any obstacles that tried to prevent them from being successful, or happy. I wanted to have that tenacity and that courage.

School was my sanctuary. It was where I excelled. It was where I received awards and recognition. Every teacher looked forward to having "Sabriel" in their class. That was nice, but not enough. What I was always lacking was genuine companionship.

Graduating from college with honors, and a Masters Degree in Literature gave me a sense of accomplishment that didn't last long enough.

"What you have achieved Sabriel is impressive. We are all extremely proud of you. This is only the beginning of a new and rewarding future," Mrs. Thompson, a psychologist/counselor said.

I am sure she was sincere, but everything I ever heard from her sounded like that Alexa program invented by Amazon several years ago.

There was always just something missing. I could never really identify what, but maybe once I started teaching everything else would make sense. And, it did for awhile.

Just like my academic success, I was also an excellent teacher. My Principal nominated me as Teacher of the Year, before I even earned tenure.Then later again, twice in my career.

More importantly than the recognition I was getting from the administration, was that all of my students were successful. Not all of them desired to attend college, but by the time they graduated, most found some direction in their life. Either an occupation that interested them, or a commitment to the Armed Forces.

Many were accepted at prestigious universities throughout the country. But, not even all these accolades seemed to satisfy me.

Perhaps more education was what I needed?

Eventually I did earn my PHD in Literature. In a very unexpected way this lead me to my future meeting with Ophelia ; the most life changing event that could ever be imagined.

But, I am now moving too fast. Past all of the essential information that you must first know before understanding how incredible Ophelia's contribution was to my world of literature.

The turn of events really began when I accepted a position at the University of New Orleans. It was just far enough away from Atlanta that nobody would know who I was, (as if anybody really cared). It was my opportunity to meet new people in a town that celebrates Mardi Gras all year. I was anxious for that spirit to flow through my veins. I was anxious to finally find a place where life would finally have meaning.

The university is located on an abandoned air field of the United States Navy, on the shores of Lake Pontchartrain. In late 1957, after a quick renovation of various existing facilities, the first classes were offered in 1958,; a year ahead of schedule. By 1969, only eleven years later, the enrollment exceeded 10,000 students.

Although the history of this university impressed me, I was particularly moved when I learned that during the aftermath of Hurricane Katrina classes resumed only forty two days after the storm passed.

I knew what it was like to overcome internal storms, but withstanding, such a devastating physical ordeal requires a definite chutzpah that is reflected daily in the attitudes of these citizens who

3

remained in their hometown. This enduring characteristic , seen everywhere, encouraged me to accept a teaching position at the university without any hesitation..

But, it was without warning, when Bradley Welch serendipitously entered my life, adding a new dimension I was not prepared for.Our first meeting was definitely awkward.

"If you are considering attending The University of New Orleans, young lady, I need to warn you that it is well known as a place where daydreamers are found lingering under magnolia trees with a cup of steaming hot chicory coffee and a bag of beignets from Café Du Monde . It is so tempting that even my early morning class has no chance to compete with that vision."

It took a few seconds for me to realize that the gentleman standing directly opposite me, behind the book shelf, was actually addressing me. I presumed that he must have thought I was a student, but before I could correct him, the mysterious man simply vanished.

It was not the first time that someone assumed I was quite younger than I really am. Once, when I was teaching a class at the community college in Atlanta, a student entered the auditorium , took a seat in the front row and began to tell me that the reputation of "this" Professor, was rated far above the average difficulty range. Naturally he had no idea that he was speaking directly to me, the very professor he was complaining about.

It was not until the lecture hall filled to capacity that I took the podium . The bewildered student in the front looked mortified. But, it wasn't until three days later that he dropped the class after I refused to go on a date with him.

Even at the age of thirty eight, I am asked for an ID when ordering any alcoholic drinks. Some find this flattering , I find it annoying.

Once I accepted the teaching position here, in New Orleans, my priority had to focus on locating a suitable apartment near the university. Nothing else really mattered. In the meantime, the Dean provide me a temporary residence at The Omni Riverfront Hotel. I am, of course grateful for the lovely accommodations. Nevertheless , I must be completely moved in my own housing prior to the start of the first semester.

My realtor assures me that there are many flats available but, this is a college town. Most college students trade their dorms for apartments as soon as possible.

I remind my realtor, that I cannot be in the same building with students. And, she reminds me that with my budget this will be a real challenge.

Then, at midnight, still searching the internet for potential living quarters , I remembered the mandatory faculty meeting, now only a few hours away.

It seemed like only moments ago that I closed my eyes when the clock alarm woke me . Instinctively I reached over, turned off the annoying sound, and fell back asleep.

Thankfully, I also wisely asked for a back up wake up call from the front desk. But, by now I have no time to waste. Arriving late, to my first meeting would not only be
embarrassing, but also unacceptable.

These mandatory meetings are all the same. Someone, usually the university President , welcomes everyone back from their summer vacation or sabbatical. This is followed by a detailed agenda . All quite worthless topics. The meeting finally concludes with the introduction of the new faculty.

Because of this academic ritual, I know that it is strategically wise to find the most remote table in the corner of the room. There I can sit unnoticed and silent until the dreadful moment when I must stand up and be recognized as one of the newest faculty members, or better known as *Fresh Meat.*

Unfortunately, even knowing the protocol this morning is not enough. Today especially, I cannot risk being late. It will only draw unnecessary attention. So, I must move quickly. I only have enough time to apply sufficient eye concealer to cover up the dark circles below my eyes.

My hair is pulled into a truly messy bun. I grab an old sweatshirt, that I use when the air conditioning automatically turns on in the middle of the night. On my shoulder is the Michael Kors portfolio bag, a going away gift from Ingrid, my only real friend in Atlanta.

Downstairs I ask the door man to please fetch a taxi quickly. If I am lucky and the traffic is light, I will arrive one minute before the meeting begins . Most of the time all the speakers are also late. Nevertheless, stopping for coffee is definitely out of the question today

Certainly there will be plenty of coffee and tea once I arrive.

The taxi pulls up to the front of the massive Colonial building. I hand him the fare, and rush up the stairs. Thankfully there are many signs leading the way to the Grand Ballroom where this meeting is being held.

Once I arrive to my destination, I open the door slightly , trying to determine the best way to proceed. Just as rehearsed in my brain, I walk with confidence to the furthest table from the front of the room.

At this moment I am not Sabriel, I am Holly Golightly, one of my role models. Proudly I am wearing, a replica of her stunning tortoise shell, brown, oversized shades.

Most people do not even know that these glasses were specifically made by Oliver Goldsmith. The purpose, of course, is to hide Holly's true feelings ,hangovers, and naturally to create an aura of mystery.

Unfortunately, the dark glasses inside a room also distorts images. I soon realize this when I collide with a tall man. He nearly knocks me over. Then, before I can react, all I feel is someone gently grabbing my shoulder, preventing me from landing face down on the carpet.

When I am able to get my balance, I lift my glasses up and see a muscular gentleman with black peppered hair, wearing jeans, and a peach colored polo shirt. Our faces are so close that I can see deep into his blue eyes. What I see there is the future. I am no longer in the present. I have somehow moved beyond this moment .Not frightening, but definitely startling.

"Perhaps you should remove those shades when traversing new terrain, Holly?"

I know this voice. It is the mystery man from the bookstore. I am impressed that he recognizes my Breakfast at Tiffany's impersonation. Truman Capote would be proud of me. Sharing the same literary image just seems appropriate at this very moment.

"My sincere apology. I am so very sorry. Early mornings have never been my favorite time of the day. It just takes me a bit longer than normal people to acclimate," I say, trying to gain my composure.

"No explanation needed. I too prefer evenings to mornings. This is why I thought that you might appreciate some of these refreshments. First day faculty meetings can be brutal."

How did he know that I would be here, at his table? If I am right, which surely I am, this is the man in the bookstore that thought I was a student? Or was that only my impression? Either way, it does not explain how he knew we would ever meet again. After he left , I did think how ironic it was. I am turning the pages of The Southern Writers' textbook, and then I hear the distinct voice of a Southern gentleman. He just must have found some way to escape from the very pages I was holding. Or maybe even, Gone with the Wind?

And, now , here we are together again. Sitting alone at the same table sipping coffee and enjoying beignets from Café Du Monde; truly a gift from heaven, as he predicted

"Welcome to The University of New Orleans, Sabriel. I am Dr. Bradley Welch the Chairman of the English Department. I don't believe that we have formally met before," he says, with a curious smile, tilting his head just slightly.

"I am sorry to have missed your interview but I was out of the country at the time. I am certain that you will find everyone here eager to help you feel at home."

Feeling at home? What was that? I have no idea how that feels.

As expected, I simply nod politely. Once the entire University staff is introduced, the room becomes silent

As I look around, most of the professors are writing in their notebooks, staring through the wall-to-wall windows, or their heads are bent, barely staying awake.

Just as the lights are dimmed and the PowerPoint presentation starts I feel Dr. Bradley reach across the table and indiscreetly pass me a folded note. It reminds me of when I was in high school and the teacher's lectures were so boring that we all would pass notes to one another. I always prayed that the nuns wouldn't confiscate mine and read it aloud to the class.

When I opened the note, just as discreetly as I received it, the first thing I noticed was the elegant formal handwriting. Like physicians, professors are well known for having unreadable penmanship. Perhaps this writing dilemma began when people no longer wrote anything in cursive. This was followed by almost exclusive use of computers to communicate. But, this note was an exception.

I find your sweatshirt quite appropriate and intriguing Have you found a suitable apartment near campus yet? If not, It would be my

pleasure to be your personal escort. There are many areas in this quaint town that you should certainly avoid. How about lunch after this meeting at The Court of Two Sisters?

B

As I looked up, Bradley Welch was attentively engrossed in the presentation, which of course I lost complete interest in after the first five minutes.

My sweatshirt? What was on my sweatshirt? I never even noticed when I put it on this morning. Oh No! Now I remember. It is my Pink Floyd Hoodie that I bought at a concert years ago.

We Don't Need No Education *is printed on the front of the shirt surrounded by a brick wall. And, now it is even. too late to turn it inside out. I can only imagine what the university Chancellor and President would think if I removed my sweatshirt , with only a bra underneath. So much for me being careful to stay under the radar.*

I decided to avoid replying to the sweatshirt comment ,and simply wrote,

No…Yes…And, thank you for such a gracious offer. I will wait for you on the veranda after this meeting.

S

Once the note was back in Bradley's hand he simply placed it, unopened in his jacket inner pocket. He accomplished this so naturally that he could be a secret agent, disguised as a college professor.

"And, now ladies and gentlemen I am pleased to introduce our newest faculty Professor, Dr. Sabriel Shelley. Dr. Shelley, please join me here at the podium so that we can properly welcome you to our university family," Dr. Monroe said, waiting patiently for me to walk from the furthest part of this large banquet hall to the front podium.

I never expected to be called to the podium. Merely standing up and waving would have been enough. But, now there is no way out. Here I am looking more like a homeless person than a professor, and of course wearing a sweatshirt that insults the very purpose we are all here for today.

Okay, Sabriel, you have been through much worse than this. You will be fine. What was I thinking of when I rushed out of the hotel

room this morning? Didn't it ever occur to me that this might happen? At least I brushed my teeth. No more hiding. It's show time.

"First I want to thank Dr. Monroe for making me feel so welcome,"(*and so ridiculous standing here with no makeup, messy hair, and my oversized sweatshirt that says We don't Need No Education, I said silently*).

"*I* am very excited to join this amazing university . And, if any of you noticed the lyrics from Pink Floyd's notorious song printed on my sweatshirt, this is why all of us are here. We are always dedicated to demonstrating how important education is. I, for one, intend to , never forget, that each student that attends my class is the future of our country. Thank you once again and I look forward to meeting all of you personally in the near future, (*but not now, please God),* " I said, waving goodbye, jogging back to my seat, carefully avoiding any eye contact.

"Good job, Sabriel. You did that like a real pro," Bradley said, grinning like a Cheshire Cat.

I ignored him. Thankfully this meeting was finally over. But, of course before I could get to the porch to meet Bradley, I was detained by at least fifty members of the faculty. All giving me helpful advice that I would never recall once they left.

Finally, out of the conference room, I found the the veranda that span the entire building. Cast iron patio tables were placed throughout, inviting patrons to sit and enjoy sipping a cool beverage during a sultry southern morning.

As I continued to walk the perimeter, still wondering if Bradley had even read my response to his note, I stopped briefly, leaned on the balcony rail, and pondered what to do next.

A few feet away, out of my view, Bradley was sitting comfortably on a Brentwood Rocker, morning papers on his lap. Patiently, I assumed waiting for me to arrive. When he removed his reading glasses I could see him at a distance.

Months later Bradley would document this meeting in his personal journal :

Should I try to get her attention, or take the advantage of this private moment to enjoy the unobstructed view that would soon pass by? Although it was only the third time that I had seen Sabriel, I now could fully appreciate what JD Salinger wrote, about being half in love

... She wasn't doing a thing that I could see, accept being here (there), leaning on a balcony railing, holding up the universe.. There was certainly nothing extraordinary about her; and, yet everything was extraordinary about her . Yes, Salinger said it best.

For a brief moment I felt as if I was Scarlett O'Hara meeting Rhett Butler at Tara for the very first time.

But, what Bradley noticed, was far more important.

There were half circles under her eyes, and other subtler signs that mark an acutely troubled girl, but none the less no one could have missed seeing that she was a first -class beauty. Her skin was lovely , and her features delicate and most distinctive (Franny and Zooey). I knew then, just as Salinger did, that this young woman was special..

"Thank you for waiting for me so patiently. It is impossible to avoid the crowds in there. I am impressed that you were able to escape so quickly. Are you some kind of a magician? " I asked, playfully.

I could sense that Bradley was tempted to take the bait, but he reconsidered his response.

What I wanted to say to her, is allow me into your world and I will show you what magic I can provide.

But, instead he said, "When you have been attending these meetings, longer than I will admit, you learn where all the closest exits are."

"These are lovely rocking chairs, I replied, already moving on to the next topic.

Walking around the back of Bradley's chair I examined it like a museum curator.

"Bentwood Rockers, you might already know, have quite an interesting history. They were designed by Michael Thonet, a German-Austrian inventor who discovered that by steaming wood he was able to create an unusual frame to the traditional rocking chair. By 1856 he was given a patent for this process."

Sometimes, often too late, I would realize I was going off on topics that nobody really cared about. Lately, I really tried the avoid this annoying habit.

Bradley however, was an exception. He was willing to listen to whatever I said for hours. He would later say that my voice reminded him of some innocent child who had command of every word I chose. For some unknown reason, Bradley said, I was eloquently entertaining.

"You, my lady have many interesting facets that I hope you will continue sharing with me," Bradley said.

No one ever before showed any interest like this in me, unless of course it was directed at literary theory or analysis. That was something that I never had difficulty expressing. Everything else to me seemed trivial.

But, it was these trivial ideas that kept me grounded. I enjoyed not having to defend why rap lyrics by Drake were as enjoyable to listen to as Mozart. Or how the artwork of Anita Catarina Malfatti, the first Brazilian artist to introduce a new form of modernism, is as brilliant as Picasso.

Bradley Welch was not only curious to learn more about me, he was eager to share with me many of his own quirky ideas.

Chapter Two

The beginning of love
is when we let those we love be perfectly themselves, and not to
twist them to fit our image. Otherwise we only love the reflection of
ourselves we find in them.

—Thomas Merton

BRADLEY WELCH

New Orleans, The Big Easy, NOLA, however you choose to
refer to the most well known city in the state of Louisiana ,
everyone agrees that there is no other place where jazz
warms your heart, and supernatural spirits runs through your veins
like ice.

After our first real encounter, at the faculty meeting Sabriel and I
decided to postpone lunch until the following week. Locating a
suitable apartment for her, we both agreed, was the priority. I had no
idea what "suitable" meant to Sabriel until we began driving around
to places that I considered to be the most appropriate neighborhoods.
This included my neighborhood, located in the very respectable, yet
slightly pricey Garden District.

Most people are not even aware of how this city is divided, let
alone the history that determines each district. Therefore, before
making this search totally futile I needed to give Sabriel a crash
course about the neighborhoods.

"First, there are really seven distinct districts in our city. Each one
has its own historical significance. But, that discussion would be so
very overwhelming that you would certainly return to Atlanta as fast
as Scarlett O'Hara, returned to Tara," I said, using my Southern
charm to make this sound easier.

"Is there any specific neighborhood that you would highly
recommend, or discourage?" Sabriel asked coyly.

"Well, yes, and no. I mean to say based on your preferences, there may be some suitable accommodations nearly anywhere. For example, The Garden District, or Uptown, like some prefer to call it, is a lovely tree lined community, near the university, with many pleasant eateries and boutiques. And, of course there is the St. Charles Streetcar," I said as we got closer to my remodeled colonial style building.

The magnolia blooms, and sweet opulent aroma of jasmine easily entices those who can afford this. It is definitely a refuge from any outside distractions.

"Quite lovely Bradley. But, isn't this where you told me you lived?"

Sabriel asked, as if a mystery was close to being solved.

"Why yes. To your right, that gigantic building, the one that looks like a white wedding cake with several layers, is my building," I said, not really knowing why I was revealing this.

"Definitely a very stately mansion. Not quite the stature of the home Scarlett and Rhett purchased in Atlanta," Sabriel said, smiling, obviously amused at her own comment.

"Perhaps another time you might ask me up for tea on your terrace?"

Now Sabriel sounded as if she was once again baiting me to play her game. But, since it was not one with any specifics rules, I chose politely not to indulge.

"Yes. What a fantastic idea. I might cater an intimate tea party for our English professors one afternoon."

I smiled at Sabriel convinced that the score in our game was still tied.

"Where to next, my gentleman escort?" Sabriel was back in her Holly Golightly role wearing her large sunglasses in spite of the cloudy day.

" I do believe that I have the perfect location. We are driving now toward The French Quarter. This area is considered The Crown Jewel of New Orleans. There is definitely a different vibe once you walk the streets. It is almost like a time machine. Like someone, or something, is spiritually with you at all times. It is a timeless portrait of what the Creole Aristocrats left for us, another generation. Among the fortune tellers at Jackson Square, juxtaposed is the vanilla cream walls of The St. Louis Cathedral ," I said, waiting for Sabriel to react. Even though the dark shades were covering her eyes I could tell that she was coming alive.

"I was quite lucky to find a parking place on the corner," I said, while, Sabriel looked up at the street sign.

It was Toulouse Street. We both looked at each other at the same time. I let her speak first.

"We need to get out of the car don't we?" She said, excited.

I just shook my head yes, allowing Sabriel to make the next move.

"How far away do you think we are from 722?"

Before I could respond, she finally realized that this stop was not merely a coincidence. I mean, really? We are both English PHD's living in one of the most infused literary cities in America. I was about to introduce Sabriel to where the famous playwright Tennessee Williams lived and wrote. At the time he was known as Thomas Lanier Williams. It was at this apartment, after trying out the name, Valentine Xavier, that he settled for Tennessee.

"Here it is? But, of course you knew this already, "Sabriel said.

I was just relieved that she was not upset at my surprise. Bringing her here to see what Williams used as the setting for his play, *Vieux Carrie,* should make her very pleased.

"If you have a few minutes to spare, maybe you would like to go inside? The house was restored into this museum. There is also a 1973 script of *Vieux Carrie* inside," I said, leading Sabriel up the steps not waiting for her to respond.

"Yes. Of course I want to visit. Thank you Bradley. I appreciate this diversion," Sabriel said, stretched up on her toes and kissed me on the cheek. I of course wished it had been a passionate wet French kiss, but it was definitely a beginning.

After spending several hours at the Toulouse Street museum we decided to take a break from apartment hunting. We left the car to find a place to grab lunch with maybe a glass of wine.

"This is a lovely courtyard restaurant. Do you frequent it often?" Sabriel asked.

Maybe I was being overly cautious, but it seemed that since that swift kiss, Sabriel was trying to discover something more about my personal life. Perhaps I was just eagerly hopeful. Overreacting to simple comments is only one of my many flaws.

"No, actually I have only been here once before, with my best friend, Emma. It was her suggestion."

Oh, that was brilliant. Now I will need to explain that relationship before she thinks Emma is a girlfriend.

"Well, you must let Emma know that she has fabulous taste. Not only is the jambalaya terrific, but, the Chardonnay you selected was a perfect choice. I hope that our date to *The Court of Two Sisters* is still happening?" Sabriel asked.

"Of course. I am available any time next week. After classes start it will be more difficult for both of us to find any free time. And, make certain that you arrange for several readers as soon as possible. The best ones are taken early," I said, grateful that Emma's name was not brought up again.

"Yes, thank you. I already have several graduate students that seem promising,"Sabriel said.

I tried not to imagine some brilliant male graduate student spending hours with Sabriel discussing the essays that they would be reading together. Every semester there was some clandestine affair revealed about professors and students. Most of the time graduate students. There was no official policy prohibiting this behavior but, it was discouraged.

"Well, I think we still have a little time to walk this district, don't we? I mean, you never really know a city unless you walk the streets and feel the pavement beneath your feet of the many generations before you," Sabriel suggested.

She was up and outside before I could respond.

The more that I learned about this girl, the more I was fascinated. We were definitely moving towards the epicenter of the unknown, which kept me interested much longer than any other relationship.

Before returning to the car we walked at least five miles. Sabriel noticed a **For Rent** sign in the window of a small quintessential French Quarter cottage.

"Oh my gosh, Bradley! This is it. My perfect house. I love it. Do you think we can walk around and look through the windows?"

This was genuine excitement. It was like a young child who discovers on Christmas morning that Santa had left her exactly what she always wanted. Even Natalie Wood, in *Miracle on 34th Street* could not compete with this enthusiasm.

Without even seeing the inside of this cottage, Sabriel called the number on the sign, told the owner she was a professor at the university and that she was absolutely sure she wanted this house.

Within one hour, while we waited sitting in the brick patio, Sabriel, had imagined where all her furniture, paintings and even her television would go. The contract was signed and money was exchanged for keys. It was the fastest transaction I had ever seen.

Inside the house, Sabriel inspected each room. The appliances in the kitchen seemed to be her favorite.

"Did you see this stainless steel fridge? Even the sink is stainless steel. I guess I will need to learn to cook. This kitchen is too beautiful for just take-out," Sabriel said, forgetting that I was even around.

"Hello? Sabriel? It's Bradley," I said on my cell phone.

Sabriel stopped, and started laughing after she realized I was being neglected.

"I am so sorry, Bradley. It is because of you that I even found this house. You really don't understand how much this means to me. Maybe someday I will share that with you, but today I am just going to let the happiness flow."

With her arms wide open I took advantage of an embrace. She hugged me back. I then whispered in her ear," I am a fantastic cook, by the way. I can make you anything you want," I said, releasing her from my hold.

"I am definitely looking forward to that, Mr. Rhett Butler. I am quite aware of how often you saved Scarlett from her many dilemmas," Sabriel said, leading me out the front door.

After leaving Sabriel off at the Omni Riverfront Hotel, I felt that I needed to talk with Emma. Thankfully she picked up her cellphone.

"Hey, Buddy. What's going on? How was your afternoon with that cute new English Professor? Not even sure what her name is?" Emma said.

"Sabriel? Oh we are just friends. I was helping her learn about the city and find an apartment, that's all," I said, making sure to sound casual.

"Bradley, listen to me. We are friends. What you need is not another friend. Stop by and let's talk. I am home for a few hours," Emma said.

"I should be there in ten. Thanks Emma."

Unfortunately, anyone who knows me understands that I have a very low tolerance level. This results in losing interest in all relationships relatively quickly. Emma, my only real friend, male or female, at the university, understands this flaw. Although there was maybe a ten minute physical attraction between us, thankfully we resolved that, and a much stronger platonic one emerged.

Nevertheless, Emma has now become my matchmaker. She continues to arrange potential partners for me. All have resulted in failure. Frustrated, Emma finally told me, honestly what she has been witnessing.

"The problem my friend, is that you are too scholarly. I mean ALWAYS scholarly! . Sometimes you need to just 'chill out '. There is nothing wrong with enjoying a pleasant 'shag' with some simple chick," Emma said, in her favorite British accent.

"You may be right Emma. A casual sexual encounter just might help me through this writer's block. It has been weeks since I have worked on my manuscript. Have any suggestions? Just remember how low my tolerance is for the status quo, and then include my unrealistic desire for change. Both are real detriments that I can't control," I said trying to be honest.

Emma looked at me shaking her head, obviously exasperated .

"Well, not being on campus for a year might have benefited you. And, of course there is a new crop of professors joining the faculty. Just please, try to control your need to be the Alpha dog. Even the bimbos get turned off by lectures," Emma said, bluntly.

"I know that you are right. Whenever, I reach a point that it appears that I am progressing, more complications arise. My expectations from a potential partner seems less realistic each day. But, then, from nowhere I meet Sabriel and my imagination begins to come alive. Sabriel offers me the intellectual stimulation that no one else has been able to achieve. It is as if she naturally understands what I need. Sometimes even before I do," I said, not even sure why I shared all this.

"Well, then my friend, get on that phone and make plans for lunch at *The Court of Two Sisters*. According to your very own research there is something that lingers at that place. Maybe, the sisters will throw a little magic dust on the two of you," Emma said, half joking.

On my way home, I stopped at the market to pick up some crayfish. Before leaving I called Sabriel.

"Hey...hello, this is Bradley Welch," I said, not believing how awkward that sounded.

Her phone message was short and sweet, like Sabriel.

"Leave me a message. If it is clever I will return a call. If not, try again."

Too late for me to be clever. I pushed the red button with the phone logo. Not a chance that Sabriel would call me back anyway. The apartment hunting is done. No need to be any more nice than necessary to the Department Chair now. Her exodus is clean and swift.

The crayfish were in the boiling water for five minutes, their heads no longer visible, when my phone began to vibrate.

"Good evening Bradley. Are the crayfish ready yet?"

It was Sabriel. *How could she know about the crayfish?*

"Well, yes they are. But…how…"

"Never mind how, darling. Is Wednesday suitable for our lunch at *The Court of Two Sisters,* around noonish? I will meet you there," Sabriel said, her voice was enchanting.

"Yes, that sounds terrific. I can pick you up if it is easier?" I offered, hoping she would accept.

"No, but thank you. You are a sweetheart. I think I will splurge and take a carriage ride. Someone told me that it will drop me off wherever I want. So Ciao darling. Until Wednesday at our secret rendezvous ."

That was the strangest conversation. Sabriel obviously likes to role play the characters that she admires, but I hope she doesn't have a multiple identity disorder. The two of us together could be very dangerous.

Chapter Three

There are more things in Heaven and Earth, Horatio than are dreamt in your philosophy.
Hamlet

BRADLEY WELCH

"Emma and Bertha Camors, were two sisters who bought this home from Jean Baptiste Zenon Cavelier in 1826. They successfully offered the wealthy Creole women a unique style of costumes, gowns, masks, and jewelry found nowhere else in the city."

I, stopped my narrative realizing that Sabriel was sipping on her Sazerac; gazed eyes, elbows upright on a flat surface, watching me, without focus, seemingly bored .

For the first time, since Sabriel arrived, I noticed that she was sitting beneath the death mask of Andrew Jackson. It was an ominous sight; one I wished I could have captured on film.

"And, by the way did you know that the *Charm Gates*, I believe that is what they are called, were manufactured in Spain?, And, blessed by Queen Isabella. I read this somewhere. Many naïve people even , imagine that touching those iron gates will assure them of love, tranquility, and, even prosperity. I am very skeptical of that idea," Sabriel said, as if SHE was the expert, not I, on the history of this most famous New Orleans landmark, *The Court of Two Sisters.*

Changing the subject quickly Sabriel asked," What is this drink, Bradley, that you ordered for me? It is quite refreshing."

Finally she was looking directly at me, attentively for the first time. The feeling was much different now, than when I was giving my well prepared lecture on *The Court of Two Sisters* . Sabriel was then obviously preoccupied.

By now I realized that her mind is designed to work at many different levels at the same time. Almost like those cell towers that are capable of reaching various stations .

Or, maybe Sabriel is just an expert at multitasking with her brain. It is really too early for me to be certain. What was becoming evident is that this young lady, sitting across from me, was an enigma that I needed to explore.

"Sazerac. That is the name of your cocktail. It is the official drink of New Orleans. But, you must already know this," I said, trying not to sound sarcastic, but it didn't work.

"No, I did not know that. But, I am sure that it has a story that YOU will tell me?" Sabriel responded, staring directly at me.

If her eyes could talk they would say, "Touché Smart Ass."

"Okay. I get it. Sometimes it sounds like a lecture, but really I was just trying to share with you how special *The Court of Two Sisters* is. I had no idea you researched it already."

Sabriel must have heard my voice change from arrogant to disappointed. She looked quite softer at this moment. More like the petals on a rose bush than the painful thorns. She then reached her hand across the table and gently touched mine. It felt as if she had just found a missing link to my body. What I saw, and experienced at that moment was so powerful that it made my hand slightly tremble.

The energy passing through each of our bodies simultaneously was unprecedented. Never before have I felt such fulfillment. And, it was all natural.

What I did not expect was what Sabriel said next.

"The creator or the creature? Who has the real power? And, who will abuse that power? Whatever is now developing, at this moment, is so much stronger than any other emotional sensation, with or without sexual stimulation."

Sabriel then released my hand. She turned her attention, to the brick wall, as if nothing special between us ever occurred. But what followed was anything but normal.

Sabriel said, "Would you mind giving me a coin to toss in the fountain? If not, I am sure I can find one. It just works better if you provide the coin, and, I am the one tossing it." It was as if she knew that this was an important ritual.

And, in fact it was. I was just once again surprised how Sabriel would know any of this. Most people who visit this city, or even those who decide to live here, never realize that Voodoo and New Orleans have been lovers forever. But, they soon either hear stories about voodoo or maybe even experience some of its power.

Voodoo was introduced here during the Antebellum era when African slaves brought with them their religious beliefs to North America. I have always studied the supernatural influences on Southern Writers in this region. So, when I learned how the slaves traditions, began melding with Haitian and Caribbean influences it was soon evident that a new religion was evolving . Naturally this effected the entire region, including the Catholic Churches. The specific similarities with Christianity includes the practices of saint worshiping, and ritual sacrifices.

After a year on sabbatical, carefully studying the effect of supernatural occurrences in Europe, I turned my attention to three particular cities, on this continent. My initial conclusion is that in these regions there is a powerful magnetic force. When identified, the results of unnatural or unexplainable events defies what we refer to as logic.

Bringing Sabriel here, to *The Court of Two Sisters*, at the very center of spiritual awakening, I was not sure what to expect. And, since my theories are still just that, I am reluctant to share anything with anyone yet. But, now maybe it will soon be possible. Sabriel's voice brought me back to reality.

"This courtyard, with the natural sounds of jazz makes me feel very different. Very alive. Almost like I have visited this before, but of course that may just be de ja vu," Sabriel said.

"I must ask you. How do you have so much knowledge about the legends in New Orleans?"

21

This time I was careful to ask, not presuming to continue with my lesson. I genuinely wanted to hear what Sabriel would say.

"There really is no mystery. I have always been curious about the occult. Not obsessed, but fascinated. Paranormal events really do not seem to have any limitations. What I mean to say, is that it spans various genres. It is the literary connections that I want to learn more about," Sabriel said.

She paused, continued to sip on her drink, and then continued.

"For example, did you know that if you take a map and draw a triangle from…"

I interrupted her immediately.

……"New Orleans, Savannah, Georgia, and St. Augustine, Florida, they are all places known to have Mojo,

" I said, completing her statement.

"Yes. Mojo. That's right, magical spirits. Not many people know this. I should have guessed that you would be an exception," Sabriel added .

"We have so much more in common than I realized," I said, hoping to sound sincere.

"Really? You are just now coming to this conclusion ? I think that connection started on the day you spoke to me in the bookstore. Remember? You then just vanished like a ghost. Nothing ever happens by coincidence. I am sure of this," Sabriel said.

She was obviously right. But it was too soon for me to realize that Sabriel is right ninety seven percent of the time. The other three percent is due to unmitigated circumstances.

"Some day, when I retire from teaching, I want a courtyard just like this one. And, inside the cottage will be a bookstore, where my guests can select a gothic, or mysterious story and sip tea outside, and eat petit cucumber sandwiches and scones." Sabriel's eyes lit up with a whimsical conviction.

"Will you invite me to join you occasionally Holly Golightly?"I asked.

"Of course Mr. Rhett Butler. High tea would not be the same without a gentleman with your stature."

This was the beginning of a most arousing, beguiling, absorbing relationship. One that I could never have imagined. Being with Sabriel was at times challenging, but never boring.

Even later, when she insisted on having her own apartment, the only time that we were not together was when we were in class lecturing or on campus during assigned office hours. It seemed entirely natural, as if Sabriel was in my life forever.

To say Sabriel completed me, would be a misnomer. There was never any completion. She kept me in perpetual motion. Sabriel gave me the ability to complete myself.

Chapter Four

Terror made me cruel...
—Emily Bronte, *Wuthering Heights*

SABRIEL and BRADLEY

*F*inding *somewhere to hide...a place where the street lights don't shine. Where it will not cast my shadow on the grass. Can't have that. No that would be a mess. Someone, probably Carter, was moving everywhere...he always finds everyone. Not this time. Not me. I learned early on that being" it" is never fun. While you are counting down, people all over are searching for hiding places,...like this one. So far nobody else knows about my secret hiding place. I am now the master at kicking the can. My friends think I am smart, but I'm not. I just know if I don't kick that can then I lose. And, I hate LOSING .*

Losing makes me feel inferior. Dumb. Menial..
"10, 9,8,7,6,5,4,3,2,1
Ready or not, Here I come."

Wait! Not yet. I can still win this game.

Stop that dreadful sound. Whose nails are scratching the chalkboard. Stop! Stop it now!

That's when I realize, now quite annoyed, that it is my ancient alarm clock screeching.

Years ago, I set my phone alarm to the new age Celtic music of Enya. Unfortunately the melodic sounds of her voice and celestial harps encourages me to sleep rather than wake. That is when I resorted to the old fashion, but reliable alarm clock.

After a few minutes of stretching, it is evident that there is no way to escape. My wish is that none of my classes would start earlier than noon. But, naturally being the "new kid on the block" all of my requests are placed at the bottom of that list. Not even Bradley dares to make those changes.

But, after a few weeks of adjusting, the classes seem to fit into place. Monday, Wednesday, and Friday I teach *Freshman Survey of Literature*. It is a large class with a waiting list for students to enroll .This is quite normal. These classes were certainly not packed because I am popular. Quite the contrary. Students just assume that a new professor will be easier since we all want those stellar reviews by the end of the semester.

I never cared about those evaluations. I am the expert. Students soon learn this. Once this is established, and respect earned, most will give me high marks anyway. Those few who don't just want a free ride.

"Mrs. Shelley, I just wanted to let you know how much I love this class. You are one of my favorites," the young coed said as she rushed out of the lecture room for her next class.

Then several other young women approached me requesting that I teach a class in *Feminine Literature* next semester .

"We have been asking for this class for a year now. Most all of the other universities offer something similar. But, we would rather not travel, or take distant learning classes. Now that you are here maybe the Dean will listen to us," a spokeswoman for this group said. She then handed me a petition with over one hundred signatures.

"And, by the way Professor Shelley there are many other petitions circulating with the same request."

Feminine Literature was always a class I considered teaching, but now this early in my tenure I was not exactly sure how to approach Bradley about it.

We were not romantically involved in any way, but there was a potential connection that both of us were trying to avoid. Playful flirtation under control is always acceptable but once that line is crossed things might get messy.

Thankfully, when classes resumed this semester both of us were too busy for even a casual lunch date. This natural distance and time allowed a more professional attitude to develop.

Our last time together was at *The Court of Two Sisters*. I could feel then that something was drawing me closer to Bradley. But, it was just for a slight moment. As a matter of fact, until just now I didn't even think about Bradley. But, I had this odd feeling that he was always thinking about me.

From nowhere there would be images flashing through my mind that Bradley and I were thinking the same thoughts. At meetings with other professors, people would comment about how my ideas sounded just like, "Professor Welch."

Working together on a University Campus is so much different than being in a corporate office where you see your peers nearly every day. Here it is very possible to move about for weeks, maybe even months and never really have a conversation with fellow Professors.

Nevertheless, in this particular situation Bradley knew where I was every day. Being the Department Chairman it was his responsibility to have this information.

But, in reality the English faculty is very independent by nature. Bradley's position was merely a formal delegation that any of the other Professors could do as well, and maybe even better. He was actually hoping that after returning from sabbatical someone else would step forward. Of course that didn't happen.

Students would share with me that Bradley often told them what a competent and energizing professor I was.

Some students even started to assume that we were a couple, even though we were never seen together.

One associated professor, whom I shared a table with in the faculty room, even suggested that he thought Professor Welch was obsessed with me.

"There are times when Bradley and I discuss a lesson and he just starts talking about how that scene reminds him of a colleague. He doesn't have to say your name. It is quite obvious it is you. All the other professors are ancient," Matthew said, a graduate reader that Bradley and I share.

"Matthew , you are making undocumented assertions. You know, like the same ones we criticize our students for making," I said, trying to ignore, his assumptions.

"Sabriel? Professor Welch always is talking in class about Holly Golightly. We all know that you are the only one on this campus that resembles that character," Matthew concluded.

Okay, I thought about this allusion that Matthew cited as specific evidence. Bradley Welch is affixed with Holly Golightly. I get it.

She is a fascinating character, created by Truman Capote. I am her biggest fan. But this doesn't mean that Bradley has me on his mind.

Many professors, including myself, become relatively close to characters that they teach for many years. Jay Gatsby is a role model of my perfect lover, if I could just correct all of those infatuations he has about Daisy.

But, as much as Gatsby was on my mind at that time, I never thought of him as real, and I never compared him to anyone I knew.

BRADLEY

Sabriel never did realize why I admired her. It is partly due to the attention she draws from her audience .This is much more than her outstanding physical attributes. It is more about how she uses those attributes From the moment I saw her at the book store, Sabriel's beauty was a blend of Natalie Wood, with some features of Audrey Hepburn, and a slight kick of Vivian Leigh. But, all of these lovely ladies combined are still not as impressive to me as the authentic Sabriel.

Regardless of her natural aesthetics, I admired her intelligence even more. Sabriel was one of the few Professors I knew had the ability to take anything complex and translate it into comprehensible data. The discussion that we had at *The Court of Two Sisters* for hours was enough for me to know that Sabriel is beyond gifted.

Personally my attraction to Sabriel became nearly obsessive. For weeks I tried to determine there was any mutual feelings . Is it even reasonable to assume that she would be attracted to me.?

"Are you serious Bradley? Reasonable? You know that emotions are never reasonable. You teach literature for God's sake. You illustrate how emotions are not reasonable," Emma said, exasperated.

"My life is not a chapter in some novel, Emma. I don't have the necessary tools to analyze why Sabriel has taken residence in my psyche. I certainly don't want to be like J.D. Salinger, constantly musing over all the young girls he fantasized . And, I certainly don't want to be one of those fools that mistake friendship for love," I replied defensively.

"Well, my amore, Sabriel is living in your mind and if you take no action your fate will be worse than Salinger's life. At least he attempted those relationships at some level. And, you know as well as I do, that we all write our own chapters. If not, then there is nothing left to live for," Emma said, walking away letting our conversation marinate.

The next day, I showed up at Sabriel's Friday lecture. At first she never even noticed me. She was lecturing with a power point and the room was dark. But, at the end of class she saw me sitting in the last row, away from the crowds. I found it slightly humorous that Sabriel appeared surprised.

When the class was over and the two of us were finally alone, Sabriel stepped down from the stage and greeted me with a pleasant smile.

"What brings the fine Gentleman from his Ivory Towers to visit me?"Sabriel said, still keeping a comfortable distance. I was obviously an unexpected visitor.

"Well, Holly, or is it Scarlett today? Any way, not important. I have requests from a vast amount of students that would like you to teach a *Feminism Literature* class next semester. They specifically are requesting you, by name," I said, taking a seat in the auditorium chair.

"I did hear that from a few students but, I had no idea that a formal request was made. And, yes…I mean, if it is alright with the administration, I would be honored to teach that class," Sabriel said, now moving closer to me.

"Wonderful. Then I will get all the paperwork in order," I said, rising from the seat, and moving nonchalantly as possible toward the back doors.

I thought that she might say something to prevent me from leaving. Perhaps just a little small talk. But nothing !

That is when I stopped at the top of the entry. When I looked back at Sabriel, the light behind her was a silhouette that looked like a transparent image.

"Would you consider being my guest for dinner Saturday night?" I said, surprising even myself..

Sabriel at first hesitated , but then responded before I exited the same door that I came in at.

"Sounds, marvelous. Looking forward to it," was all I heard.

Without turning around, I replied,

"Fantastic. I will text you with the details."

And, then it was all over.

Once, Bradley was gone, I reflected on what just happened.

That was certainly an odd encounter. Maybe I misinterpreted what I felt at The Court of Two Sisters...No, there was definitely some energy flowing between us. I guess I will see on Saturday. This is probably no more than a business meeting to discuss the details of the new class. I will prepare a syllabus tonight to give him tomorrow.

Minutes later I heard my phone ringing. It was Bradley. His text said.

I will pick you up at 7:00 pm tomorrow night. Dinner at my place. I hope you like lobster, if not text me back.
B

His place? Maybe it is an informal department meeting? People around campus say that Bradley likes to keep everything low key. But, lobster doesn't sound casual to me. I guess I will just need to wait until tomorrow.

Chapter Five

He wanted all to lie in an ecstasy of peace; I wanted to sparkle and shine like a jubilee. I said this heaven would only be half alive; and he said mine would be drunk; I said I should fall asleep in his; and he said he could not breathe in mine.

—Emily Bronte , *Wuthering Heights*

SABRIEL and BRADLEY

"Do you ever get so involved with a novel that at times you think that it may be real?" I asked.

The wine was making my mind rather murky, although I was careful not to expose too much, too early.

Bradley was still putting the leftover lobster away in the kitchen. He refused to let me help him with any cleaning.

"Give me just five more minutes and we can talk philosophy over a glass of brandy," Bradley said, from the well stocked kitchen.

I was definitely impressed with the gourmet meal that Bradley insisted he made all by himself. And, once I saw his kitchen with all the latest gadgets I was convinced that he really does do all his own cooking.

Bradley Welch was definitely a conundrum. Although not boastfully handsome, he easily could be mistaken for a GQ model. His shirts are always pressed, even the polo one he is wearing tonight. And, his jeans are just tight enough to admire his well rounded buttock. But, what was most attractive about Bradley was his dark black hair with just a few silver streaks strategically painted naturally to appear distinguished.

I could sit here and just watch him do these domestic chores for hours imagining that when he was alone he would do them all in the nude.

"Bradley? Do you ever multitask naked," I asked, playfully.

Just then I heard the dishwasher starting.

"Sorry about that, Sabriel. I couldn't hear a word you said," Bradley apologized carrying in two brandy snuffs and a bottle of Cognac.

I was relieved that he never heard my sexual innuendo. It was a wonderful dinner. We were alone, not like the group that I imagined, yet, it was not intimate. This was a friendly evening between two people dedicated to teaching.

Nothing more than that. At least nothing more yet. But eventually Bradley is going to remove those barriers and let me in.

"Sorry about taking so long with the dishes. I am rather an addict at keeping things clean. Not, like crazy nuts but dirty dishes in particular make me nervous," Bradley said, finally sitting down at the opposite chair from her.

"It is certainly good to know that my boss is a control freak early in our working relationship. I will do everything in my ability to meet your expectations," I said, pleasantly.

Bradley simply smiled, poured the Cognac and replied, "Sabriel you have already superseded all my expectations."

Was Bradley flirting with me or was this just my imagination running wild again. It is better to put out a few more feelers before I respond . It has been some time since I have played this mating dance with anyone. Hell, I have never been attracted to any man, or woman for that matter to ever want to play this game. Most of my past relationships have been only physical. You know, with men that offered potentially good sex, but nothing more. This was much more confusing. First, Bradley is the one that I theoretically report to. His evaluation of my teaching performance will be considered highly by the administration. I am confident that I will do well in both physical and intellectual performances, but, it might become a little "sticky " if we become intimate.

Secondly, Bradley is probably in his late forties, maybe even fifty.. Why isn't he married? Or, in a long term relationship? I really don't know anything about this man. What I do realize is that whenever we are together something begins to change inside of me. It is as if he is the keeper of my next challenge, my next movement. He is the Maestro and I perform the music he decides to conduct. I am not yet sure if I enjoy being in his orchestra, but I am enjoying the prelude thus far.

"Sabriel?... Sabriel? Have I bored you to a state of ambivalence? You seem to be in another universe?"

I barely heard Bradley's voice.

"Oh...,no Bradley, forgive me. I am just enjoying the moment so much that I must have been mind wandering for a few moments," I said, fairly convinced that this was a safe explanation.

"Mind wandering? That is a clever phrase. Is it anything like daydreaming? Because, if it is, I have been doing much of that lately," Bradley said, lifting his brandy snifter and clinking it to mine.

This was a definite invitation to respond flirtatiously. Game on Dr. Bradley Welch.

"Well, that all depends on the subject. My mind wandering can happen when I see a flock of geese that reminds me of Mary Oliver, or it can be initiated by the gesture of a Southern Gentleman's expert culinary skills." I said, deciding to leave the next move to Bradley.

It was still fairly obvious that we both were merely trading one of our pawns for the other. When they were all gone the true talent would surface.

"Nicely stated Dr. Shelley. Mary Oliver is one of the most neglected contemporary poets of our lifetime. It doesn't seem to matter that she won The National Book Award and Pulitzer Prize in 2007. Her poetry is rarely taught in any university curriculum. Maybe you can include her in your Feminism Literature Class next semester?" Bradley asked, but it really sounded more of a sincere request.

His response to my hook reply was definitely strategically planned. He was not prepared to relinquish any defense until there was some certainty I would reciprocate accordingly. I may have underestimated Bradley's experience with the art of courtship, or maybe it was all me wanting to believe that this evening would be the beginning of something more intimate? After all Emma seems to enjoy her platonic relationship with Bradley. Maybe that is all he is capable of.

While I was mind wandering again, Bradley was turning pages in a book that he had retrieved from his bookshelf.

"I am sure that you are familiar with this poem by Mary Oliver, but would you mind me reading it aloud. It is one of my favorites?" Bradley asked.

Which one of us were rehearsing now ?

"Yes, of course…please read it to me. I absolutely enjoy listening to poetry read aloud. I think all poems should be heard not only read," I said, fluffing the pillows behind me and stretching out on the couch as comfortably as possible for Bradley's performance.

The Geese, by Mary Oliver

You do not have to be good.
You do not have to walk on your knees for a hundred miles through the desert repenting.
You only need to let the soft animal of your body love what it loves.

Bradley paused at that line and looked directly into my eyes. It was the first time I had noticed the intensity; the sheer power of his stare made me feel his desire to inhale my entire soul. It was no more than a few seconds, and Bradley returned to the words on the page.

Tell me about despair, yours, and I will tell you mine.
Meanwhile the world goes on.

By this time Bradley had the book on his lap and he was reciting. Each word sounded like a new opening to a very private life of a complex human.

Meanwhile the sun and the clear pebbles of the rain,
are moving against the landscapes,
over the prairies and the deep trees,
and the mountains , and the rivers.
Meanwhile, the wild geese in the clean blue air, are heading home again.
Whoever you are, however lonely,

The world offers itself to your imagination
Calls to you, like the wild geese, harsh, and exiting-
over and over announcing your place
in the family of things.

Bradley closed the book, that he never really needed, waiting for my reaction. When tears began to form in my eyes and the drops started leaving a trail , Bradley moved to the couch.

First, without a word, he began to kiss the tears away. His lips were so light that it felt as a feather was not only wiping my cheek but caressing my entire face.

Then, once Bradley was certain the tears stopped he held my face in his two hands. When his tongue entered my mouth it felt like it belonged with mine. After a few moments of our mouths delighting in discovering one another, I could feel my body being lifted into the air. It was the very first time that I felt safe, truly wanted, and alive simultaneously.

What happened the rest of our night together sealed our future. This was the man I was going to grow old with. Nothing ever before, or that I could imagine ever after, would compare to this evening. It was so much more than sexual intimacy. I can only describe it as emotional accessibility, or synchronization. This is when emotional openness and responsiveness , tender touch, and eroticism all work together like an opus.

Bradley and I for the very first time in both our lives were able to allow the physical limitations we had with intimacy, to relinquish into the emotional security we now discovered concurrently..

We never discussed how this happened or why our paths crossed. That night could never be repeated or attempted. Haley's comet circles every seventy five or seventy six years. I can only imagine our experience similar to that phenomenon. What neither of us knew on that day was how little time was left.

Chapter Six

To live in this world…
You must be able to do three things. To love what is mortal; to hold
it…against your bones knowing your life depends on it.
And when the time comes to let it go,
Let it go

—Mary Oliver

SABRIEL and BRADLEY

"I have a surprise for you this morning," Bradley said, whispering into my ear that was carefully placed beneath a pillow. My eyes hidden from the sunlight with another pillow.

When Bradley got no reaction, he lifted one of the pillows off of my head gently, and turned up *Queen* singing *We Will Rock You*.

"Really Bradley? You know I have a class this morning. A class that you scheduled knowing how I HATE MORNINGS," I said, reaching for my eye mask on the bed stand.

"Wrong, Princess. Today is Friday. Day off for us both. Now get that cute ass out of bed and let's try to get to Le Monde before all the hot fresh beignets are gone," Bradley said patting my butt for encouragement.

Now I remember why Bradley could not convince me to give up my adorable cottage. There I could sleep as long as I wanted to on the weekends. And, of course I loved decorating my own space with my own style. Then there were also the idiosyncratic neighbors with their dogs that physically resembled them, only with much more flair.

For example, Martha with her Irish Setter, Alex. He shared the same auburn colored hair as his mistress. And Martha, with a cigarette hanging out of her mouth, while Alex always marched

35

around with his two tennis balls in his mouth, makes a memorable vision.

But, my favorite is Guinevere. Yes, that really is her name. And, she, always has her white poodle, Godiva, dressed in some elegant pink outfit. Around her neck is a collar with her name in rhinestones and a crown.

"Sabriel? You up? We really need to leave here in ten minutes or there will be no surprise."

Bradley was yelling but he was not angry. There were times when I knew he was upset, but screaming in anger was never the way he expressed his frustration.

"Yes, Darling. Ten minutes, I promise," I said, now curious about what this surprise could possibly be.

Although I refused to move in permanently with Bradley, in his fashionable garden condo (where everything is always neat orderly), one of us was always in each other's bed at least five out of seven days a week.

"You have to agree Holly , that if you simply moved in with me you would get used to our routine much easier," Bradley said, quite seriously.

" OUR Routine? Don't you mean YOUR Routine? This situation seems to be working just fine thank you, Rhett Darling," I replied kissing him as we walked out the door.

I realized that refusing to move in with Bradly was something that we would need to discuss in more detail soon. But, after only three months, honestly I didn't want to abandon my independence. Unlike many people, I really do enjoy the hours by myself. It allows me time to think, imagine, and mostly relax without any expectations.

For awhile Bradley also enjoyed his own private world. We were both creatures of habit. So, we compromised and kept our own private spaces while spending nearly every night together in one of our two beds. But things were now moving more swiftly..

After that infamous night, eating that lobster aphrodisiac , drinking Cognac, and reading about Geese, sleeping alone made it even more difficult to stay apart We were now branches connected by the same tree.

In the beginning, we really did make an effort to keep our relationship, do I dare say "under the covers." But, soon, it became very obvious to the entire faculty that Dr. Bradley Welch was not the same. He was more joyful, and playful than usual. But, most of all he was always smiling.

"You have been shagging haven't you Professor? And, don't deny it to me Bradley. I have never seen you this glowing before. If you were a woman, people would say you were pregnant," Emma finally said one day.

After that there was no use denying our relationship.

"So, I give up Bradley. Are you going to tell me where we are going," I asked, anxiously.

"After our coffee and beignets, I promise," Bradley said, smiling.

That smile was really irresistible. It felt like the sunshine kissing my face.

"Okay, but, you do know that the longer you make me wait, the more I will want to know," I said sipping my coffee trying to be patient.

Bradley reached under the table, touched my knee and said," You know what happens to the curious cat, don't you?"

"No, not really. Are you going to tell me?" I asked, now truly curious, eager to hear his response .

" Well, my dear, that cat became the cat in the hat that lived in Wonderland," Bradley said, leading me out the door.

I was tempted to point out that the Cat in the Hat never visited Wonderland, but I knew by now that he would somehow spin that story into a believable scenario.

"We are here." Bradley said nonchalantly with no other explanation.

"The Hotel Monteleone. Are you feeling adventurous, Miss Holly?"

Bradley always called me "Holly" when he was in a playful mood. This is how our adventure for today began.

I knew already that this hotel, like so many others in New Orleans, was notable because authors like Ernest Hemingway, William Faulkner, and Tennessee Williams all spent time at The Carousel Bar.

But, if was Truman Capote who actually spent time here as a young child. He often reminisced about his mother locking him in a room whenever he did something annoying. Which apparently was quite often.

"Are we going to drink some mint juleps at The Carousel Bar, Mr.Butler?" I asked, now eager to role play in this historic setting.

"After we visit one of the suites. I was granted permission to take you to The Truman Capote suite. Some claim that this is where he first was inspired to write, *Breakfast at Tiffany's*. I thought, since you wrote your thesis on Capote, that this might be a great starting point," Bradley said.

"This is marvelous, darling," I said in my best Holly Golightly voice.

"But, what could possibly be better than standing in the room where my creator first gave me life," I added.

Arranging the head scarf that I always wore when Bradley chose to take his classic 1955 BMW 507 convertible out for a spin. Leaving my *Breakfast at Tiffany's* glasses on, added just the right vibe when the doorman let us in.

Bradley stopped briefly at the front desk, where he was given a key and we headed toward the elevator . Only a few people turned around to take a second look at me. I really was not planning on wearing my London Fog raincoat, but it did add just the right touch to my costume.

Inside, there was a brass plate placed on a round table that identified this as The *Truman Capote Suite*. What I first noticed was how spacious this room was. The parlor looked like about 430 square feet; half the size of the entire room.

The ornate chandelier was hanging directly over the dining table with four gold brocade chairs, that matched the gold brocade drapes. This was definitely a fashion statement that reflects Capote's desire to appear elegant, while still chic. His personality often demonstrated much of his bohemian life style. This was exactly what attracted me to his writing. It spoke directly to me, as if I was his only audience.

Bradley could see how consumed I was with all the specific details. On the coffee table were copies of *Other Voices Other Rooms, Answered Prayers, The Unfinished Novel,* and, of course, *Breakfast at Tiffany's.*

It really appeared as if this room was a replica of a Hollywood movie soundstage. Nevertheless, there is no dispute that Capote stayed here, and may have even lived in the hotel with his mother for a short time. The very fact that this talented, and troubled man would even choose to return to a place with such difficult memories is what fascinates me most about Truman Capote.

"Some people believe that it was in this hotel room where Capote first thought about *Breakfast at Tiffany's,*" Bradley said, interrupting my imagination.

"Do you know that in 1981 a reporter from *People* Magazine once interviewed Truman Capote on a bench in Jackson Square? He asked him why he returns to this city that holds so many skeletons. Capote's answer was, ' I get seized by a mood and I go. I stay a few weeks, and I read and write, and walk around. It's like a hometown to me.' When I read this I immediately believed that by returning here allowed him to purge some of his demons," I said, examining *The Breakfast at Tiffany's* copy one last time.

"I did hear that about him. In that same article he spoke about places that he enjoyed, from *The Caribbean Room* at the Pontchartrain Hotel, to the local cemetery. And, of course Gunga Den, the Bourbon Street burlesque club."

Bradley always impressed me how he was able to connect the dots that I would start about any literary topic. He truly is a genius, or somehow has found a way to read my mind.

"Yes, you are correct. In 2007 he included, *Portraits and Observations ,* his essay, on 'New Orleans 1946'. It was because Capote considered New Orleans, 'a secret place'. His detailed descriptions of characters and scenes from the French Quarter, was one of the many reasons I wanted to live here," I told, Bradley.

"Well then, I should be very grateful to Mr. Capote."

Bradley walked close to me and kissed me gently.

"Maybe a quick sexual tryst on Capote's bed, Holly. I sometimes fantasize what that would be like," Bradley whispered in my ear, holding me close.

"My, my Mr. Butler, what would Scarlett think of that," I said. Our eyes were now fixated on one another.

"You are certainly correct. My fantasy must remain just that. Do you want to see any other literary suites? There is a suite for, Tennessee Williams, William Faulkner, Ernest Hemingway, and, Eudora Welty?" Bradley asked.

"No, I don't think so. I want to let all of this settle in. Thank you so very much for such a considerate surprise," I said, walking toward the door.

"Well, I am pleased that you enjoyed this, but we are just beginning our journey ," Bradley said, feeling very satisfied that this day was moving perfectly as planned.

The Carousel Bar, downstairs, was now a great pit stop. On September 3, 1949 the hotel introduced a unique design where the cocktail lounge subtly rotates every fifteen minutes. Originally, the Swan Room, a popular nightclub, offered legendary acts like Liberace, on piano, and Louis Prima, playing Jazz on his saxophone.

"This is the same bar where Tennessee Williams alludes to in *The Rose Tattoo and Orpheus Descending.* And, even more contemporary, Rebecca Wells refers to this bar in *Divine Secrets of the Ya Ya Sisterhood ,* and *Little Alters Everywhere, "* Bradley said, trying to avoid lecturing.

"Is there anything that you don't know about New Orleans literary history?" I asked. This time sincerely impressed.

"Forgive me, please Sabriel if I start going off on a tangent. Sometimes the literary trespasses into the supernatural that I am researching. Anne Rice for example, includes so much voodoo, and vampires in her novel, *Interview with the Vampire.* Did you know that she was born right here in the Irish Channel section of New Orleans? She may be the main reason I started working on this project," Bradley said.

"Anything that you share with me is always eloquent. I am still not sure why you are attracted to me,"I said.

"Never doubt how much you contribute to this world, Sabriel, and to me. Have you ever had moments where the characters you are researching, come alive?" He asked.

"I never heard anyone else admit this, but yes, I know exactly what you mean. So far, those characters have kept there distance, but I know they are always nearby. Almost like they are waiting for me to make the first move."

What I was confessing to Bradley I never admitted to anyone else. It sounded crazy. And, it might be.

"When the time is right and you are ready, those characters will evolve. Always accept the energy that flows through you. That energy will soon open a truly new perspective of life," Bradley said, seriously.

The rest of the afternoon now felt like we were moving in tandem. There was less necessity to speak aloud and more internal sensations.

After finishing my Vieux Carree, the Carousel's most famous cocktail, created in 1938 by Walter Bergeron, I was a little light headed. But, it was time to move on.

Bradley refused to give me any clues , but once we left the city it became even more mysterious. I didn't have to know much about the terrain to realize that we were moving toward a wooded area.

"This area is known as *Honey Island Swamp.* It is one of Louisiana's last preserved wetlands. It is only accessible on a flatboat that will take us to an ancient Cajun Village," Bradley said, parking the convertible in an empty lot.

"Must not be a very popular tourist attraction. It looks empty,"
I said, reluctantly.

"Well, my Dear, that is because we have a private tour," he said, winking.

"This isn't going to be like that novel written by...? I don't remember his name. But it has that famous banjo scene?" I said, watching Bradley secure the car as if we were planning to be away for a very long time.

"*Deliverance?* Is that what you are alluding to? It was written by James Dickey. And, in 1972 a motion picture was released . That scene you remember is, '*Dueling Banjos'.* Anyway, in answer to your question, no, this will not be the same. That novel takes place on the fictional Cahulawassee River Valley, in Georgia."

Bradley was careful not to sound like he was lecturing.

"That is a relief. But, tell me more about this trip," I said, now genuinely interested.

"*The Honey Island Swamp,* was given that name because of the honeybees that could be seen swarming on a nearby island. It is not only one of the most pristine swampland habitats in America, it also is over twenty miles long. In addition to all the typical swamp animals, like alligators, raccoons, owls, wild boars, etc. it is also where 'Tainted Keitre' lives."

Bradley paused, waiting for me to respond.

After a few minutes of silence I could see we were nearing the dock where the flatboat was waiting. That was when I finally asked,

"Okay. You win. Who is this Grendel creature that lives in the swamp?"

"Similar to the legendary *Beowulf* manuscript, written anonymously around 1025, and, found on the British Isle, our creature, according to folklore, is a group of chimpanzees that escaped from a traveling circus and interbred with the local alligators . Those who have recorded sightings say that our *Grendel* is seven feet tall, with grey hair and, yellow red eyes. It also leaves a disgusting odor behind, similar to a skunk," Bradley said.

"And, please tell me once again why you brought me here to visit alligators, and swamp creatures?" I asked.

Bradley, put his arm around my waist, and said, "Because, my dearest Holly, if you are going to be a local you will need to learn about all the haunting and supernatural spirits that are with us daily. There is also a small cabin at the outskirts of the Creole Village that few know about. We have a lunch date with Aunt Katie Brown. No one knows how old this legendary voodoo priestess is, but some believe she is related to Aunt Julie Brown, from the Manchac Swamp who is well known for predicting hurricanes."

This was all very difficult to absorb. Bradley stopped with his story when we were greeted by the captain of this rather strange looking flatbed. It did have a sheltered seating area in the middle, but no other amenities were obvious.

Does it even have a bathroom? And I cannot see any life jackets. Like that would even matter once the alligators found you floating around.

"Welcome to *The Jean Lafitte* . She will be bringing you to places on earth that few have ever visited. Bradley, is a frequent visitor and has as much information as I do. So come on down the steps, find a comfortable seat, and NEVER put your hands outside of the boat."

The captain didn't need to go into detail about about keeping my hands inside. As soon as the boat began to move we were surrounded by alligators.

I didn't have to say anything to Bradley. My silence said it all.

About forty five minutes later the captain steered the boat to a very small homemade deck. We were greeted by an elderly woman wearing an apron over a gingham printed dress, wet boots, and a bandana on her head.

It was a silent reception. Nobody said a word, but Bradley guided me into the wood cabin that was sparsely furnished, but comfortable, and welcoming. On the round table was a loaf of homemade bread, bowls with jambalaya over grits, and cups of hot tea.

I was obviously here as a spectator, but it was also another way that Bradley was letting me in to his complicated, intrinsic life. Listening to him and Kate speaking Creole was fascinating. I had no idea that Bradley was able to understand, or even speak this French language.

Some people consider Creole, incorrectly, broken French, but in fact it is based on a blending of West African languages brought by the slaves and the French dialect. It is not easy to learn. Bradley must have spent many hours with someone who speaks Creole to have learned it this well to communicate.

I wasn't sure when it would be appropriate to ask him about this skill, or if I even wanted to know. What ways becoming quite obvious is that I was now traveling in one direction with no return. The longer I spend time with Bradley, the more questions I have. But, I also know that none of the answers would ever change how my feelings are now bond to his.

Chapter Seven

On days such as this, Death's long shadow hung like a broken halo over everyone—a sign of things to come.

—RW Patterson

SABRIEL and BRADLEY

Bradley:
"You're lease is about to expire soon? Am I correct?

Me: "Yes, I suppose it will. I wasn't really giving it much thought ."

Bradley: "Perhaps now is a very good time to consider it."

I lowered my reading glasses and placed the essays I was grading on the coffee table. Saturday mornings, if we had no plans during the day, was reserved for getting current with the academic part of our lives.

Before I was able to respond to Bradley's odd question, he was out the front door for his early morning jog. Whenever we spent the weekend at his condo the routine was consistent. Not regimented, but definitely organized by someone who is a creature of habit.

The Oxford English Dictionary does not provide the meaning of this idiom, but it does offer an interesting definition for creature.

"One who owes his fortune and position to a patron; one who is actuated by the will of another, or is willing to do his bidding; an instrument or puppet."

I also remember reading during my Linguistics Class that Sir B. Brodie, a respected psychologist in 1862, said, that if we use the term "creature of habit" as an analogy, the idea is enslavement, or victimization by a habit.

Is this what I was allowing to happen? The pre Bradley months, as I like to refer to them , were very unconventional; even Golightly, as in Holly. I was a free spirit. My gypsy lifestyle led me to many new adventures. That wandering desire led me to Bradley. But, now I have acquiesced to Bradley's traditional lifestyle. How did that ever happen? And, why did I ever let this happen? Not sure, but I am guessing it happened that first time we had sex. Since that moment I started to change my priorities, and really changed who I am. The only real trace of the old Sabriel is somewhere in my cottage home.

"Hey, there? Are you finished with those papers, cutie," Bradley asked.

He didn't wait for a response, but headed directly to the shower.

Another Bradley routine.

"Whatever you are grading must be real intense. You didn't even here me come in," Bradley said, from the nearby bedroom.

"Not really. I was just reflecting on this pathetic life I now have. This is what I am dwelling on," I said, knowing well that Bradley was already in the shower, not hearing anything that I said.

A few minutes later, Bradley appeared, with only a towel wrapped around his waist, his hair still wet, and the scent of fougere , the French word for fern. It was a natural fragrance that was very well suited to Bradley's pheromones (scented sex hormones).

"Did you have time to consider what we were discussing before I left for my jog, " Bradley finally said, taking a seat next to me on the couch.

"No, not really. But, I will soon," I said trying to ignore the strong androstenol scent.

This extreme sexual drive that was pulling me toward Bradley's half naked body was impossible to resist. Before I could get my natural instincts in check, I was straddled on his lap, he was the willing victim, and I the aggressor.

There was nothing about this that resembled "a creature of comfort." I was moving up and down Bradley's well oiled penis like it was my own personal vibrator.

Even Bradley's mouth sucking my breasts could not stop me from changing my position slightly. Now my legs moved to Bradley's shoulders. I was now the owner;

I was now in control, and the harder he became the deeper it went.

45

Time was irrelevant. It seemed non stop. And then, the climax came for us together, and I remembered why nothing else mattered in my life but him.

"Wow. Whatever it was that I put in your tea this morning I will have to do this more often," Bradley, said picking me up and taking me into his bedroom for the next act to this play.

It was now early afternoon, two hours later, when we finally stopped trying new positions . Each was more exciting than the previous one. But, it was not just the sexual satisfaction that kept both of us intense Something inside of our minds was developing. A new understanding for each other. A new appreciation for each other. It was as if something previously lost was now found.

"Will you please consider moving in here with me, Sabriel? You need to admit that what we have is truly special. When you are not here, neither am I. And, you must feel the same as I do," Bradley said, not willing to concede on this topic.

I got on my knees and moved slowly toward him, but, he stopped me half way, before I could answer. Both hands cradling my face, looking at me with those blue eyes, that said in my mind:

You are my freedom, intuition, faith and wisdom. Without you my life is shallow. Take me in; let me give you the relief needed to breathe the air, and inhale my spiritual soul.

I knew after that Bradley was worth relinquishing any fear or doubts about my future. He was my future.

Two weeks later, I gave my notice to the landlord that I was not going to renew my lease. That decision was not easy for me. I never let anyone get this close. The only time I ever shared my space was when I was forced to in the orphanage and my college dorms. Both places were extremely difficult for me to accept. They were also places that I had no choice but to accept. Since that time, I have always made certain that I have complete independence. That is my security; counting only on myself.

But, now it was time to accept that someone else was more important than me. It was a major, critical, and frightening decision. It was an unknown world. Waking up every night with someone only inches away. Accepting that person's peculiar habits, and asking him to do the same. Learning how to negotiate; knowing when to gracefully concede.

"I thought we might go out tonight to celebrate our first real night together as a couple. You know, a committed couple," Bradley said. I could tell he was genuinely excited.

Any commitment, other than to my academic career was new territory. I was not really even sure if I could be committed. I don't mean that I would ever cheat on Bradley. My love was never an issue. But, there are so many other ways to be unfaithful, and I would try not to be lured into that dark abyss. *God help me. God help us both.*

Chapter Eight

Between stimulus and response there is space. In that space is our power to choose our response. In our response lies our growth and our freedom.

—Vicktor Emile Frankl

SABRIEL

On July 7, 2017 Bradley and I became engaged. This event was one of two resolutes that I had made. Never to be engaged and never to own a dog. Both of those pledges were broken. Not intentionally I may add.

It was now nine months since I made that major leap to move in with Bradley. People in the college community did not seem surprised. Emma was ecstatic. She took all the credit.

"If it wasn't for me Bradley, we would still be having sushi every Wednesday night together until the end of our lives," Emma announced when Bradley told her the news in the faculty room.

I was quite glad that nobody else made any overtures about our relationship. Life just seemed to move on very much as before. Only now Bradley was making dinner for me almost every night and I was doing the laundry for two instead of one. No doubt, I had the best deal.

Then, when finals were over, Bradley asked me to go with him to Savannah for a few weeks. He was going to rent a beach house on Tybee Island and do some research in Savannah about the supernatural events that seem to connect somehow to the Creole voodoo in New Orleans.

Savannah was always someplace I wanted to visit when I was younger. After I read the novel by, John Berendt, *Midnight in the Garden of Good and Evil,* it was a place that I had to see. I was only fifteen years old then, still living in the Atlanta Orphanage.

The eccentric characters and the Southern Gothic tone, kept my interest, but it was the Hoodoo, West African folk magic, that Bradley was most interested in exploring.

"Hoodoo is a traditional African American spirituality. It is a mixture of several West African religions. The Gullah, are also known as African Americans that live in the Low-country, Georgia, Florida, and South Carolina. Their descendants still live in both the coastal plain, and the Sea Islands."

Bradley stopped to make certain that I was paying attention.

"Is all of this history lesson boring you, darling? I hope you will forgive me, it's just that I have spent several years gathering evidence to support my theory that there really does exist a 'Mojo' triangle, and that it is intentional, not merely a natural phenomenon," Bradley said, eager to get started.

"You have nothing to apologize for. I only wish that I had as much knowledge as you do. Being able to speak to Aunt Kate in her native Creole language is such an amazing accomplishment. And, although I might be a distraction to you while you are researching, I plan on doing some research myself, in downtown, Savannah," I said, arranging the straw hat that Bradley bought for me just for this trip.

" Well, you definitely look quite like a Southern Belle, I must say. More like Scarlett than Holly this morning. And, just to clarify any misconceptions, YOU NEVER are a distraction, unless I want you to be. We are actually the best couple I know," Bradley said, kissing me goodbye.

"Good luck on your ghost hunting. I will meet you back here at around five. Just in time for Happy Hour somewhere on this Island," I said, as he was walking toward the door.

"Every hour with you is my Happy Hour. And, I have dinner reservations taken care of, so you just have a fun time sightseeing in Savannah," Bradley said, before I could ask where we were going for dinner.

Most of what I brought was casua since Tybee Island is a beach resort town. But, if I find anything downtown Savannah that is perhaps a little more dressy I might splurge and buy something for this evening.

Tybee Island is eighteen miles from downtown Savannah. When Bradley decided to make reservations here, rather than in the city, I questioned his reasoning . But, he told me that he wanted us to enjoy being on the beach, unwinding after a long semester, and that Savannah is a charming city to visit, but there is just nothing more meditating than being near the ocean, hearing the waves at night. He was right. I never lived by the ocean before. But, just stepping out of our back door and feeling the warmth of the sun penetrating through the grainy sand convinced me why people spend a fortune to live here.

In Savannah I chose to hire a horse drawn carriage rather than the touristy tram. Since I was by myself it really did feel like a private tour. Marty, my tour guide, lived here his entire life, and shared with me personal experiences as well as the historical details.

At Forsyth Park , Marty explained to me, the Confederate Memorial was designed to be in the middle of the park with the pathway wrapping around it.

"Marty, is it possible to make this a literary tour? I know that you didn't advertise this in the pamphlet, but I will be glad to pay you extra?" I asked, sincerely hoping to see more than the traditional monuments and landmarks.

"Certainly. Miss. Pepper and I will be happy to accommodate any special requests. As a matter of fact, the literary tour is our favorite. Many of these authors I taught in my classes at Savannah High School, many years ago," Marty said.

"That would be wonderful. Thank you for being so kind," I said.

I chose not to tell Marty that I taught Literature at New Orleans. Hearing his narration would be much more authentic if he doesn't feel as I am testing him.

The morning with Marty lasted nearly three hours. It was a fascinating time listening to him add his personal reflections while showing me where Flannery Connor lived as a child, and a more current author, Chris Fuhrman, author of *The Dangerous Lives of Altar Boys*. That novel, I learned, was set in Savannah. Marty also shared with me that Fuhrman was born here in Savannah in 1960.

"Unfortunately, Chris died in 1990 of cancer. While he was attending *Blessed Sacrament School,* here in Savannah. We were acquaintances. Not really friends, but sometimes we were with the same groups," Marty added , while showing me his home.

There were so many other wonderful locations that Marty took me to, including the famous *Bonaventure Cemetery* mentioned in

Midnight in the Garden of Good and Evil. Marty added that the Bird Girl statue, pictured on the cover of that novel is now in The Telfair Museum. This is where Marty and I parted. I wanted to personally see the statue. Not sure why. Maybe just to know that I was able to, was enough without further explanation..

"Make sure that you visit E Shaver Book Seller at 6 East Liberty Street. There are some good choices of books by authors who have chosen Savannah as a setting. It is also a favorite local place to sit and sip a good cup of tea in their parlor," Marty said, as he and Pepper left, on their way to a shady place for a well deserved lunch break.

Bird Girl statue was actually more impressive than I expected. It is cast in bronze and stands fifty inches tall. The image of a young girl , with a sad expression, wearing a simple dress, head tilted , provokes a melancholy atmosphere. Her elbows propped against her waist holding two bowls almost appears sacred.

A curator leading a group through the museum explained that the original statue was made in 1935 by an artist known as Sylvia Shaw Judson. That statue is in Illinois , at her summer estate. It only achieved fame once it was used on the cover of *Midnight in the Garden of Good and Evil.*

There were only four statues made from the original plaster cast. This one, now in the museum, is the fourth and most famous. Originally it was located at the Trosdal family plot in the *Bonaventure Cemetery.* But, due to so many people curious to see the statue, it was removed by the family and loaned to the museum.

Since it has been such a long time since I read that novel, I decided to buy a copy and read it while we are staying at Tybee. It might be an interesting way to experience the events by visiting the landmarks that Berendt alluded to in the novel.

Finding the E.Shaver Book Seller was very easy. Everyone knew where it was. When I arrived I understood why is was so popular..

First, I was greeted by a lovely cat, whose name I later discovered was Bartleby . Named after, I presume,
Bartelby the Scivener, by Herman Melville. Then,. Jessica Melbourne, the bookstore owner, led me to the section that included regional novels set in Savannah. *Midnight in the Garden of Good and Evil,* was showcased. I found a copy, without disturbing the

display. Then I noticed another cat, with a collar around his neck that identified him as Mr. Eliot.

T.S Eliot has always been my favorite poet to teach. But, this Mr. Eliot was curled next to a few books in the back. I reached for a copy, and Mr. Eliot mewed as if he was approving my choice.

On the cover of this novel was the Tybee Lighthouse. The title was, *Destiny Revisited,* by an unknown author, Eleanor Tremayne. As I read the synopsis the story it sounded interesting. After all, Mr. Eliot recommended it.

When I went to the register another cat appeared from nowhere. When I asked Jessica who her helper was she said, "This is Skimbelshanks. Are you familiar with the musical *Cats?"*

"Yes, of course. He is the very bright and energetic orange tabby that lives on the mail trains," I said.

"I am impressed. Most people have no idea who he is, even after I tell them he is a character from the musical," Jessica said

"T.S Eliot is a favorite of mine. As a matter of fact he suggested I read this book, *Destiny Revisited.* I decided it was a good choice since we are staying at Tybee Island for a week," I said.

"Eleanor was here last year for a book signing. I understand that she lives in St. Augustine, Florida, now. Only a few hours from here. If you have never visited St. Augustine it is well worth the drive," Jessica said, handing me my purchases.

I wonder if Bradley knows about St. Augustine? Maybe if he finishes his research early we can take a scenic drive to the oldest city in America. I bet that ancient town has some interesting stories to tell.

I looked at the time on my watch. It was 3:30pm.

Oh my. It will take me thirty minutes to drive home and another hour to get dressed. No time for shopping. Hope wherever Bradley made dinner reservations is casual dress.

Then I saw it. In the boutique window right in front of where I parked was the most perfect little black dress that I have ever seen.

I walked in, told the salesperson I wanted that dress in the window. She informed me that it was the last one available.

I looked at the size. It may be a little snug, but what the hell. I had to have it.

"Okay, I will take it," I said, and handed her my credit card.

Five minutes later I was in the car driving back to Tybee Beach. I have never purchased any clothing that fast. I never read books more than once. And, I never buy books from authors not recommended, or that I at least read a review on.

It must just be something about Savannah.

Chapter Nine

We are confident , I say, and are willing rather to be absent from the body and to be present with the Lord.

—II Cornithians 5:8
(Inscription on pedestal of Bird Girl)

BRADLEY

Savannah's enigmatic energy is captured in the cobblestone streets, neighborhoods with moss laden trees , and the bloody fields where soldiers died during The Siege of Savannah, in 1779. Add to this the 1820 Yellow Fever epidemic that took a tenth of Savannah's population and, it becomes much easier to accept why many people have determined that this city is haunted.

It is this paranormal activity that begins in New Orleans, travels to Savannah, and continues flowing to St. Augustine, Florida that I have been tracing for the last two years. Each of these cities are breeding grounds for spirits. There is no debate on this.

But, why? Why do these spirits seem to travel in this triangle? Every visit I feel that I am getting closer to the answers, yet, I am unable to support my thesis with tangible evidence. It isn't easy to convince spirits to come out of their closets. Those supernatural spaces are also where they feel safe.

The conundrum is, that the few spirits that have appeared to me enjoy the companionship; the connection to life, but they have no desire to return permanently. When they first started appearing, I thought that they were restricted on how often or how long they could remain. Later, when they became more comfortable with me, a bond of trust began to form and I learned that it was the Spirit who controlled the length of their visits.

Including Sabriel on this trip was a challenge and risk. I have no idea if any Spirits will surface once they know we are together. I am not aware of any being jealous of my relationships. Nevertheless, this is a chance I have to take.

Distractions due to Sabriel seems to be quite the contrary. Since she has moved in with me, the spirits are determined to include her in our supernatural activities; internally rather than externally, as I have experienced.

During my meeting with Kate on the Bayou, now nearly a year ago, she strongly advised me to visit a place known as the *The Magic Mushroom* in Savannah.

"This is the place where you will find many answers to your questions about Sabriel. Some answers you may not want to know, but Jada will tell you the truth boy, if that's what you are searchin' for."

Kate's words were still fresh in my mind when I approached the small strip mall looking for this Voodoo haven. Most of the other businesses appeared to be normal. There was a tattoo shop anchoring this small lot. Next to that, was a barber shop, dry cleaners, two vacant spaces and a pub. *The Mellow Mushroom* was lit up on the outside but all the windows were darkened not allowing any sunlight in.

But, then again all this makes perfect sense. If you are harvesting mushrooms they do best in the dark.

I parked directly in front and noticed that the only other two cars were near the pub.

Either this strip mall is slowly dying or the Savannah residents haven't discovered it yet.

The inside of the establishment was as odd as the outside. It took me a few minutes to adjust my eyes to the darkness. But then the first thing I saw was a blonde girl that looked Creole with long dreads. She was standing next to a life size poster of *Screamin Joe Hawkins* with the words:

"I put a SPELL on you…

beCAUSE you're MIIIIIIINE!"

Now I knew I was in the right place.

"Excuse me. Do you know where I can find Jada? A friend of mine from the Bayou said I could find her here?" I asked , not getting much of a response.

I looked around to see if there was anyone else that could help since this dreads girl was not responding.

As I expected, the room smelt of incense and herbs laced with a few aromatic lit candles. There was also some bookshelves that offered patrons methods of self medicating their problems by using various oils with specific spells written out to follow at home.

Just as I was thumbing through one book with an exotic cover resembling a skull surrounded by feathers, an African American woman with the deepest blue eyes appeared from behind the beaded curtain. I have seen many Creole Cajun ladies from Haiti to Paris but none ever looked this provocative.

It was with her eyes alone that made me follow her every move. After what seemed like a lengthy time of silence, she took my hand and lead me to another room behind the screen. It was filled with greenery. There were even large trees with moss hanging from branches. It felt as if we had entered Eden and I was being led by a glorious serpent.

"You are here to seek advice? If so, understand that Jada cannot see the future. She can only tell you about the present, and how it will effect your future. Do we understand each other?"

I cleared my throat and answered

"Yes, I fully understand."

The ceremony now begins. A familiar Christian prayer comes from some unknown speaker. Then the drums play syncopated rhythms with guitars. Cymbals, and flutes are introduced. To my right is a screen that shows people dancing in a circle around a pond with a fountain in the middle. Then a woman, with a mask, collapses in what appears to be a trance. Another woman goes to her knees, removes the mask and I notice that the face revealed is Sabriel. I stand up and begin objecting to what I am seeing.

"How have you found Sabriel? Why is she here in this condition. I refuse to let you harm her."

I realize that my voice is now loud and threatening.

"What you are watching is what is happening. But, not in the way you are witnessing it. It is Sabriel's spirit that you see, not her physical being. It is an honor for Eizula, the great mother spirit to fill Sabriel with a Loa, or blessed spirit. If she is to be your other half she must learn the power of the Gullah-based tradition here in the Low Country which is considerably different than in New Orleans," Jada said, trying to reassure me.

Although, it was comforting to know that Sabriel was not experiencing this ritual physically, I was not even confident that she would accept my marriage proposal.

"What happens Jada, if Sabriel rejects my offer of marriage. How will all of this effect her?"

"First, Bradley it is to your advantage to make this happen, but regardless if you are with Sabriel or not, she has her own inner Loa apart from you. There is a pantheon of spirits that some gifted people attract. Sabriel is still learning how to appreciate this," Jada said.

Our session lasted over one hour. When it was completed I was gifted the *lingua Franca,* a common tongue among many isolated plantations. How I chose to use what I was given in the future was my decision.

When I left Jada I finally understood that the physical interactions, both intimate and social, have advanced between Sabriel and I to a level of mirroring one another. Jada just confirmed that the time was now to move to our next stage of relationship.

Since Sabriel may soon experience sightings like I have, I must let her know what to expect. Then she will decide if she is ready to accept this lifestyle.

Tonight, we move to that next level. Tonight I will propose marriage, after I explain to her what she may expect. Waiting any longer makes no sense. I fell in love with Sabriel before I even saw her. In that bookstore, eighteen months ago, it was her enchanting eyes that held me in her power. Feeling her body during our first sexual encounter, I knew she was more Spirit, than human. Now I know why.

Chapter Ten

THE POT CALLS THE COFFEE POT...

Hey, Cajun
and you, Creole
how come you call yourself white
or black? Who gave you these names?
We are the descendants of the French, the Spanish, the Africans,
the Indian, the Acadian, the Haitian,
and all the other Gombo People who came to Louisiana. These
spices made the Gombo.
Our rich culture serves as our common bond.
We are the same Paprika blood, and that blood connects us with the
world...
And, all the worst for those who do not like what we are. How long
can they look at us and tell us we don't exist?...

—Sybil Keon, *Gombo People*

SABRIEL

I wasn't running away from anything when I decided to move to New Orleans from Atlanta. But, I also wasn't trying to find a permanent base. Do you know how many people never leave their hometown because that is their safety net? I am just the opposite.

It is not because I spent time in the orphanage either. Although that might contribute to why I have no roots. There has just always been this feeling inside of me that there is something better right around the corner.

Anticipation motivates me more than any other factor. My best, and only childhood real friend, Debbie, she prefers Deb, used to call me a gypsy. I am not quite a gypsy yet. It is more accurate to say that I am a gypsy in training.

Anyway, whatever I am at this moment, I do admit that I have never known what it feels like to belong.

I prefer large groups. I don't ever need to spend much time with anyone alone. I feel the most comfortable standing in front of a podium speaking to large crowds who are sitting at a distance. That is my perfect setting; my comfort zone.

New Orleans. It was a perfect place. I could just fade in and out whenever I chose. The ethnic, social, and economic tapestry of diversity, was just what I needed. This is truly the melting pot of our nation.

Then I met Bradley. It was just going to be a casual professional relationship. Absolutely nothing sexual. And if it did end up sexual, not permanent.

Now, eighteen months later I am in this lovely cottage on Tybee Island waiting for the man I am in love with to return home so that I can share all my new stories about Savannah.

We drove here in my Jeep Cherokee , because I refused to go 642 miles in Bradley's sports car even if it is a classic BMW. And, once we arrived here, we needed to rent another car so that Bradley would be able to move around without worrying about me during the day.

Thankfully, I was back to the cottage in plenty of time to be ready, even a few minutes early.

I poured a chilled glass of Chardonnay that we opened last night, and moved to the outside patio to watch the beach walkers and ocean.

"I'm back, sweetheart. Just going to take a quick shower. I promise to be ready in ten minutes," Bradley said, moving to the only bedroom.

It must be nice to be able to take only ten minutes to get ready. I would never complain about the few times Bradley has ever been late. He is a perfectionist and time freak. But, he has never complained about my tardiness.

As promised, Bradley was ready in ten minutes, exactly.

"You look marvelous, Holly. Where did you find that 'little black' dress? How was Savannah? Tomorrow I can go with you and maybe fill in any of the gaps you may still have about the city," Bradley said, grabbing his sports coat.

"I will tell you all about my day at dinner, and can't wait to hear about your meeting. I have been curious all day where you are taking me for dinner," I said, tossing him my car keys.

"*The Old Pink House,* downtown Savannah. Did you happen to see it while you were out today?" Bradley asked..

"Yes, I did as a matter of fact. Marty told me all about it," I said, coyly.

"Marty? It didn't take you long to find a replacement for me," Bradley said, smiling keeping his eyes on the road.

"Well, if you must know the truth, Marty isn't your competition it is Pepper. He is the one that stole my heart," I said.

"Then you know all the history and ghost sightings by now. To be honest there are not many places in this city that don't have some supernatural story. But, *The Pink House* also has some wonderful southern dishes that I know you will enjoy," Bradley said, finding a parking place very close to the restaurant.

"We are so glad that you could join us this evening, Dr. Welch. We saved your table, facing the garden. We have had a great crop of fireflies recently. They should provide you with an entertaining show tonight."

"Thank you, Sean. I appreciate you saving me the best table tonight," Bradley said, pulling out my chair for me to sit.

From my vantage point I could clearly see the lush grass surrounded by a variety of fern, and blooming magnolias. This was truly a beautiful setting after a busy afternoon.

"Thank you so much Bradley for including me in this trip. I have enjoyed visiting the literary district and talking to many of the locals. Oh, and I bought a novel that I never heard of before, *Destiny Revisited.* I don't recall the author's name, but she lives in St. Augustine, not far from here. Did you know this?" I asked, curiously.

"Yes, of course. I was going to tell you about this tonight as a surprise, but, as I am getting used to it now, you somehow have found a way to capture not only my heart, but my head," Bradley said, reaching for my hand.

It was the first time that Bradley was saying what I already knew. Whatever has happened between us, and I have no idea what that is, I am glad that Bradley has now addressed it.

"Regardless, there is one surprise that I don't believe you are ready for."

Bradley reached into his pocket, took out a brilliant diamond ring, and placed it perfectly on my finger.It took my breath away, and I was speechless.

Finally, after several moments of silence, Bradley said,

"I love you Sabriel, for always and forever. You are my reason for living and without you life will never be the same. Please be my wife," Bradley said, waiting patiently.

"Yes. Yes. Of course I will be your wife," I said.

Bradley walked over to my side of the table, and we kissed, while from somewhere unknown I heard, *Moon River,* playing in the background and the entire restaurant was clapping and cheering.

The remainder of the evening was a blur. I don't know what I ate. Not even sure when we returned home. After dinner Bradley took me to several jazz bars where we met some local professors. He introduced me to them as his "fiancée.

The celebration continued all night with plenty of champagne. So much champagne that I only slightly remember Bradley lifting me from the car and carrying me into the house. This is all I remember. Everything else went blank.

*The next morning I was laying next to my fiancé. A wonderful man that chases ghosts and spirits during his pastime. And yet, for the very first time in my entire life I felt whole. Then this movie I saw years ago, **Jerry Maguire,** flashes into my mind. It is a specific scene I see in my memory. Jerry says, 'you complete me' to describe how much he loves Dorothy, the Renee Zellweger character. Does Bradley complete me? Do I need to be completed? Why do I need to be completed? Why did I say yes so quickly? And, what happens if today I say no? Damn it! Why did Bradley make this so complicated?*

"Good morning, darling.No regrets about last night? I mean other than having a bad hangover this morning?" Bradley asked, cuddling next to me.

Feeling the warmth of his body, and his breathing on my neck while cradling me in his strong muscular arms I knew that this was real.

Bradley did so much more than complete me. To complete me suggests that I was empty without him. And, if I lose him will that make me a hollow person? Jerry Maguire might feel that Dorothy completes him, but It is I that will be Bradley's Maat, the Egyptian Goddess of Justice. Together we will balance the truth, honesty, love, and passion that completes us both.

"Well, my head does feel like someone used it as a soccer ball. But, not even that will change my answer from last night. I am afraid that you now will have to share the rest of your life with me," I said, whispering .

Bradley, jumped out of bed, like he was a sprinter.

"Perfect. Now let's get some coffee and check out *Moon River,* Holly Golightly. It should make you feel right at home."

Before I could even respond, we were showering together, cleaning each other's body. It felt like a baptismal ritual. There was no sex. What we were experiencing was so much more. Our lips were now one. Our hands were now together as in prayer. At this moment it was only God that was with us. We both felt blessed.

I was now ready to start enjoying life. I looked at the engagement ring on my finger. It was the first time that I noticed the size of the center diamond. It had to be over two carats.. The round halo cut was sparkling so bright that there were images that looked like stardust on the windows.

"I hope you like the ring?" Bradley said, noticing how preoccupied I was.

"If you prefer selecting your own, I really won't mind," Bradley added.

I reached across the passenger side of the car, placed my finger on his lips and said, "This ring is perfect. Nothing that I would ever choose could compare to this ring. It must have cost you a fortune Bradley. Now I know why everyone was holding my hand last night. You will never need to worry about any other man ever hitting on me. This ring can be seen fifty feet away," I said, adding some comic relief.

"If only it was that easy. You have no idea how charming you are, Holly Golightly. Truman Capote once wrote, 'Never love a wild thing ...if you let yourself love a wild thing , you'll end up looking up the sky.'"

I chose not to respond to Bradley's last comment, instead, I changed the topic.

"Are you going to tell me all about *Moon River,* and what makes it so important to the movie?" I asked, enjoying the Savannah landscape.

"Oh no. You're the Capote scholar. I'm just the driver. I expect that you will share with me what you know," Bradley said.

I wasn't sure if I believed him, but I did tell him what I knew. And, Bradley filled in the historical notations.

Henry Mancini was commissioned to write a song that Audrey Hepburn would sing as Holly Golightly. No one ever expected that when Johnny Mercer added the words that the result would be not only mesmerizing but lasting.

There is no one who has ever watched the scene where Holly is singing *Moon River,* while strumming on her guitar on the fire escape without feeling melancholy.

But, today that mood was not going to consume us. Today we were going to rewrite the ending to *Breakfast at Tiffany's.*

Chapter Eleven

*Ashes to Ashes, dust to dust; all lie down around the Mulberry Bush
London Bridges falling down; heavy rain, heals all pain.*
                                                    —Destiny Revisited

SABRIEL

O
n our drive to St. Augustine I remembered the novel I picked
up at that quaint book store in Savannah. The one with all
the curious cats named after literary characters.

Destiny Revisited. An interesting title. Not sure why anyone would,
or even want to revisit their destiny, but I was about to find out.

"Why exactly are we going to St. Augustine, Bradley? " I asked,
thumbing through the novel on my lap.

"Well darling, as I recall, it was you that suggested that we go.
Something about that author and the book you are reading," Bradley
said, keeping his eyes on the road.

"Yes, that is what I said. But, you told me that you were planning
on perhaps going there anyway," I said.

"St. Augustine draws millions of visitors from around the world
for various reasons. It even has its own lighthouse, much more
haunting than that one on that cover of your novel." Bradley pointed
to the Tybee Island Lighthouse, on *Destiny Revisited.*"

"But, for us, I think it will be a great place to complete our Mojo
triangle tour and explore the ancient city," Bradley, said.

I decided to put aside my reading for when I return home to New
Orleans. It will be a good souvenir and memory of our engagement
in Savannah.

Not knowing anything about St. Augustine, I asked Bradley to
give me some highlights. Naturally, that encouraged him to begin his
lecture. It was about a two hour drive but, by the time we were a few
miles from our destination I knew almost all about the historical
details, and even a few interesting literary lessons.

First, St. Augustine was established in 1565, by Pedro Menendez de Aviles. According to all historical accounts, Pedro was responsible for easily defeating the French garrison who occupied the fort, mercilessly slaying anyone, who refused to convert to Catholicism. It was a massacre so horrible that in memory of all those killed, that site just south of St. Augustine was named, Matanzas , Spanish for Slaughters.

After hearing this, I was rather apprehensive of what I might see. But, as we entered the ancient city, Fort Matanzas was the first visible sight, in contrast to the calm setting of the Marina. Docked in the harbor was an assortment of wealthy yachts, sailboats, and speedboats. And, directly across the street were numerous buildings that reflected another time period in the architecture.

"What do you think, Sabriel? Is it what you expected?" I heard Bradley ask as I saw a lovely horse drawn carriage pass by.

"I am not certain what I was expecting but, I am feeling like this is another world. Like that musical, *Brigadoon,"* I said, still in awe of my surroundings.

"That is a very good analogy, Holly. I always feel the same way when I return. Thankfully, unlike *Brigadoon* , where the villagers are not allowed to leave, we may visit as often and as long as we like. And, there is so much supernatural, or what many locals like to call haunted, to explore that I return here as often as I can," Bradley said.

Before I could ask how long this visit was going to last, we were pulling into an alley that was leading us to a small parking lot behind a quaint building that looked like a cottage, from a fairy tale.

"Welcome to The St. Francis. It is where I stay whenever I want to learn more about paranormal activities. We are here in the center of town, yet excluded from any personal visits from the spirits. I hope you will find it as charming as I do," Bradley said.

I wonder how many other ladies were guests here with Bradley? It is not something that I would ever ask, but it was something that came to my mind almost instantly.

"Good afternoon Dr. Welch. We are so glad that you are visiting us. It has been a while…at least a few years?"

"I think you are correct, Marge. I have been preoccupied in New Orleans with classes, and…of course my most lovely distraction, Dr. Shelley."

Marge extended her hand to meet me. I was curious if Bradley was going to add that I was his fiancé, or leave it at just another paramour he was impressing.

"Pleasure meeting you Marge, please call me Sabriel, it is certainly less formal," I said, trying to be quite natural while feeling awkward.

"Yes, of course Marge, you can also refer to Sabriel or ' Holly'. That is my affectionate name for her. I can share that now, since we became engaged last night in Savannah," Bradley said, proudly.

Marge looked relieved, and genuinely happy for both of us.

"Oh, Bradley, that is such exciting news. I am sending up a chilled bottle of champagne to your room. I just hope none of your other lovers will mind you sharing a bed with such a beautiful human," Marge said, laughing.

It did take me a few seconds to understand that Marge was joking. She must have noticed the strange look on my face because she added,

"I assume that Bradley has shared with you the paranormal activities that our hotel is known for? Actually, the whole town is home to many ghostly apparitions."

"Thank you, Marge for informing Sabriel of your permanent boarders at *The St. Francis,*" Bradley said, as we began to walk through the airy lobby.

"Nobody knows how old Marge is, or how many years she has been the proprietor here. There are many interesting theories that I won't bore you with," he said, unlocking the door to our room.

"Oh, and just to reassure your curious mind, no, I have never brought anyone else here with me."

I looked at Bradley thoroughly confused and yet relieved.

"Can you read my mind, Bradley?" I asked.

"Not any more than you can read mine," Bradley said, kissing my forehead gently.

Obviously not wanting to discuss this topic any further, Bradley took my hand and led me to the outside balcony. It was an interesting view that overlooks St. Francis Park.

"This view is certainly not as impressive as the one from *The Plaza* of Central Park. But, there is a certain charm knowing that you are experiencing the tranquil ambiance of a place where echoes of the past can be heard and sometimes even seen," Bradley said, sharing this moment with me.

There was definitely a different sense of being; almost as if I was in a different time zone. If I were to write this in my journal I would compare this feeling as to stepping out of my modern world as a visitor to the sixteenth century. Very much like Mark Twain's novel, *A Yankee in King Arthur's Court.* I was ready to expect many different emotions in the next few days ..

"Marge mentioned that there are ghosts that still roam this Inn. Have you personally seen any?" I asked, so that I could prepare myself if any appeared to me.

Bradley, uncorked the champagne that was sent to our room, poured each of us a glass, and took a seat across from me on the plush settee.

"What I can assure you darling, is that I have never slept with any ghosts, and that none of the ones I know will be jealous of you," Bradley said, taking a sip of the champagne.

"That isn't really what I asked but, it is good to know. What I am really curious about is why do these ghosts remain here. Is there a reason why their spirits are not able to rest where everyone else goes when they die?" I asked.

"That is a very astute question , my Holly. You surprise and impress me every moment we spend together. I can't wait until the world knows that I married the wisest woman on this planet," Bradley said, reaching over and kissing my hand.

"Am I going to get an answer Professor, or just flattery?" I asked.

What came next was a Paranormal lesson that hopefully would prepare me for future sightings. Although, there was no way that Bradley could prepare me for what would happen eighteen months later.

I did learn some important differences between ghosts and spirits. Bradley, showed me on his lap top the following quote by the late Hans Holzer, Professor of Parapsychology and, author of one hundred and nineteen books on this subject.

As I read on, Holzer states:

"Ghosts are similar to psychotic human beings, capable of reasoning for themselves...Spirit's, on the other hand, are the surviving personalities of all of us who pass through the door of death in a relatively normal fashion."

"What I have found is that ghosts often times don't even realize that they are dead. I cannot even begin to explain how often these ghosts will talk to me about events that to them occurred yesterday, but historically it happened several hundred years ago. St. Augustine, because of its historical location, and being the center of so many years of activity, is by nature a place where ghosts remain," Bradley said.

I was fascinated, and yet slightly uncomfortable. Surrounded by all of this natural beauty, and four centuries of legends wherever I walk makes me truly feel like an invader.

"You never need to feel like that, Sabriel. The spirits that are also here will always make you feel welcome, if you don't fight it," Bradley assured me.

Bradley was right. While he was busy with his research I spent my days walking the one hundred and forty four square blocks within the St. Francis Inn. Besides the striking architecture and the narrow brick paved streets, there were numerous museums, galleries, antique stores.

What I enjoyed most about this ancient city was discovering so many secret alleys that would lead to alfresco dining among arbors of flowering jasmine, or tea shops that invites you to take a few sips faraway from the "maddening crowds".

Our final dinner at St. Augustine was at *Collage*. It was a magnificent restaurant, intimate, and relaxing. The perfect place to end a perfect vacation.

"Have you enjoyed this preview of what to expect? If not, I will totally understand. My life is definitely abnormal," Bradley said waiting for my response .

Abnormal? Bradley has no idea how abnormal my life has been for over thirty years. What I should be telling him, is that his fiancé is anything but normal. But, I think I will let him discover this for himself. Anyone who spends their free time searching ghosts, may just be able to accept my flaws.

"Sorry Professor Welch, it looks like you are stuck with me. And, you were right about St. Augustine. It is like no other city that I have ever visited. I love New Orleans, but St. Augustine with its magic and beaches has captured my heart," I said.

"As long as there is still room in your heart for me, I won't object. We will return often and you will learn to love it as much as I do."

Months later I would remember those words. The next time that I would return to St. Augustine, I would be carrying Bradley in an ornate urn, recalling the words on that first page of Destiny Revisited...Ashes to ashes, Dust to dust...

Chapter Twelve

For life and death are one , even as the river and the sea are one.

—Kahlil Gibran

BRADLEY

Sharing my Mojo Triangle trip with Sabriel, our engagement, and knowing that we would be sharing so much of our lives together forever gave me such peace that it seemed that finally I had found the missing link to my reason for living.

Our wedding was small, and private. Sabriel had no family to invite, and I only had Emma. I asked her to be my "bestie". I needed her that day more than I realized.

Sabriel, invited Ingrid, her only close friend from Atlanta to be her "Best Maid".., and other than the non-denominational pastor, the photographer, and two couples, we didn't even know, who were vacationing at the same resort that was our wedding group..

Neither Sabriel, or I desired to turn our wedding into a public spectacle. Everything that day was going to be quite spontaneous, like both of our personalities.

During our winter break. we were looking forward to visiting somewhere exotic and relaxing. After that busy fall semester spending a few weeks off, at the Bahamas was ideal.

"I have a good friend, actually a movie producer, who lives in Hollywood that bought a lovely home in Nassau. Martha and I have visited it there often during the holidays. If you want to stay there I will give him a call?" Blaine offered.

Blaine was one of the few professors outside of the English Department that I occasionally spent time with. He was a Sociologist also interested in the occult. We would share our research, and often talk about collaborating what we discovered and co-publish. Although that never happened.

"I know that you and Sabriel are planning some rest and relaxation away from this 'battlefield', but Nassau also has some great places to investigate the paranormal," Blaine added.

"I don't know about the paranormal activities during this visit with Sabriel. We spent a few weeks doing the *Mojo Triangle*. She was a good sport, but I don't want to push my luck. If you could ask your producer friend if his property is available, and send me any pictures you have, I will share the idea with Sabriel," I said.

The next evening Blaine sent me pictures. They were labeled "*Nirvana Oasis*".

"It is available for two weeks during Christmas and New Years. Check out the pictures. The name says it all. You won't be disappointed my friend."

And, Blaine was right. These pictures were unbelievable. The house was magnificent. Six master bedrooms, four additional bathrooms, one located outside in the beach cabana, next to the infinity pool, that was directly overlooking the most varied colors of blue ocean that I have ever seen in this world.

Somewhere I recall reading an article about a Canadian astronaut, Chris Hadfield, who was asked about his "spaceship's-eye" view, from The International Space Station. He claimed that the most beautiful sight for him was the Bahamas. Hadfield said that he was mesmerized by the "vast glowing reefs of every shades of blue that exists."

I of course already knew this and agreed with every word. The Bahamas offered Sabriel and I an opportunity to escape a few weeks and regenerate our tired souls.

When I finally shared the video and photos that Blaine sent me, Sabriel was delighted just like a young child being told she could choose any gift she ever wanted.

"I have never in my life seen such a magnificent view as this one, and we can see it everyday, all day for two weeks? Can we afford this, Bradley? I mean two weeks in Paradise, or 'Nirvana' might cost us a fortune." The stars in Sabriel's eyes began to fade away.

"No worries, sweetheart. This property belongs to a producer friend of Blaine's and it costs nothing. It even includes a chef that prepares our meals, and a driver who will take us wherever we want. So, what do you say? Shall we spend the holidays in the Bahamas 'man'," I said, dancing my best reggae interpretation.

" Oh yes, Bradley!...But, wait. What about Emma? You always spend the holidays together. And, I already invited Ingrid to stay with us during one of those weeks." Sabriel said, now confused with the excitement of complications.

"This estate has six bedrooms. Ingrid and Emma can join us. We can all celebrate together," I said, proud that I found the solution.

"Oh, Bradley. I just had the greatest idea. Let's get married at the Bahamas on New Year's Day. It will be perfect. Both our best friends will be there, and we will start the New Year truly in a memorable way," Sabriel said, waiting for me to respond.

"Perfect. I will leave all those details up to you and the girls. My responsibility will be the flowers, music, and reception," I said, embracing my beautiful Sabriel.

We were both busy the two weeks before our vacation with the details of the wedding and finalizing all of our university duties. But, it was an exciting time of the year, watching everyone prepare for Hanukkah, Christmas, Los Posadas, Kawanzaa, and any other celebrations I may have missed.

While Sabriel and Emma were out every day shopping for the "impeccable, perfect" wedding dress, I was researching the venues at Nassau for the best place to consummate our marriage.

Since Blaine and I were both very familiar with the Bahamas area I included him in my search.

"Have you considered the *Atlantis* on Paradise Island? They have a great location, and the food is superb. But, they may be booked on New Year's Eve already," Blaine suggested one afternoon when we met for beer at *Famous Door*

"*Atlantis*, is a beautiful place to visit, and I definitely intend to take Sabriel there for lunch, drinks, or maybe a show. But, I am really searching for something more intimate. We don't want the New Year's gala to overshadow our special moment at some extravagant party," I said.

"Then you should definitely check out *Compass Point Beach Resort*. It is on the waterfront and it is surrounded by Junkanoo huts that look like a traditional Bahamian parade and celebration," Blaine said confident that this would be the place.

I opened my laptop on the bar, googled the name that Blaine gave me. The images were just as he described. I particularly liked the idea of taking our vows at midnight on the beach, with the moonlight, Reggae playing in the background accompanied by the sounds of waves. It was the ideal place.

"Oh, are you planning a visit to the *Bahamas?*" The bartender asked. I noticed his obvious accent.

"Well mudda sick! That's my home maan," he added.

After a few minutes with, "Jimmy" the bartender's affirmation on my choice, I was confident it was the perfect location for our wedding. I returned home to immediately complete the reservation process.

I was fortunate to speak to a marriage consultant that arranged all the details. My plan was to have an early pre wedding dinner at the famous *Graycliff Restaurant.* This would be followed with drinks at *The Compass Point,* where the bride, groom, and members of the wedding party can retreat to their individual cabanas until the wedding begins.

"Sabriel, Ingrid, and of course you, Emma, will all have your wedding attire already delivered, along with all the extra things you ladies might require . When you are ready Emma, you can visit me in my cabana and try to calm my nerves assuring me that I have not lost my mind," I said

Emma was the first, and only person I could trust who would keep this a secret until the day of the wedding.

"I am very impressed Bradley, but not really surprised. You are such a perfectionist that I can't even imagine that you would leave anything undone." Emma said scrolling through the pictures and videos that I was proudly showing her.

"I know that Sabriel has a few surprises for you also on your wedding night. I feel so special being the keeper of all these secrets," Emma said.

"Sabriel surprises me all of the time. I still cannot believe that she agreed to marry me. A fifty year old bachelor, ten years older than her. She is not only brilliant, she is more beautiful than she realizes," I said, truly amazed.

"Oh, Bradley...You have always underestimated what a great man you are. But, I must admit that Sabriel has used her special *mojo* on you, and it has made you even a better, more sensitive man. The two of you are an impeccable couple, and I am so excited to know you both," Emma said.

Emma was right. Sabriel and I were as perfect for each other as any writer could have created. There were times that I was like Henry Higgins , the stubborn professor in the musical, *My Fair Lady*. Presuming to know so much that a lowly flower girl could never teach me anything. Other times, I resembled Rhett Butler, stepping out of the pages of Margaret Mitchell's novel, *Gone with the Wind*, obsessed by Scarlett's naïve charm.

But, the real truth is, I am Bradley Welch, a man like every other man, who must at last accept that he is falling into the ocean, drowning in the depths, for a woman he loves more than life itself.

Chapter Thirteen

"Alice laughed. 'There's no way trying,' she said. 'One can't believe impossible things.'
'I daresay, you haven't had much practice,' said the Queen. 'When I was your age, I always did it four times a day. Why, sometimes, I've believed as many as six impossibles before breakfast.'"

—Lewis Carol

SABRIEL

I never dreamt to be a princess. Being a bride was non consequential. Daydreaming, at times, was pleasant, but never ended the way I wanted it to. And, even in-spite of Dr. Dollittle's impression on me, I always left the imagination game to others.

Perhaps that is exactly what attracted me to Bradley. He believed that there really was something in this strange person, called Sabriel, that also held a spirit like Holly Golightly. He made me believe that I had some magic ability to transform this mundane life into one that "sparkles with imagination."

The first time Bradley said this to me, I laughed at the thought that anyone would find me imaginative.

"But that is exactly why it works for you. Don't you understand Holly? It is because of your naïve innocence that imagination sparkles so naturally that you are never aware of it," Bradley insisted

"My darling Bradley, for some very strange and unknown reason I believe that you are a victim of some ancient sorcerer who has placed a nasty spell on you. You fell in love with a very common frog and imagined her a princess ," I said in reply.

"There it is, PROOF, at how extraordinary you are Sabriel. You are able to turn my attention of the unknown with the confidence that everything is possible. Even a princess masquerading as a frog," Bradley said laughing.

"Do you think that Lady Guinevere ever imagined that she would be the Queen of Camelot? Or that Scarlett O' Hare would ever be in love with Rhett Butler? Or, what about Holly Golightly? *Breakfast at Tiffany's,* would make no sense without her. Just like my life is meaningless without you," Bradley said , sincerely.

The following morning we were on a nonstop flight from the Louis Armstrong Airport in New Orleans to Nassau, Bahamas for our destination wedding.

Bradley kept all the details a secret. All I knew was that he was able to reserve the beach house in Nassau, and that Ingrid and Emma would be arriving two days before Christmas.

We had all agreed to only one gift each. Being here together was the most important gift. The memories would be captured on video and film throughout our stay. And, of course on New Year's evening Bradley arranged a local photographer to capture all our wedding details professionally. I would never have been able to accomplish what Bradley arranged. The entire event was masterly orchestrated, like everything that Bradley ever does.

"Are you sure you don't want me to go with you to pick up Ingrid at the airport?" Bradley asked.

"Absolutely, I am sure. You stay here and do what you do best. Organize the evening events. I am leaving you in charge of him, Emma. Don't let him get too crazy," I said grabbing my cellphone and the small Gucci bag Bradley found on sale downtown.

I was never into designer brands before, but this small leather handbag with the cute Gucci clasp was very appealing.

"Oh, my, gosh ! Sabriel? You are glowing! I can't wait to meet the man who melted the Ice Queen," Ingrid said embracing me with her arms full of shopping bags from familiar Atlanta stores.

"I can't wait to show you my gown, and get caught up on all the recent gossip," I said, grabbing her hand and giving her bags to Desmond, our personal driver.

"The only real gossip for weeks were about you Sabriel. Everyone wants to know how this Dr. Bradley was able to win your heart. When you left Atlanta you insisted no husband, and no dog," Ingrid said, laughing.

"All, I can say, is that life offers us some very strange choices. You will love Bradley. He is everything that I never knew I wanted," I said, surprising myself.

"Well, whatever Bradley did to change your mind, has made this transformation amazing. You are just 'sparkling'," Ingrid insisted.

There's that word again, sparkling. Why does everyone notice this but me? I am very happy, but I don't see sparkle when I look in the mirror.

Christmas morning was better than anything that I could have ever imagined. When Emma and Ingrid agreed to come before Christmas, it made this seem like a true family gathering.

We all agreed to only exchange one gift each. Nobody, of course, limited their gifts as agreed. But, it was not until after all the gifts were opened, and the tree now surrounded by bright shiny holiday foil, when Emma was the first to notice that something was moving in a packages left under the tree.

"Oh, my goodness...Bradley? I think some creat...." I stopped talking as I watched a caramel colored fur ball with four feet wobble directly toward me, as if he was being controlled with a remote.

When I reached down to touch this live fur ball, he almost jumped in my lap. His brown eyes reminded me of chocolate drops, and around his neck was a red collar with the rhinestone letters: **B A I L E Y.♥** .

By this time, Bradley was sitting next to me and Bailey. Both of us were loving him together.

"When I first saw him, I thought he looked like the Bailey Crème you enjoy in your coffee. If you want to change his name it isn't too late," Bradley whispered in my ear, as if he didn't want the puppy to hear him.

Bailey...yes, that is your name. And, you will always be my best Christmas gift. We will learn how to love each other more each day.

Bailey, nuzzled in my arms and began to sleep peacefully.

"This has been an incredible year for you Sabriel filled with unexpected blessings; a great way to end this year and celebrate a new beginning. Thank you so much for inviting me to be included in this beautiful real life Fairy Tale," Ingrid said, smiling at me.

It was Bradley that responded.

"Sharing the beginning of our new life with both you and Emma are the enchanting elements needed to make our wedding event a true celebration," Bradley said.

Bailey and I were inseparable every day. He found a comfortable spot with his head on my pillow between Bradley and me every night.

"How are we going to have a private wedding night, with Bailey invading our space," I asked.

"Don't you worry about that my Holly. I guarantee that Bailey will have a responsible surrogate during that time.

"Why would I ever worry about that," I laughed. "You are my perfect hero. This pre wedding is beyond what I could have ever imagined," I said.

"Well Sabriel, now is the time to unleash all those suppressed daydreams, imaginations, and unrealistic expectations. From this time on everything is possible. I promise you," Bradley said, confidently.

And, he was right. My life was changing and it would never be the same again.

On December 31, the day before my wedding, I did one last fitting at a local bridal shop where the dress was sent directly from New Orleans. It was weeks since I had tried on the actual wedding gown. I wanted to make certain that everything still fit in the right places. It was a very slim gown and to get the perfect effect it must fit perfect.

"Oh my goodness, Sabriel! This dress looks amazing. Audrey Hepburn might have invented the first 'little black dress' when she walked down a deserted Fifth Avenue in New York, sipping coffee and munching on her pastry in front of Tiffany's, but you are rewriting the end of that short story by Truman Capote. You, Sabriel are the WOW factor," Ingrid said, seeing me in the gown for the first time.

"You don't think it is too over the top, do you, Ingrid? I mean, I don't want to ruin this day by making it seem like a mockery, or a cheap Hollywood act," I said, now having second thoughts.

Several months ago, after hours of searching for what would be the best dress for my special day, I finally found "my gown" in a catalog. It was an exact replica of the gown worn by Audrey Hepburn in *Breakfast at Tiffany's* .

"Do you think that I can have this gown made in white?" I asked the bridal consultant.

"I don't know why not. It is a very famous gown, yet an easy pattern. Let me see what I can arrange for you, Sabriel."

Several days later I was called into the small bridal shop downtown, measurements were taken, and my gown was completed in ten days.

Today, when I came in for my final fitting, the reflection in the mirror looked so much like Holly Golightly that it was difficult to believe I was looking at myself.

Well Dr. Bradley Welch here I am, your very own Holly. I promise never to disappoint you, and to always love you.

Chapter Fourteen

Never fear shadows. They simply mean that there's a light somewhere nearby.

—Ruth E. Renkei

BRADLEY

The moment that I saw Sabriel walk toward me, on our wedding day, wearing that magnificent white satin gown, paired with matching long gloves, the strands of pearls I gave her the night before, I finally knew that my life was now starting; it was no longer on cruise control. Sabriel was at last allowing me total access to a world I was afraid to enter by myself.

There really was no exact turning point that I can now recall. But, without warning, all my research on the supernatural mojo triangle began to make sense. What I was writing became organized, exciting, but most of all it was now evolving into real experiences.

It may have started on our trip to Saint Augustine, when the spirits seemed to appear regularly to me whenever I was close to Sabriel. She never experienced a sighting or even a sense of any apparitions, but they were always surrounding her.

Thankfully I learned much during one of my visits to Cassadaga, a well known and respected *Psychic Capital of the World*. It was a short drive from St. Augustine. Sabriel, I was told, is what some spiritualists refer to as a paranormal conduit. That is a person that attracts spirits without knowing or ever seeing them. I was also assured that those spirits would never do any harm to her.

"The very worst that could possibly happen is that Sabriel might experience some blithe spirit that will play some silly games with her. You know, like moving objects in the house, or hiding her car keys. You don't need to ever worry about the spirits hurting Sabriel. She is gifted. Most people never know of this gift," Thomas said.

Thomas is a respected Psychic that lives in Cassadaga Spiritualist Camp and offers Psychic readings, seances and meditations.

"Is this your first visit to Cassadaga Bradley? If so, I would be pleased to give you a brief historical tour of our fascinating town," Thomas offered.

I knew most of the important facts about Cassadaga , but hearing from a local resident is always an interesting perspective.

"You might be interested to hear about Arthur. He is our resident hotel ghost, at The Cassadaga Hotel. He tends to be more active when conduits, like Sabriel are present," Thomas said.

"Yes, I do remember once hearing his story. Arthur is an Irish descendent who truly enjoys his gin and cigars. Some people have seen him moving chairs to the window, or even actual glimpses of Arthur in mirrors. This is what you would consider, friendly spirits. Correct?" I asked.

"Yes, exactly Bradley. We just consider this a normal sighting."

What I learned from this short visit is that this community , known throughout the world as Cassadaga, is a spiritual "vortex", where the imaginary shroud between what we refer to as the "real" world and the "spirit" world is as vulnerable as any other community. The few residents that have chosen to live there and practice their strong belief in the supernatural also are welcoming to any of us who have open minds.

Sabriel and I were learning also how to balance our daily lives. I was especially impressed how Sabriel was learning to accept my excessive organizing while I continued to be amused at all her peculiarities.

One particular habit that Sabriel has is insisting that our personal items in the bathroom are separated by an imaginary line. Whenever it is necessary for me to use the only outlet on her side, I have to be careful not to disturb any of her bottles and jars of makeup magic.

What I find particularly ironic about this obsession is that Sabriel's bathroom is the only place she is organized. If you open her drawers, glimpse into her closet, or are a passenger in her car you will experience a chaotic disaster. Once I suggested that perhaps she should consider streamlining her personal life. Sabriel's response was,

"That's very much on my schedule, and someday I'll get around to it; but, if it happens, I'd like to have my ego traveling along. I still want to be me when I wake up one fine morning and have Breakfast at Tiffany's."

"Alright, Holly," is all I said. Whenever Sabriel quotes anything from *Breakfast atTiffany's* it is always my sign to back off. And, I do.

The real truth is that nothing that Sabriel could ever do would make me regret living with her. I am always grateful that she is willing to ignore all my faults. This is what everyone says assures a perfect marriage.

Then, without any warning I began to realize that there was something wrong with me. It was a strange feeling. I tried to ignore all the signs. One evening, while we were having a lovely dinner on our patio admiring the Magnolia trees were in bloom during sunset, that feeling returned. As always Sabriel had set our table with the *Desert Rose* china, crystal wine glasses, and Michelangelo silverware that we received as wedding gifts from various people.

On weekends, we always opened a variety of different wines that paired nicely with our meal. Sometimes it was Filet Mignon, that I grilled to perfection. This was always accompanied by a Cabaret that we purchase directly from our favorite winery, *The Oak*. It takes its name directly from the street it is located on.

This is a seductively tempting establishment that I can spend hours (and have), listening to Patrick, the general manager boast about how the pallet is begging for the "stones and acid" or perhaps the, "Smokey herbs" that flirt with the natural oak flavor. Whenever Sabriel and I wander in for a small plate of appetizers we leave with several bottles of *The Oak* recommended favorites.

On this particular Saturday evening, Sabriel had prepared a fabulous salmon Creole, with grilled asparagus, saffron rice, and tossed green salad. The Chardonnay was chilled and the New York Symphony was playing on our Echo creating the most pleasant ambience.

But, then it started. I reached for the wine opener and my hands began to tremble uncontrollably. It took Sabriel a few moments to notice what was occurring. She was able to rescue the wine bottle from my hands only seconds before I released it.

"Are you alright, Bradley?" I heard Sabriel ask. But, I wasn't sure how to respond.

"Bradley!...Bradley…?"

Sabriel's voice sounded as if she was in an echo chamber.

The next thing that I can remember is two strangers in white shirts, lifting me from somewhere, and carrying me out on what must have been a stretcher outside. Before I was put in the ambulance, I noticed that the moon was a blood orange. And…then nothing.

When I finally woke up, there were tubes everywhere. Nothing appeared familiar, or even real, except for Sabriel's hand linked to mine.

She must have felt my fingers moving, because I noticed her eyes opening.

"What happened? Why am I
here?"

Before Sabriel could say a word another group of white figures rushed into the room, and Sabriel was rushed out.

"Dr. Welch? Look into this light and follow it for me, please."

I was too tired to argue, or even ask any questions. All that I could do was follow this person's instructions.

After several more routine examinations, Sabriel was allowed back into the room. Her eyes looked hollow. It was as if I was looking at a distorted picture of my beautiful wife.

"Please sit down, Mrs Welch. Bradley, you are just waking from a medical induced coma. You have been sleeping for three days. Do you remember what happened before you were brought here?" The Doctor was asking.

"No…I mean, not really." I looked at Sabriel for some definite answers. But, she was silent.

"Well, three days ago you were brought here in an ambulance by the Paramedics. It appears that you might have had a stroke, but I will not be certain until we do an exploratory exam."

"What does that mean exactly, Doctor? What will this require?" Sabriel asked, nervously.

This was the first time I heard Sabriel speak. Her voice was fading.

"It means that we will need to schedule your husband for brain surgery as soon as I can get our team together. We need to be certain that there is no tumor or internal bleeding," the doctor answered.

"And?…And, if there is? Then what?" I asked, now very skeptical.

"Well, Doctor Welch, it all depends on what we discover. What I can assure you, is that time is of the essence. I will return once the operating room is ready."

The Doctor was gone before I could ask any further questions.

Sabriel returned to her designated chair next to me. I reached for her hand. We looked at each other, speechless. Sabriel obviously was as confused and concerned as I was. Finally I was the one to break the silence.

"When was the last time you slept, Sabriel?" I asked.

"I have been resting here. The nurses prepared a bed on the couch. Emma is taking care of Bailey for us. She has also been here several times."

It was clear that Sabriel was trying her best to sound like everything was under control. But, her eyes showed something else.

"Listen to me carefully, Sabriel. In my wallet is the name of my attorney. If anything should…"

Sabriel interrupted me.

"Nothing is going to happen Bradley. The doctors are going to take care of whatever this is. You will take a semester off to finish your book, and everything will be back to normal."

There was no use continuing. I realized that it would only make things worse. Emma knew all about my financial arrangements. If the worst was to happen, I knew that Sabriel would be well taken care of for her entire life. That was arranged days before our wedding.

Those next few hours while the preparations were taking place, Sabriel and I discussed the bookstore that she always dreamed about, after retirement, my Mojo Triangle Supernatural book, our trip to Savannah and Saint Augustine, and of course our wedding. It was as if everything that meant the most to both of us was being rewound for a second viewing.

When we were finished with our dreams and memories, the attendants entered, right on cue, as if the film director was in total control. Sabriel and I were only actors waiting for our next scene.

For some odd reason as I was being taken to the operating room the last words through my mind was, " *All the world's a stage,*
And all the men and women
Merely players;
They have their exits and their entrances,

And, one man in his time plays
Many parts...

Chapter Fifteen

"Once upon a time, when women were birds,
There was the simple understanding ,
That to sing at dusk,
And, to sing at dawn was to heal the world thorough joy.
The birds still remember
What we have forgotten,
That the world is meant to be,
Celebrated."

—Terry Tempest Williams

SABRIEL

He is DEAD! Bradley is dead. If I refuse to admit that he is dead then he is still alive. Is that reality! Death! It is such a definite, final statement. The word doesn't even reflect the distinction between one person and another. One might even say that Death is the natural equalizer to life. When Death enters a room , it overpowers all the signs of life that are present. It is as if, Life and Death have a secret pact. One that humans will never be allowed to enter.

And, there is little comfort in knowing that we all will eventually die. It is not the actual death that is disturbing. It is not knowing when Death is coming to wrap his arms around you, removing you from earth forever, with no regards for those who remain without you. How will they survive? How will I survive?

"Oh, we will survive. Even you Sabriel. Bradley and I shared a special bond for many years. Not like the brief one that the two of you had. And when I say brief it is not to make your time any less important than our relationship. Bradley truly believed you were his soul mate," Emma said.

Soul Mate. Those words seemed so insignificant now. Bradley and I were so much more than that cliché. We somehow completed each other. I did not know how, but we did have that intrinsic ability to meld into one. And it happened on several occasions.

The first time this happened was when I was on my daily walk with Bailey, about three months after we were married. It was a lovely wooded area with a winding path around a small pond that sometimes attracted geese. I could always tell when Bailey's tail went up that he was prepared to jump into that pond and retrieve one of those birds, if only I would let him.

But, on this afternoon, just as we crossed the bridge I could see myself across the pond waving.

I felt rather light headed, but not faint. It was as if my spirit was being transferred to another body, but that other body was my own.

Somehow it was Bradley with Bailey now on the bridge and not me. When I realized what was happening, I sat down on a nearby bench trying to make sense of all that just occurred.

"I thought you were at the University Chancellor's meeting? How did you get here?" I asked.

Bradley, took my hands in his. They felt like ice. My entire body felt as if it was melting, mid summer in New Orleans.

"It's okay, Sabriel. The first time that this happens it can be very confusing, even disturbing. But it is only a natural reaction," Bradley said, as if nothing had really happened.

"What do you mean, NORMAL?"

I said nearly screaming.

"My body just moved into yours without any warning. I mean, Bradley, one minute I am on the bridge with Bailey, and now I am here where you were standing. We totally switched physical beings," I said terrified.

"Everything in this life has a practical explanation, even these moments that challenge us to look beyond our own comfort zone," Bradley said, without any hesitation or even doubt.

"Has this happened before to you? It must have, since you are so sure that you know why and how it happens," I asked, still unconvinced.

"Yes, and no," Bradley continued to say, but now sounding like an authority on the subject.

"This phenomena is known as Twin Flames. It is often confused as Soul Mates, but that really is only a myth. Twin Flames have parallel lives in the same soul, or spirit. If we had never met, our separate lives would have continued on similar paths regardless. I knew that you were my Twin Flame when the polarized energy between us surfaced after our first meeting at the University Bookshop. That theory was verified when we had our first sexual encounter. I chose not to share this with you until you experienced it also. Today you finally evolved."

Bradley said this to me while holding me in his arms. But, I was not feeling that same sensation. Finally later that evening, Bradley decided that it was essential for me to know as much as possible about how this enlightenment would effect our lives. He then removed a copper red leather book from the bookcase. It appeared quite old and used. It surprised me that I had never seen it before. Many evenings I chose to seek new reading material from that very same bookcase rather than to read something on Kindle. The pages turning in a real book somehow just makes me feel like I am connected with the author, and especially the characters.

"This book was given to me by a close friend who passed away a few years before you arrived here to New Orleans. The gentleman was my mentor. His name was Dr. G. C Colby. No one ever knew what the G or C stood for. We all just called him Colby. Anyway, his life is another chapter in mine, one that I will save for another day. What you need to understand about our Twin Flame relationship begins on the first page of this book."

Bradley, opened the book to the beginning and handed it to me.

Out of the original unity of being there is a fragmentation and dispersal of beings, the last stage being the splitting of one soul into two. And consequently, love is the search by each half for the other half on earth or in heaven.
Sufi writing, 12th Century

I handed the book back to Bradley not knowing how he expected me to react.
Who was Sufi? Or was Sufi writing a philosophy? I was now more confused than before.

"Am I supposed to now understand what all this means by reading this quote by some 12th Century writer? Seriously, I need to know more. What am I to expect? Is this Twin Flame also an Eternal Flame that binds us forever?" I asked, immediately regretting how that sounded.

Bradley retrieved the book, replaced it in the same place and sat down across from me. The expression on his face was solemn. Now that I reflect back, I wonder why I couldn't see through his eyes the pain he was feeling. My flame, if I had one, must not have been as strong as his.

Later I learned that most of the time, we were never totally in each others body. The times that we did blend into one, became less often.

Now I am convinced that Bradley wanted to spare me from the critical end that he knew he was approaching.

What Bradley did leave me with was a cache of his knowledge that I acquired from our unity. He provided me with so much more than I had to offer him.

When I would share with him how guilty I felt about my experiences , Bradley would say to me,

"You are my Holly Golightly, Sabriel! Without that Huckleberry attitude; without your wanderlust desire, I would never know what joy is."

Does this mean that part of me also died with Bradley? Or was his flame still inside of me? Through my pain It felt like he was trying to lead me out of my depression. Death was not new to me . When my Baba died, and I was an orphan, at only ten years old, the pain was so numbing that it never left until I met Bradley. I almost feel guilty that I don't feel that same grief now.

But, now it was time to search the boxes that Emma gave me. Her instructions from Bradley were specific. Do not deliver until after the Memorial Service.

Bradley had insisted that he wanted something small, simple, and speedy. The three S's he liked to call it.

Although I did try my best to follow his instructions, the St. Patrick Church was standing room only . Sitting in the front with me was only Emma and Bailey I had no idea how many people were there. That is until the usher led us out first. When I turned around I was stunned.

"Who are all these people, Emma?" I asked, while being led to the fellowship hall, where everyone was to meet briefly for the final farewell. Since Bradley wished to be cremated, there was no need to move to a graveside.

"Bradley knew many people, Sabriel. Before you arrived, he was involved in many civic groups including *Friends of the Homeless.* Bradley would arrange local restaurants to donate food three times a week and volunteers were responsible for serving those homeless people who felt safe enough to meet in the park. And, this is only one of the groups he worked with," Emma said.

I did not understand why he never talked about this or any of the other charities. For however close I thought we were, Bradley had many secrets. Some of those secrets were now in this cardboard box.

As I carefully removed the duct tape that sealed it, there was an envelope directly inside with my name on it. This caught me totally off guard. Emma made it clear that Bradley gave her the contents of this box five years before we met, and never did he ask for it back.? Not even Emma new what the contents were.

Shortly after the Memorial Service it arrived, via some carrier service.

How could Bradley have written me a letter five years before we met?

I felt a slight chill move through my veins, as I removed the contents from the envelope.

"Smile my Holly, what you are about to experience will be such a wonderful adventure that I wish that I was able to join you. But, I have left you in good hands. Soon you will meet someone very special who will teach you all about those mysteries you could not discover in all the literature you have read and taught. When you have completed this tutorial it will be time to write that Great American Novel that you have always wanted to attempt.

In this box you will find some interesting notes that my good friend Dr. Colby left . Later, once settled in your new home , you will need to take a drive to a very enchanting village known as Cassadaga. Once there, check in with Abigail at the Hotel. Oh, and make sure you bring my ashes. Abigail will take over from there.

The money that I have left you will be enough for your bookstore and tea shop. I am certain that it will be a success. There is also

money that is being invested. I have arranged for Mr. Jackson, my
attorney, to provide you with any funds that you will ever need.

I know that all of this has come very quickly and that you are very
confused. Trust me it will all be clear in time. You are now and
always will be my Twin Flame. Trust your instincts and trust in our
love.

—*Bradley*

I folded the letter and placed it back in the envelope. Bradley was right. I was confused. But, no longer afraid. Taped to the notebook beneath the envelope was a postcard. It said on the front;

Welcome to Saint Augustine, Florida the oldest city in the United States established September 5, 1565.

Chapter Sixteen

The world is a book, and those who don't travel read only one page.

—Saint Augustine

SABRIEL 2019

*I*t is important to find just the right place. Not too much light.
*Lights create shadows, and shadows help them locate you. When
that happens. it is too late. You are 'it'! And, everyone knows
it's never fun to be 'it'.*

*I am a master at kicking the can. Not because I am so much
smarter than anyone else, but, because I HATE losing. Losing makes
me feel inferior. Dumb. Not smarter than my opponent .*

*Knowing where to hide is only one important strategy. You also
must be sure that your timing is right. If you are too early 'it' will
catch you and that is never good.*

" 10, 9 8 7 6 5 4 3 2 1! Ready or not, here I come!"

Rrrrrrrrrrrrrring!
Buzzzzzzzzzzzzz!

Wait a minute! I can win this game!!
It was happening again.

My body begins to stretch out like one of those silly putty animals
with distorted limbs. I reach for that annoying phone and finally turn
it off.

Why don't I just pick one of those clever songs, like *Wake me up
before you go go* , *by* George Michael and Wham? Because, I would
just rollover , put the pillow over my head, and go back to sleep.

Before I met Bradley sleeping was a luxury that I never
experienced. There were so many action dreams that when I did

wake it always felt as if I was the star character in a *Mission Impossible* movie with Tom Cruise.

Once I was married, thankfully all this stopped. Sleeping with Bradley made me feel safe; secure. There were no more conspiracies to discover, or helpless victims to save. My life was finally complete. Until that day. That day I officially became a widow at the age of thirty-five.. Now those sleepless nights have returned.

It was not clear to me when, or even why Bradley chose Saint Augustine for me to open my bookstore. We only talked about this idea briefly, maybe once or twice, but never chose a location.

Naturally, I was always free to make my own decision. There was really no restrictions on when all this would happen. The university, graciously offered me my teaching position whenever I chose to return. But, honestly once I opened that cardboard box that Bradley left me, I knew that there was some reason, unknown to me now, that I needed to begin my relocation at Saint Augustine, Florida, and as soon as possible.

Although I was impressed at my first visit to St. Augustine, at that time I never intended to relocate permanently. I was determined to research as much as possible, about this unique town before the actual move.

Reading 'real' books, you know those outdated printed 'dinosaur' models, always seemed more reliable. That is why I chose to spend several hours in the university library, rather than search the internet.

"Of course you know Dr. Shelly that the internet has so much more available on Saint Augustine, than we do here," Sarah Whiting, the chief librarian said one day.

"Yes, of course you are correct, Sarah, but sometimes there is nothing that can compare to an actual book. I will just check out these three, please. I should have them back to you by next week," I said, signing my name on the outdated form used by all the faculty.

Sarah, offered her condolences for Bradley's passing, and said I could take as long as needed to return the books.

I remember our first visit to the Ancient City . It was the day after we were engaged. The lovely St. Francis Bed and Breakfast provided me with such wonderful memories. The location allowed me to wander freely through the cobblestone streets of Aviles , to some of the most curious shops hidden in secret passages.

What I really wanted to know was some of the historical background. If I was going to call St. Augustine my home then I definitely should know as much as its current residents.

The first book that caught my interest was titled, *The City of God: St. Augustine of Hippo.* I already knew that Pedro de Menendez de Aviles was the Spanish Admiral who founded St. Augustine on September 8, 1565, but, why it was named this and the significance never seemed to matter until now.

Apparently , it was on August 28, the feast day of Saint Augustine , that the fleet led by Menendez first saw the land and chose to anchor off the tidal channel, known as the River of Dolphins by the French. Naming this land after the Catholic Saint was all that I knew at this time.

But, now, thankfully to this small book I selected, the first important note. It was that St. Augustine lived most of his mortal life in Hippo, a seaport city in North Africa , now known as Algiers. It was during the early 400's , as a priest, bishop, and theologian, that lead him to be recognized by the Catholic Church as a Saint.

But, why? What did this very humble man do to be immortalized? Not only as a Catholic Saint, but as the Patron Saint of an ancient city with so many secrets?

As I continued to read I discovered that Augustine was not always a follower of Christ. There was so much, that he doubted that he began to look not only at the Christian doctrine but, began to experiment with other philosophies, and perhaps even the occult.

At his lowest level of despair, Augustine questioned why his desires of the flesh were dominating his spiritual needs. He asked God to help him reconcile and allow him to understand.

This complete desperation was something that I could honestly relate to lately. Not ever being a faithful follower of any religious denomination, lead me more towards the road of agnostic. But, since meeting Bradley, and even more so after his death, I have felt that my soul was losing energy.

Was Augustine feeling this also, maybe?

As I continued reading, according to what is known, Augustine heard a voice speak to him that said, "Tolle, lege" which translated means, "pick up and read in Latin". Not only did Augustine follow those instructions but he devoted his entire life to sharing what he learned in all his powerful writing .

Augustine is credited for being "the crucial turning point in human consciousness from classical to modern ways of thinking,." According to Thomas Cahill, a respected historian.

How is it that I earned a PHD in literature and have never come across anything about Saint Augustine ? Whatever the reason, I am convinced now, like Augustine, that a stronger power is leading me to this new life. Without any safety net, moving to a place that I only visited once, with no friends, does require some faith in God, even from a skeptic believer.

The last note on this page said, "Pope Boniface the VIII canonized in 1303 Augustine as the patron saint of brewery , printers, and theologians."

I wonder if I can stretch this idea of sainthood to also include struggling writers, and wayfarers searching for answers?

Reading all of this it becomes more apparent how the naming of St. Augustine continues to be appropriate to this ancient city. I learn that this town, like its namesake, has experienced its shares of struggles, and, true to its namesake, St. Augustine connects the old world to the new.

Naturally, this is why Bradley wants me to live here.. All of this now makes sense. He may be physically gone, but he has not left me. That Twin Flame, or maybe more accurately soul mate connection, will forever exist , and I will take it with me to our new home in St. Augustine.

Chapter Seventeen

"For last years words belong to last years language,
And next years words await another
Voice.
And to make an end is to make a beginning."

—*Little Gidding,* by TS Eliot

SABRIEL

❝Oh Emma…I so much wish you could come with me. Just tell all of your students that you are going on an African safari and you don't know when you will return," I said, taking a quick inventory that everything was in my Jeep before I started on my eight hour drive.

"I already used that excuse when you and Bradley got married in the Bahamas and I extended my vacation by a week. Don't you worry about a thing. You are Holly Golightly, remember? There is nothing that can stand in your way," Emma said, waving goodbye.

For some reason, I felt that this would be the last time I saw Emma. It was the same way I felt when Ingrid left after Bradley's eulogy. I was moving really away from everything I knew in the past.

No one has called me Holly Golightly since Bradley. I felt much more like Alice who just jumped into a cracked mirror with no way out.

Although it was only 9am if I drove the entire eight hours I would be in St. Augustine by 5pm. I made the decision to stop for one night at the Alabama Gulf coast shores. It would give me an opportunity to take the drive slowly and make it feel more like a vacation than an escape from reality. All I wanted to do was walk on the beach, sit on the sand, and feel the salt on my tongue like I did in Tybee Island with Bradley.

Emma made the hotel reservations for me , and Bailey. Mostly because my mind was not functioning with all of its neutrons. What I really needed was someone to put my dog and me in the car, and assure me that we would both make it alive to our destination.

This was the very first time Bailey was going on a road trip. He would go with Bradley and I often to our classes and was always well behaved. But that was not an eight hour car ride to a new home where nothing would be familiar.

Not ever owning a pet, and really never wanting one to be responsible for, made all of this more difficult. But, what I soon learned after Bradley's death , was that Bailey was also grieving. There was no way to explain to him that Bradley was not returning. There were times that I would look into his eyes and see his pain.

It was only the two of us now. But, we both knew that we needed each other. Bailey was now my best friend, and he protected me wherever we went. He was not aggressive, but definitely cautious.

"Here is your itinerary Sabriel. I have programmed your car and your cell phone. I don't suggest you go to sleep, but theoretically your jeep is on autopilot, from here on. Even Bailey can take over if necessary. Just don't wander too far in the shores and you should be just fine," Emma said handing me my Automobile Trip-tic in case anything went wrong.

Bailey and I arrived four hours later at The Lodge at the Gulf State Park, a Hilton property. I was glad that we had stopped at a small dog park about thirty minutes before to allow Bradley to relieve himself.

The car valet was very pleasant, taking my bag and Bailey's back pack. I had to assure Bailey that this was okay. Just like traveling for hours in the car was new to him, so was checking into a hotel.

Emma assured me that we would not have any problems, and she was right. Even the bellman had doggie treats available.

Thankfully the elevator was close and my room was on the seventh floor, ocean front. Once inside the spacious room, I walked to the glass doors that opened to the patio, and checked that the railing was high enough to prevent Bailey from falling over. I felt like an overprotective mother . That must be why people have dogs before they have children.

The outside view of the ocean after a four hour drive with an anxious Bailey, was very relaxing for both of us. We sat out there for a very long time. The sound of the ocean waves was mesmerizing. It also made me question what was happening.

Was I running once again from my demons, or was I running towards them? Why couldn't I learn to just adapt to situations, like death? Neither Bradley or I had enough time to adjust to living together, before he was gone. I try to play various scenarios in my mind? What does Holly Golightly really do once she leaves "Fred"? Why can't I just leave Bradley, and send him a postcard from Brazil? Oh...yes, Bradley is dead.

Or, maybe I should be more like Scarlett O'Hara and just ignore Rhett's anger and say, " Tara is my Home. I'll go home and find some way to get him back! After all tomorrow is another day!"

Tomorrow is another day, and although I am unable to get Bradley back, I am able to find my own way back. Saint Augustine, will be where I find who I truly am.

Bailey sticks his wet nose between my shoulder reminding me that it is now time to take him for a walk on the beach. He was only a puppy in the Bahamas and never really remembers a beach or the ocean. Or, maybe he does?

The beach never disappoints me. By this time all the sun worshipers are getting ready for an evening out on the town. This leads us to an almost empty beach. There are a few children, maybe age five and seven who are busy putting their final touches on a sandcastle with sea shells adorning the tower.

Bailey looks at the duo, considering a short visit but I am sure that he will get too close and that sandcastle will turn into a sand pancake. Thankfully, Bailey turns his interest to the flock of sandpipers challenging them to a race. I have to use all my strength to pull him back on his leash. In the past few months this furry ball of cuteness has now fully grown into a ninety pound Golden Retriever. His natural instincts tells him to fetch those cocky birds. But, I have read the strict policy posted on the entrance to the beach. With no exception all dogs must remain on a leash. I am not in the mood to argue with any beach patrol.

But, before we head back to our room I do let Bailey into the ocean. The leash is long enough that I am not totally emerged . What I don't expect is that Bailey catches a fish. As soon as I see it I know he is going to bring it to me like a trophy.

A man nearby, with a sophisticated looking fishing pole, starts to clap.

"I've been here for an hour and no fish," he says, showing me his basket.

"And, now your dog is here ten minutes and just look at that whopper in his mouth?"

While I am jumping around trying to decide what to do with that fish in my dog's mouth, the stranger takes a picture of Bailey.

"Give me your email, lady. I will send you a copy."

Before I can determine if this is safe or not, I quickly do what he asks. In the meantime when Bailey realizes I am not taking the smelly fish from his mouth, he drops it in the man's bucket.

"Huh? This might be the only fish I get all day. Thank you. Good boy," the man says petting Bailey's head

We say our goodbyes and start back to our room. It surprises me that Bailey was so friendly with the fisherman. Maybe he just felt sorry that he had no fish.

I decided it would be much better to eat in our room tonight. Bailey had a very long day and trying to control him even on an outside patio restaurant may be asking too much.

Back in the room Bailey was already stretched out across the king size bed finished for the evening. Even when my dinner arrived thirty minutes later, Bailey showed little interest. Maybe he was dreaming of future fishing expeditions, but after today it was clear that he will need some dog training classes. I want to keep him near me when I finally find my bookstore, but Bailey will need to learn how to be hospitable or we won't have any customers.

Tomorrow was another adventure. We should arrive at The Hotel Casa Monica, in downtown St. Augustine by 2:00pm. Emma assured me that it is the best hotel in town, and Bailey is welcome.

Bradley and I saw this hotel when we were there during my first visit to St. Augustine, but I really don't remember much about that hotel. I certainly never thought that I would ever be checking in with my Golden Retriever, rather than my husband.

When news went out about Bradley's death, several people from St. Augustine sent gifts to the Memorial. We arranged them all according to Bradley's request. It included donations also to the Cassadaga Spiritual Association.

The proprietor of The St. Francis Hotel, where we stayed during my engagement visit, offered me a room while I was searching for permanent living quarters. But, there were just too many memories that I wasn't ready to face yet. But it was Bradley's friend that suggested to Emma The Casa Monica, and the accommodations seemed perfect.

I was hoping to rent a small house downtown no later than two weeks after I arrived. Everything that I was bringing, now in storage, should fit in a 1700 sq. ft. house. But, the location was more important to me than the size. Since it was only Bailey and I this should not be difficult to find. Yet, as I was closing my eyes, hoping not to have any more reoccurring nightmares, realistically I knew to be prepared for anything. Life has never been easy for me.

I reached over to put my arms around Bailey, who seemed quite content, and thanked God that another day passed without tragedy.

Chapter Eighteen

"Ophelia is a little walking owl, bewitched by her unconscious femininity, her father, and what "they say". She never finds her own voice. She never finds her own body, or her own feelings and therefore misses life and love in the here and now. Gradually the waters of the unconscious to which she is "native and indued" swallow her."

—Marion Woodman

SABRIEL

T he reason I have always been attracted to strong women characters in literature is because I am constantly searching for answers to my own insignificance as a woman. Regardless of my recognition as a Professor, in my own psyche I am only Sabriel, widow of the brilliant Dr. Bradley Welch.

As much as I try to be The Wife of Bath, from *The Canterbury Tales,* by Chaucer, or Janie Crawford, in *Their Eyes Were Watching God,* by Zora Neale Hurston, I am always Holly Golightly, from *Breakfast at Tiffany's,* by Truman Capote, running away from my problems or trying to rewrite who I am.

When I was researching and preparing for the Feminist Literature Class , now canceled, once I decided to leave New Orleans, I became very interested in the character Ophelia, in Shakespeare's, *Hamlet.* There are, volumes of literary studies about Ophelia, but most of them never seem to really capture who she is or even why she is included in the play, except to act as Hamlet's love interest.

However, I did find two exceptional interpretations that would have been excellent for my class. The first one was, an article titled, *The Most Beautiful Ophelia: The Duality of Femininity in Shakespeare's Hamlet,* by Emma McGrory. Two of her interesting observations are what I also noticed in my studies.

First, Ophelia is early portrayed in the play as a "pinnacle of innocence, or a figure of cunning sin." This image of women throughout society has not changed. Once Ophelia, like many other women, are expressed in this "duality of societal perception" it becomes easy to dismiss their importance. Like Ophelia, we fade into the background of whatever setting we are placed in.

The next fascinating point is that everything related to Ophelia, revolves around sexuality. If we agree that Ophelia is a symbol of all women, like Eve, then we recognize how sex determines our fate. We are either perceived as innocent virgins, unable to compete with men, or we are the wonton temptress that lure men away from logic.

Perhaps if my bookstore is not sustainable I can try my Feminist Literary Course at Flagler College. It has a good reputation for the humanity classes, I understand.

My morning reflections are interrupted by an early phone call from my realtor, Anna Hanna. Her name was so easy to remember, I had to ask her if it was somehow made up, as an alias.

"No, Sabriel unfortunately not. My parents thought it sounded 'cute' and I have never forgiven them. I suppose I should be thankful that they didn't name me Hanna Barbera Hanna. People might think then that I am a cartoon," she shared with me at our first meeting.

It is difficult to tell how old Anna is. She reminds me of a cross between a hippie from the sixties or a gypsy. Her hair is a lovely auburn with streaks of gold that appear natural from the sun. It is always neat and hangs loosely bellow her waist.

Anna also has some obvious tattoos that appear quite proudly on her arms and back. Although, I am sure that she would be delighted to tell me what each image means, I have not asked because I enjoy using my own imagination.

"Good morning, Sabriel. How are you and Bailey enjoying Casa Monica?" Anna asked.

"It is a magnificent hotel. The rooms are so spacious that it almost feels like an apartment. Oh, and the location could not be any more perfect," I said.

"I am sure that you have had an opportunity to read the background of this landmark hotel by now. There is so much history in this town that every day you will learn something new. I feel as if it is a living museum that stays alive because of the diversity of our residence. You will fit right into this community, Sabriel."

"Thank you, Anna. As lovely as Casa Monica is, I am anxious for Bailey and I to find our own abode. Have you found any interesting properties yet?" I asked anxiously.

" I have several for you to view this afternoon, and I have an excellent dog sitter for Bailey, Her name is Chloe and she can't wait to meet you," Anna said.

Bailey has never been left with any sitters or kennels, with the exception of Emma. But, I did realize, for practical reasons he would need to go with Chloe . It would be impossible for me to leave him here in the room, so it was time for Bailey to learn to adapt like all of us have.

"Okay, we will be ready at 12:30pm," I said.

When Bailey met Chloe in the hotel lobby, he acted as if he already knew her. It was love at first sight

"I'm not sure if Bailey will even want to return to me. I have never seen him react to a stranger like this," I said, handing Chloe the leash.

"Chloe is St. Augustine's official dog whisperer. I have never seen a dog who doesn't like her," Anna said, reassuring me.

"You have nothing to worry about, Dr. Shelley. By the end of the day Bailey will be happy to return. I have plans to introduce him to the city. It is a very dog friendly community where Bailey will find plenty of treats," Chloe said, as she waved her hand from behind.

"Ready to begin your search," Anna asked.

"Yes, Ma'm ready as I ever will be," I said not really knowing what to expect.

Anna took me to several properties that bordered the Ancient town that were within my specifications, but none of them really moved me. When, Anna finally asked me if I would consider a property that included my book store and my house together I hesitated.

"Do you mean like an apartment upstairs over the bookstore?" I asked, not certain how that would work with Bailey.

"Not exactly Sabriel. I just got a message that a property downtown became available. It is very rare that commercial buildings have any vacancies, but this store front has an unattached house with four bedrooms and a yard directly behind. From what I understand a gate separates the two properties but they are being sold as a single unit. Interested?" Anna asked, again.

I wasn't sure how I would like living in the center of town. It is of course a beautiful town, but with all the tourists surrounding you all day and evening it might be too much. But, I was willing to see it.

When we arrived and Anna parked the car in front of the house I thought I was looking at a cottage in the Cotswolds

"My goodness Anna, this looks like a Bed and Breakfast Inn you would find in England," I said, definitely impressed.

"Well, from what I understand that is exactly what it was for many years. But, I am not certain what the business located behind the house was," Anna added.

Walking through the home I began to imagine how my furniture would fit. By the time we went through the backyard patio garden, it didn't even matter what was behind the oval wooden gate. I felt like I was walking into a novel by C.S. Lewis.

" It is odd that you say that Sabriel because the name of this inn was Narnia,"Anna said.

"Oh my, I don't think it is a coincidence that you brought me here. Let's move on through the *Narnia* gate and see what we find.," I said.

As anticipated, there was a spacious courtyard that lead us to the main building. It was two stories with a wood staircase leading us to the second floor. Upstairs was more of an open loft. Through the railings you could see below, and through the opposite window there was a view of Matanzas Bay and The Castillo de San Marcos Fort. That must mean that this building is located on a corner lot of Avenida Mendez, the main avenue leading directly into town.

"I think this building was a costume shop for all the locals that dress in period costume. It is a thriving business here. Not sure why the owner chose to sell it. Also I think it included vintage clothes and antiques. Not necessarily my style, but very popular among locals," Anna said.

As we walked through the empty rooms there was a strange aroma that seemed to follow us. It was not unpleasant, nor was it very strong. Just a pleasant combination of jasmine, vanilla, lavender, and maybe a hint of rosemary.

"I must say, whatever fragrances this shop offered was very pleasant. They must have vacated rather recently since I can still smell the essence," I said, following Anna into another room.

"No, not really. From what I have been told, this building has been vacant for at least a year. It was once known as The Hamblin House and prior to being a dress shop it was a restaurant pub. That must be why this room still has a kitchen and a counter. I can't imagine that it would be that difficult to renovate, actually," Anna said, continuing to examine the structure for any obvious warning signs of damage.

I wasn't quite sure what I would do with the loft. It definitely offered a large amount of extra space. Perhaps, because of the excellent view it could be used as a sitting area.

Regardless of any renovations needed, this was beginning to resemble exactly what I always imagined my book store would look like. By the time Anna found me sitting on the steps of the stairs I had sketched out a preliminary blueprint of what I wanted the interior to look like.

Anna sat down next to me.

"I had no idea that you were also an architect, Sabriel. This drawing is quite impressive. I presume from what I am seeing that you will want to make an offer on both properties?"Anna asked.

Before I could answer, I felt a slight tap on my shoulder. It was very light and fast, but definitely a spiritual sign. My first thought, of course is that it was Bradley's spirit assuring me that this was the place we had both discussed in the past. But, then I found some lavender branches placed neatly beside me. They were not there before, I was certain of that. When I picked them up to show Anna, she didn't seem surprised.

"These strange occurrences might be odd to you Sabriel, but those of us whom have lived here for awhile notice it all the time. You just need to keep an open mind and never be surprised. We do live in an Ancient city that is still very much alive," Anna said, touching my hand.

"Nothing really frightens me anymore, Anna. My husband, Bradley spent many hours and travels researching the occult. He always assured me that in most cases any spirits that we attract are kind and are here for a purpose. As a matter of fact, once every thing here is settled, I need to visit Cassadaga with Bradley's ashes," I said, reluctantly.

I was not certain how much Anna actually followed the paranormal world.

"If you want someone to go with you Sabriel, I know several spiritualists personally that reside at Cassadaga. I would be happy to join you," Anna said, kindly.

"That is very thoughtful of you, Anna. Especially since I really don't know anyone in this city. I don't know anyone anywhere any more, except Emma who lives in New Orleans, and Ingrid in Atlanta."

It was the first time that I must have realized this reality, because I sounded rather distant, even to myself.

"Well, you have selected the right city to live in. Many of us are here because we were tired of living in places that were just too confining. We needed space to flourish and St. Augustine allows us to do this. And, don't forget, you know

Chloe ," Anna said, now hugging me.

A few hours later we returned to Anna's real estate office, that was also located downtown under a massive oak tree. It was clear that whoever built this small house did so with the tree as the major focal point.

"Do you have any idea how old this office is, Anna?" I asked, sitting across a large oak table. An oak tree with an oak table?, I just found this quite ironic.

"Not really Sabriel, but you will find a variety of beautiful country homes around town. Many of them, like *The St. Frances*, have been made into popular Bed and Breakfast establishments. Almost all have special stories.," Anna said, while preparing the loan documents.

Thankfully to Anna's expert negotiating skills, I was able to buy both properties for a reduced price. After a substantial down payment, it left me just enough for some minor renovation and money to buy furniture and books.

Chloe, the dog whisper, introduced me to her boyfriend, who owned a construction company. Since they both loved Bailey, I was able to get a great rate.

Chloe also was able to fill me in a little about the previous dress shop. What I learned was that not only did it provide period costume for those actors working in town, but also for a group of storytellers that perform literary "gigs" as Chloe called it.

"I have attended some of these impromptu events and they are very entertaining. There are also a few starlets hoping to get discovered, that move around town in Victorian costume. Not sure where any of these people are shopping these days, but the inventory was more than likely bought up by several local stores," Chloe told me one afternoon while we were eating lunch at *Harry's*.

Harry's is a restaurant bar really only a few feet away from my bookstore. When Chloe first brought me here for lunch, immediately I knew that I was going to copy their courtyard. It was directly outside of the main restaurant and offered alfresco dining surrounded by lovely magnolia trees and small party lights in the trees that twinkled even in the daylight. It reminded me of *The Court of Two Sisters* in New Orleans, but there was definitely a different vibe.

Harry's is quintessential St. Augustine. It attracts both locals and visitors with a variety of seafood, steak and Creole. But, it is the music that adds just the necessary atmosphere to the Creole, French, Spanish blend.

"This is what I want, Chloe . I want people to distinguish my bookstore from any other one. When I was in Savannah, there was this quaint book store in the center of town that made you want to stay there all day. I feel like this at *Harry's* and I want people to feel the same way when they visit me." I shared with Chloe .   "When Alex is finished with the blueprint you gave him, this store will be like no other in this town. I can't wait to see the final results," Chloe said.

Everyone was actually waiting. And I was beginning to get nervous. Strangers were asking me not only when was my opening scheduled but, what name had I chosen. There was no name yet.

Anna, Chloe , Alex, and evening Bailey, offered their suggestions. Nothing sounded right.

One evening, when Alex was finished, with the loft, elevator lift, book shelves, the café, and the outside patio, I walked through the finished store. Upstairs in the loft, Alex had removed the windows, and extended a wooden deck with a retractable roof that could be used during inclement weather. There were several tables with comfortable swivel chairs, and sectional sofas that were modular; easily moved when needed. The antique lighting and Havana ceiling fans created a welcome sitting space for various book clubs or simply conversation.

When Alex showed me sample staircases, I chose the dark wood wide spanned staircase for downstairs. It reminded me of a miniature version of the staircase at Tara in *Gone With the Wind*.

Would anyone else feel that same resemblance?

On the ground floor, the wall to ceiling windows provided the natural light penetrating through a variety of stained glass hangings. Each represented literary characters from well known plays and novels. The upper glass portrayed a famous replica of Ophelia, from the play *Hamlet*. The next one, was Scarlett O'Hara, from *Gone with the Wind*. Near by, on the bottom window was Alice, from *Alice in Wonderland*. Next to Alice was Holly Golightly, from *Breakfast at Tiffany's*. I also purchased several metal mermaids, starfish, turtles, seahorses to provide a nautical theme.

Although there were plenty of books placed in all of the bookshelves, there was also assorted seating available, welcoming anyone wanting to bring their own book to read.

Finally there was the indoor café that offered tea, coffee, juices, and fresh pastries . The seating outside resembled a comfortable lounge that you would find at any resort. Alex decided to also include speakers everywhere. This made It possible to stream music everywhere in the building.

It was the first time that I saw my bookstore completed. What I was witnessing was truly an amazing accomplishment. Now all I needed was a name that would do it justice. And, I only had five days left before opening day.

Chapter Nineteen

If you have been up all night and cried till you have no more tears left in you – you will know that there comes in the end a sort of quietness. You feel as if nothing will ever happen again."
—C S Lewis *Chronicles of Narnia*

SABRIEL and CARCOSA

C **ARCOSA** : I chose not to include book store or café. I left the purpose of this building to be a work in progress, without limitations. People are welcome to gather for any reason, with books to inspire, and an imaginative café that includes quotes from classical novels, dramas, and poems.

My intention was to offer whatever the community needs, or wants related to literature. I carefully selected my staff. They represent retired teachers, current students from Flagler College, Storytellers, and any other bibliophile who wish to join our family.

It is the beginning of a new era for me that is filled with the unknown. But, for the very first time I felt really alive.

Many people have no idea why I named my business **CARCOSA.** It is not any easy name to remember, since most have never heard it before. But, it was my goal to make everyone in St. Augustine know what **CARCOSA** means and want to visit often.

Two days prior to my grand opening, Alex reminded me that if I intended for him to post the name of the store over the door, I had to decide today.

"Without a name Sabriel, this is like a baptism without the baby," Alex said, anxiously.

"Well, your analogy is not really correct, Alex. The "baby" is ready for its celebration, he just doesn't have a name. But, I have finally decided," I said.

I could see Alex's eyes sparkle, because if I was going to be honest, this was his "baby" also. Without his talent there would be no need for any name.

"**CARCOSA.** That's it. That's the name," I said, waiting for his reaction.

"What the hell is **CARCOSA?** Nobody is ever going to remember that. They are going to call it **CAR!**" Alex said, sounding confused.

"Well, my good friend take a comfy seat right here on this new chair. And I will share with you what **CARCOSA** means."

Alex sat down, but wasn't eager to learn any lessons, so I gave an abridged version.

"On December 25, 1886 Ambrose Bierce published a short story,*An Inhabitant of Carcosa.* This is a fictional ancient, and mysterious city. There is a city in France, that Bierce may have alluded to known as Carcassona. It has been inhabited since the Neolithic period, and links the Atlantic to the Mediterranean Sea. Are you recognizing any similarities?" I asked

Alex just shook his head no, and went to work on the large wood sign that needed to be prepared by Monday.

What I didn't share with Alex was that in Ambrose Bierce' story, a man from CARCOSA awakens from a sickness induced sleep to find that he is in an unfamiliar wilderness. St. Augustine was no longer a wilderness, but to me it was still unfamiliar. I related to this idea. And, what I wanted was to have my place be a welcoming stop for anyone that feels the same.

I would not have time by Monday, but in a few days there would be a short summary of Ambrose Bierce's story. It would be my job to make sure everyone knows what **CARCOSA** means and why they are welcome.

Monday morning Anna, Chloe, Alex and I all met early in the café, where I had catered for all my staff, a great selection of bagels, cream cheese, lox, and fruit from *Shmagels,* a delightful family owned business located on Hypolita Street.

For the opening day, we prepared special gifts. There were book marks, mermaid pens, and notepads with **CARCOSA** stamped across the top. It took Anna and I most of the night to do this, since it was a last minute decision.

Alex spent the rest of the evening completing the Moniker that could be seen from the street. Since the former Hamblin House faces

The Plaza de la Constitución , Alex wanted to make certain that customers could see the sign from a distance without resorting to cheap neon lights. And, it was truly an artistic storefront signature.

The name was in large black letters that appeared to be three dimensional. In the evening, at dusk, **CARCOSA** shined as if each letter was surrounded by moonbeams. What I found specifically inviting were the words below that say in very elaborate but clear cursive:

Enter the land of Enchantment
Exit with a joyful spirit

On one side was a white dove, On the opposite side was a bluebird.

"That was Chloe's idea," Alex said.

"I love it! Everything is so perfect. The white dove, the bluebird, the moonbeams and especially the script. The two of you truly captured what I always dreamed about."

The three of us were hugging each other together, while Bailey kept nudging his way in between.

"That's okay Bailey. We also put a decal on the front door welcoming all dogs," Chloe said to Bailey.

CARCOSA was open from 9:00am-8:00pm. And, from the Grand Opening it was a success. Everyone at some time during that week stopped by to visit. Even a local journalist from *The St. Augustine Record.*

Many people met for tea or coffee before going to work, while others gathered to sip a cold ice drink and check out what new Indie novel was being featured.

From the beginning, I decided that I would showcase Independent book writers from across the country. Many started visiting St. Augustine, and I would invite them for book signings. Any local writer was also invited to organize a book club or even start writing workshops.

Naturally the bookstore also included classic literature and a few contemporary novels that readers asked me to order. There was also a section of used books that were donated by people who were downsizing with no longer any room available for all their books.

"Excuse me. Are you Sabriel Shelley, the owner of **CARCOSA?**" A tall man asked. His sandy blonde hair, reminded me of a slightly older surfer. There was something very familiar about his smile. But,

I just couldn't figure it out. Before I could answer this pleasant stranger, Anna, took my arm and lead me outside for some promotional pictures.

Later, she told me that the gentleman that she tore me away from was Eric Pacetti, a local reporter. He left his card, asking me to call him tomorrow.

"Eric and I went to school together. He is a nice, but mysterious guy. Always has been. But, you should follow up so that we could get some free local advertisement," Anna said.

I took the card and slipped it into my desk drawer.

My house, that was separated by the Narnia gate, was not yet ready for entertaining. Anna invited me to stay with her while I waited for the final renovations . I was thankful for Anna's offer since, Casa Monica was lovely but also costly.

Since the bookstore was my priority, my personal residence was still in need of much work. Alex promised that when he completed his current job, across the bridge at Anastasia Island he would begin work on my house.

When I finally did move in I just lived with loose wooden floors, a small kitchen and purple walls. Most of the time, when I was awake, I was either at the bookstore or in my own private oasis outside, enjoying the music streaming from *Harry's*.

I had no desire to move any further than the circumference of my property. Everything I wanted, or needed was here.

"Okay, Sabriel, I understand that you are still in mourning over Bradley. But soon you will need to face the community beyond your own business. And, only five miles away is the beach, For goodness sakes girlfriend, there is a beautiful world out here just waiting for you," Anna said one afternoon.

"I know you are right, Anna. Even my friend, or I should say Bradley's friend Emma says the same thing. It will happen. When the time is right, I will know it," I said, trying to reassure myself.

The one thing that I regretted was not spending enough time with Bailey. Oh, don't make any judgements about me yet. Bailey is a very pampered pooch. Chloe takes him for several walks during the day, and he is the resident "greeter" at **CARCOSA.** When he isn't in the café patiently waiting for treats, he is lying upstairs in the loft, in the special bed that Alex designed just for him. It is a hand made wooden base with a down filled mattress that is so fluffy that it could be used as a comfy cushion. Which it is , by Bailey. And, just in case there is any doubt who sleeps there, Alex carved Bailey's name quite boldly on the front of his bed frame.

Nevertheless, my time spent with Bailey seems to be rare. That was when I decided to leave **CARCOSA** early one night and take Bailey for an evening stroll on the beach. Bailey jumped eagerly into my Jeep as soon as I opened the door. Although the beach access for vehicles is closed at sunset, Anna's brother was on beach patrol this evening and I knew he would let me in, as long as I didn't stay too long.

Once I saw *The Oasis* Restaurant I turned onto Trace Avenue and drove to the end of the road, where a guard railing prevented any cars from entering . After a few minutes, I saw the headlights getting closer. Todd flashed the lights alerting me that he was opening the gate. My Jeep was a four wheel drive, so the sand would not prevent me from getting stuck on the beach. When I finally decided to stop, Bailey was anxious to get out and run.

Todd followed in his dune buggy, and parked right next to me.

"You picked the perfect evening, Sabriel," he said, opening my door to let me out.

"Can I let Bailey off his leash? He is well trained and won't run off," I asked, while Bailey waited, his mouth drooling, ready to chase whatever he might find.

"As long as you can keep him from roaming into the dunes, it should be fine," Todd said.

Once Todd left, I let Bailey free, and grabbed my beach chair. Then I began to walk as close to the waves as possible. Todd had briefly mentioned how special the sea looked, but I had no idea until right now. The ocean was sparkling with neon colored gems. It was as if someone had chosen to empty a treasure chest of various precious stones in the middle of the ocean. When the waves ebbed, there were different shades of teal, opal, ruby, diamonds, aquamarine, and golden ember.

After a few minutes Todd returned to sit with me.

"What is this Todd?" I asked, mesmerized.

"What you are watching is known as the sparkling ocean phenomenon by most people. When I first witnessed it, I thought it was like the auroras, are also known as northern lights. And, in fact they are similar. Auroras are formed by disturbances in the magnetosphere caused by solar wind. While what you are seeing, is the natural chemical process known as bioluminescence . This allows living things to produce light in their body."

"Do you mean that all that sparkling is coming from sea creatures?" I asked, still fixated with what looked like perhaps a clever editing by a cinematographer.

"Yes, exactly. Some very lucky fish, squid tiny crustaceans, and algae produce these chemicals to confuse predators, attract prey, or even to invite possible mates," Todd said.

I was impressed. There were so many different elements surrounding me. The ancient city of St. Augustine, with five hundred years of stories echoing everywhere, was only the beginning. There was also paranormal, and supernatural events that cannot be ignored. And, of course the mysterious ocean that attracts us like a magnet. Everyday offers me a new experience, a new invitation to appreciate this ever changing life.

Bailey was ready to return home for the night. I thanked Todd for the marine biology lesson, and letting me have a private sighting of the sparkling ocean.

"I will follow you out, just to make sure you are safe. Every once in a while some homeless dude likes to wander in and spend the night. They are harmless but we have to escort them off," Todd said.

I was quite familiar with the homeless population of St. Augustine. Several of them were regulars at **CARCOSA.** Thus far they caused no problems. They would just stop by for a cool place to rest, and we always had something leftover from the early morning bakery. A few would actually use the computers. Nobody seemed to object.

Before returning home, I decided to check with Anna about the evening business. Usually, Wednesday's were slower, for some reason. But, Anna had a few promotional ideas that she thought might attract more people. One idea was to have a charades night. Publicize the game night on Wednesday's with a small entry fee, and prizes for the winners. I told her that I would stop in for a few minutes to hear about her ideas. Anna was a wonderful assistance that worked at the bookstore with me whenever she wasn't selling houses.

"I have sent you several ideas that have all the details included. When you have a chance we can go over it together," Anna said, as I headed through the back garden to my paupers house.

"Oh! Wait! Sabriel. I almost forgot. This very beautiful, but odd young lady came in just before we closed and asked specifically for you. She asked me to give you her 'calling card'. And, Eric Pacetti also called, twice," Anna said , handing me the card that said:

Ophelia requests an audience with Sabriel Shelley. Please meet me for high tea on Friday at The Corazon Theatre .

"Do you have any idea who she is?" I asked Anna.

"No, but she looked familiar. Just can't quite place where. High Tea with Ophelia, sounds quite intriguing. I can't wait to hear what this is all about," Anna said.

I waved good night, anxious to fall asleep dreaming about the sparkle sea.

Chapter Twenty

You can never get a cup of tea large enough, or a book long enough to suit me.

—C S Lewis

SABRIEL

Several years ago, while visiting London on a solo vacation, I decided to spend one afternoon learning all about the iconic art of tea that the British are so well known for.

Although I already had experienced a few tea afternoons at *The Kensington Hotel,* where I was staying, I really never knew why the British had such high regard for this practice or that there was even several different types of tea occasions.

So, one rather typical wet London morning I asked the very regally dressed door man to fetch me a taxi. Riding in a London taxi in itself makes one feel royal. Motorized Hackney cabs, as they are sometimes referred to, are usually painted black. What fascinated me the most was when I learned that taxi drivers are required to pass *The Knowledge* test prior to being licensed.

"If you don't mind, will you explain to me what this *Knowledge Test* requires? I am from across the pond, and everything about the British culture interests me," I asked my driver one day.

"Of course, Ma'm. I would be happy to share that with you. We are expected to decide on the proper routes immediately at a passengers request, or due to traffic congestion. We are not allowed to depend on any satellite technology, or ask a controller by radio. We are the pilot and navigator of this vehicle, and every passenger must be assured that we have passed all the requirements for their safety and enjoyment," the driver said, very formally.

Apparently, this *Knowledge Test,* I learned, required an in-depth study of pre set London street routes, of all the tourist attractions, as well as residential neighborhoods, and the business district. It is the world's most demanding training course that was initiated, without significant change, since 1865. Those applying must pass at least twelve appearances. These are periodical oral one-on-one examinations that require approximately thirty four months to pass. I realized now why riding in these black cabs always made me feel safe and secure.

When I gave the address of where my tea lesson was being held, the driver immediately recognized the establishment.

"Camellia's Tea House is an excellent place to learn all you ever want to know about the tea industry. But, if it becomes too technical you might want to also try, *Bridget's.* It is considered a much more practical choice, if I may be so bold to suggest," James, the driver, said.

As it turned out, James was correct. Although I did enjoy the tour that *Camellia's Tea House* offered it was definitely designed as a tour and not a real class with hands on learning. So, I took James advice, and was now on my way to *Bridget's Tea Cottage.*

When I arrived, a few minutes late, like I always do everywhere, a very pleasant lady, greeted me. She was dressed in a Victorian pinafore with a lovely crotchet apron designed with various herbs like rosemary, mint, and thyme. Her name was also neatly sewn in the center of the apron in script. *Gigi.*

"We are just waiting for a few more students. Please help yourself to some pastries, and coffee or tea." Gigi pointed to the items neatly placed on the Buffet.

I found it almost sacrilegious that coffee was offered in a tea house. But, then it was also well known that many Americans still prefer coffee over tea.

Once all of us were seated in the parlor, Gigi returned to lead us into the official classroom for this afternoon. It was a lovely atrium with wall to wall glass windows that featured a lovely British rose garden, and very traditional, yet a modern twist that juxtaposed the old with the new. It was fascinating to see how the landscape created an atmosphere outside, that promoted the lovely art of serving tea inside.

First on the agenda was a brief history lesson on the afternoon tea ritual. Apparently, we were told , that in the nineteenth century Anna, the seventh Duchess of Bedford is credited for establishing the idea of having afternoon tea. After complaining of feeling a lack of energy in the afternoon, the Duchess began to request tea be served in her boudoir with a light snack.

Later the Duchess found that inviting friends made this experience even more delightful. When she returned home to London, the summer practice that began at her Woburn Abbey continued. Soon all of the other social hostesses began to send out formal invitations to their friends, using calling cards. Tea was often followed by a walk in the gardens to enjoy the visual and aromatic display of a variety of rambling roses, Delphiniums, Hollyhocks, Peony, and Lavender, just to mention a few.

Our narrator, naturally took advantage of the outside garden that surrounded us to make her point.

"If you ever wondered what distinguishes high tea from any other tea, it is quite simple. It is the height of the table." Gig waited for any questions before moving forward.

"I am not sure if I understand," I asked, what might seem like an obvious question.

"Do you mean that the only distinction between regular tea and high tea is how tall a table is?" I asked, genuinely surprised

" Well, yes and no. The reference to the table is that it is the height of a dinner table, rather than a small tea table found in a Drawing Room. It also includes more substantial food, such as warm scones with clotted cream and freshly made finger sandwiches, a variety of homemade pastries and of course a wide selection of teas," Gigi added, as a footman, dressed in a traditional black and white short waisted suit began to deliver all that Gigi had just described.

Then another guest asked if there was any other distinguishing fact about high tea.

" Actually, yes. There are very refined and specific social rules that aristocracy expects guests to follow. First, it is customary for the person hosting to serve the tea. In high society this was done by the footman initially. The teapot spout always faces the host. Then the proper manner to drink tea is to raise the tea cup to your lips. And, never extend your pinky finger."

Gigi demonstrated for us. And, we followed her instructions.

Next, we were told that the correct order to enjoy the food is "savory to sweet." This meant sandwiches first, then scones, and pastries last.

"A few other tea rules if you want to be absolutely correct, is to avoid calling High Tea and refer to it as Afternoon Tea. This is just protocol that not many follow any longer.

Next, avoid over stirring, and always stir, if you must, from 12 o'clock to 6 o'clock. Always use a strainer, not a teabag. Obviously this practice is now outdated, although still used in Buckingham Palace." Gigi was now taking questions.

"Is there a proper method in actually making British Tea?" The same lady who previously spoke, asked.

"Although you might get many different opinions on this, preparation of tea, it is almost always the same. You must start with boiling water; and never tepid. After you pour the boiling water into the tea pot, you will not be able to reuse the remaining water. If you need more you must start over. The one important note is how long you will steep your tea. The longer the stronger, but always remove before it becomes bitter. Also use porcelain, ceramic, or glass cups to serve the tea. If there are no further questions ladies, let us enjoy our own afternoon tea," Gigi said, pouring the water as she just instructed.

Since that visit to the British Isles, I never really thought about afternoon tea, until Anna handed me the invitation from this mysterious young lady, named Ophelia. I also might talk to Anna about arranging Afternoon Tea at the **CARCOSA.** I was not familiar with any other places in town that offered this event. Anna did mention that she and Alex found a tea house at Jax Beach called *Ashes.* Maybe a short drive there would give me some ideas on how to include something similar at **CARCOSA.**

When did The Corazon Café and Theatre begin serving High Tea? I would try to stop by there several times a month to support my local businesses. But, never did I see anything about any Tea being served. Maybe, I should make a call before I waste my time on what just might be a practical joke.

"Good morning. This is Sarah at the *Corazon Café and Theatre.* How may I direct your call?"

I knew Sarah, from my previous visits. Like me, the owner at *The Corazon* hired students from Flagler College . They were all very dependable, and friendly.

"Good morning, Sarah. This is Sabriel from the **CARCOSA.** I received an invitation yesterday from a young lady, whose name is Ophelia to meet her at *The Corazon* for afternoon tea. When did you start having this event?" I asked, trying not to sound too suspicious.

"Oh we haven't. But, this young lady with a British accent asked us if we could offer High Tea on this one occasion. She said that she would provide everything, and that all she needed was exclusive use of one theater for a few hours. It did sound odd, but the manager agreed. So, I guess we will see you at 3:00pm."

"Yes, of course. I guess we shall all find out what this mystery is about in a few hours. Thank you, Sarah."

I put my cellphone down and looked out the front window.

It was a beautiful September morning. The tourists were mostly gone until November when the annual *Night of Lights* will bring them back for the holidays. Business was slowing down, but steady with the locals and visitors from Jacksonville.

An afternoon of tea with a visitor from the British Isles just might be what I need to get refreshed from all the other loose ends in my life.

Chapter Twenty One

A s Hamlet said to Ophelia, "God has given you one face, and you make yourself another." The battle between these two halves of identity…Who we are and who we pretend to be is unwinnable. "Just as there are two sides to every story , there are two sides to every person. One that we reveal to the world and another we keep hidden inside. A duality governed by the balance of light and darkness , within each of us is the capacity for both good and evil. But those who are able to blur the moral dividing line hold the true power.

—Emily Thorne

OPHELIA

E ver since 1504 when Jacopo Sannazaro wrote a poem titled *Arcadia,* writers of all genres, throughout the centuries have attempted to understand who I am. How weak or strong my character is, my mental state, and every other possible thesis that you can imagine.

In sixteenth century a little girl lost her balance while searching for flowers near a mill pond and drowned. This girl was Jane Shaxspere, possibly a relative of William Shakespeare, who was only five years old at the time of this accident. Be assured that I am not the ghost of that child. This is a mistake many people who have had the privilege to meet me first believe.

"Oh, you must be the ghost of Ophelia visiting here from the supernatural world."

Or:

"Since Ophelia, in the play Hamlet, drowned then that must make you a ghost traveling on earth to avenge your untimely death."

Believe me when I tell you that I have heard some remarkable explanations on who I really am and why I am on earth visiting. This is definitely why I am now much more cautious about who I reveal myself to.

Many people merely assume that the great William Shakespeare created me to be the love interest of his most acclaimed tragedy *Hamlet.* But even the bard never realized that his characterization of Ophelia would be studied and interpreted for hundreds of years. Even my dear friend William could not have foreseen the changes to my original personality. I truly am a work in progress.

For those of you whom may have forgotten the original Ophelia in *The Tragedy of Hamlet, Prince of Denmark,* this play is set in Denmark and depicts a son's obsession to revenge his father's death at any cost. Naturally, there is much more to this plot, but it really is my role that is essential for you to understand. How else will you realize how I have developed into who I am today and why I am visiting.

In the original play, I am almost always depicted as a fragile feminine pawn used by my father, Polonius, my brother, Laertes, and of course, Hamlet. That role may have worked well for the sixteenth century Elizabethan audience, but thankfully there have been many other creative voices that know how much more there is to me, than a crazy maiden consumed with the symbolic meaning of, Rosemary, Fennel, Pansies, Columbine, Rue, Canker Rose, and , Violet.

There have been so many discussions about this scene in Act V, that in the nineteenth century John Everett Millais, the artist, depicts my dead body floating in the lake surrounded by those very flowers that I earlier gave away in my mad scene.

Although, I definitely understand all of the attention scholars, artists, and even musicians give to my relationship with Hamlet, it is rather annoying that they are also unable to consider that I might be much more intelligent than to commit suicide over my father's death and Hamlet's rather awkward rejection.

Fortunately I am not the only one to have noticed this. Playwright David Hays, the National Theatre of the Deaf, presented in 1993 a new version of *Hamlet* called *Ophelia.* In this version I am given the opportunity to explain what really happens. Although, I do find it quite ironic that I am mute, and must use many gestures to support my story . What I particularly enjoyed was that this writer gave ME the famous lines, "*To be, or not to be…* ".

This just makes so much more sense, since Hamlet really never understands what those words mean. For me, throughout all of my different visits historically, the idea of "to be" is always why I am here. "Not to be" isn't even an option. Although, I must admit there are many people wandering this earth in the state of, "not to be."

Then there is Rachel Luann Strayer's version of my life, that I found quite creative and amusing. In this one act dark comedy, I am primarily used as a the heroines past intrusion into her current life. In other words I am seen and heard only by Jane, Strayer's disturbed character that has an obsessive life.

This storyline has me portrayed as a literary character that chooses to take residence in Jane's head. Rather preposterous to me, but nevertheless this writer creatively attempts to use me as the annoying reflection of Jane's personality.When I start to sing obnoxious songs about death and valentines Jane fears that I am the one sabotaging her relationship with her boyfriend, Edmund .

Unfortunately, what Jane is forced to face is that she is allowing her past to intrude dangerously on her present. This also reminds me of another character friend of mine, Gabriella Girard. Like Jane, she has many literary voices residing in her subconscious that she must learn to control. During this visit to St. Augustine it will be a perfect time for Gabriella and I to reconnect once again.

Well, I could spend endless hours talking about me, and how people think they know who I really am, but it is much more pleasant spending time with mortals. They are fascinating. At least some are.

Sabriel and I will become good friends, I predict. She has the ability to have an open mind, which will be imperative, especially as the others start arriving. Oh, yes, there will be others, like me who all have the same purpose. It is not customary for more than one character to appear to a human , but there are exceptions. St. Augustine, an ancient city that has so many voices from the past melding with the present is a perfect scenario for us to share our stories to a new generation.

A few days ago, Flagler University Theatre presented *Ophelia's End.* It was a very ambitious task, that was well received by the community. Similarly to the Deaf interpretation, my character is a strong woman faced with obstacles that I overcome. This play gave me the motivation to approach Sabriel, and to offer her an opportunity that few scholars are ever granted.

My first meeting with mortals always needs to be well planned. Can you just imagine me walking up to anyone and saying, " Hi there. I am the living, breathing Ophelia from that well known play *Hamlet* , by William Shakespeare."

Most, if not all, people would ignore me, think that I was an advertising gimmick, or that I was truly insane, like the original interpretation of my character. This is why I always make my first appearance private.

In this situation I found it quite easy. *The Corazon Theatre* will be the perfect place for our first meeting . What better scenario, than an afternoon tea? Who doesn't enjoy High Tea as a temporary way to escape from reality for a few hours?

Since I did my homework on Sabriel I know that she is a Literature Professor, who recently moved to St. Augustine when her husband suddenly died. The supernatural and the occult are not frightening to her. As a matter of fact she embraces those ideas. But, perhaps one of the most compelling arguments for our group to meet with Sabriel is that she needs us to move her in the right direction. Sabriel has a future, and that future involves me and the others that are to follow.

Now that Sabriel will soon be arriving I must make certain that this small theatre is secure for the private showing of my own video adaptation of the original play *Hamlet*. It is quite a brilliant montage of all the cinematic videos that have ever been recorded and of course some scenes that are reserved only for those few mortals that I visit. It is a premiere and preview of what Sabriel will experience when she chooses to move forward.

I am truly excited about this meeting. Not only do mortals have this unique experience to meet with some of the most fascinating characters in literary history, but we also learn how we have influenced them. It becomes a symbiotic relationship that can influence all of our lives.

The setting is ready. Let the performance begin!

Chapter Twenty Two

It is the unknown that excites the ardor of scholars , who in the known alone, would shrivel up with boredom.
Wallace Stevens

SABRIEL MEETS OPHELIA

*W*ho could this Ophelia be, and why is she asking me to meet her for tea in such a formal manner?

These thoughts were flooding my brain for the past forty eight hours. No one in any of the tourist attractions could recall any visitors that looked like they were from the Renaissance.

"Sorry Sabriel, but most of the tourists that come here are either dressed like pirates or want to buy pirate paraphernalia," Jeremy, said standing outside the very popular St. Augustine Pirate and Treasure Museum, and he should definitely know.

Jeremy is the Ambassador to this landmark that houses forty eight individual exhibits and over eight hundred artifacts. Everyone that works there at the museum, is in period costume. It is not unusual to see pirates eating breakfast or lunch at a local diner.

"Maybe she is a new member of the Colonial Quarter on George Street. Sometimes they restructure their programs and include new members," Jeremy suggested.

"I'm not sure. It just maybe my overactive imagination. I guess I will soon discover who this mysterious lady is," I said, walking back to the **CARCOSA.**

It was a perfect September morning. The heat wave was now gone inviting more residents to enjoy all the wonderful tourist sites that are now back to normal and more accessible. The walk back to my place was only about fifteen minutes but I noticed how empty the streets were this morning.

Once inside the **CARCOSA,** I decided that since Anna was the only person to have seen this Miss Ophelia, maybe she could give me more details.

"Really Sabriel she was only here for a few moments. But, I can say she definitely is an attention getter. Not in a flamboyant way, much more subtle. As soon as she walked through the door it was her sheer violet printed summer dress, that went right above her ankles, that caught my attention. Then, as she almost seemed to glide toward the kiosk, I noticed her laced sandals, perfectly paired to her violet attire. And, on the crown of her waist long blonde flaxen hair was a headband made of assorted dried flowers . If this was anywhere other than St. Augustine she may have looked totally out of place, but you know how many women of all ages, around here dress in Bohemian garb. We have so many that look like Gypsies or hippies from another world. Local vintage stores are some of our most lucrative businesses," Anna said, not really sure why I was so curious.

"Well, hopefully this tea will reveal what Ophelia has to offer," I said.

"Just have a good time, Sabriel. Enjoy your afternoon tea and be open minded to some of the possible suggestions. We have many creative people living in this city," Anna said.

With that advise I returned home to prepare for my clandestine meeting. Thankfully Alex finally completed most of the house remodeling. Inside the four bedroom cottage all the wood floors were refurbished, new tile was replaced in the three bathrooms, and the master bathroom even had a claw style tub and separate shower. Although the kitchen cabinets were all updated, I insisted in keeping the original antique oven that looked like it belonged in a forest cabin.

But, it was the wrap around porch outside that I loved the most. I found a variety of wicker rocking chairs and sofas with overstuffed cushions at a variety of thrift shops. Now all I needed was to invite my neighbors and friends to enjoy a pleasant retreat from a busy world. Unfortunately I only have a few friends. But, I was hoping that they would enjoy visiting.

Alex also created a fairy tale back yard with mini party lights, a lovely water fountain and my own *Alice and Wonderland* stone creatures hiding between the southern magnolia trees and hydrangea bushes. There is even a variety of rose bushes that the gardener planted in the side yard. Anna says it is my own personal English rose garden.

Such a magnificent living area inside and out with nobody to share it with. Moments like this I miss Bradley even more than usual. The grandfather clock that I moved from New Orleans reminds me to stop daydreaming and get ready for my tea party with Ophelia.

What does one wear to a tea party these days? Actually, to be more accurate this is quite an intimate afternoon tea with some unknown person that goes by the name of Ophelia. Well, since I have nothing similar to the *Downton Abbey* attire, I will improvise the best I can.

After about thirty minutes trying to mix and match a variety of different outfits I soon realize that time is running out. Even if I decided to drive to the Corazon, which is only about five miles away, the traffic sometimes is unreliable. I absolutely did not want to be late for this event. So, I finally chose a mid calf pleated skirt with a simple white eyelet peasant blouse. On the way out, I grabbed a favorite straw hat to accentuate the Bohemian look.

Thankfully the Corazon has parking behind the theatre, and it was relatively empty, since typically it is closed on Monday and Tuesday. I was still curious how Ophelia was able to arrange this event. I suppose I will soon find out soon enough.

"Glad to see you Zoe. I can't believe how long it has been since I have been here," I said not sure what was next.

"Welcome, Sabriel . We have missed you also. Business must be booming at the **CARCOSA** . Every time I walk by there I see something new going on. Your hostess, Ophelia is in the first theatre waiting for your arrival," Zoe said, smiling.

Most of the staff were students at the local Flagler College. They were always friendly and very helpful during the many events that the *Corazon* offered. Not only are there three separate cinemas, but on different days of the week there are story tellers, poetry reading, and Trivia nights. These are very popular with the local community.

As I entered the first theatre the tables, chairs, and love seats normally arranged for dining during the movie were moved to the side of the room. As I walked toward the one large round table in the center , I noticed the profile of a young lady instructing the video technician about the lighting, and sound for the video that apparently was on our agenda. A rather odd afternoon tea, but nothing seemed normal about any of this.

I stood silently waiting to be noticed, when almost naturally this most magnificent creature turned toward me with a smile that I am certain has melted many unsuspecting men of all ages.

"Oh my gracious, Sabriel, forgive me for not greeting you properly when you arrived. I must have gotten carried away with the last minute preparations. Allow me to formally introduce myself. I am Ophelia, and I am so looking forward to our becoming the best of friends," she said, extending her right hand.

I of course reciprocated by politely following proper etiquette. But, I could not stop staring at how perfect this young woman was. Although her voice sounded relatively mature with a slight accent that I could not identify, she appeared to be no older than fifteen. Yet, she carried herself as a sophisticated lady, and her eyes revealed a deep chasm into some unknown world.

"It is of course my pleasure to meet you, Ophelia, although I must admit I have no idea why I am here. Have we ever met before? Perhaps years ago in London? I must say there is something about you that is very familiar. Yet, I simply have no clue," I said taking a seat at the side of the table.

"I have prepared a short film montage that I hope will help explain who I am and why I have arrived at St. Augustine at this time. After the showing, we will enjoy a wonderful afternoon tea prepared exquisitely. The Queen of England would be proud of such an assortment of specialties. Then we can discuss our future arrangements."

Ophelia signaled for the lights to be turned off and the movie to begin.

Just as Ophelia had promised, the film included a variety of movie clips. What I did not expect was that they were all different versions of *The Tragedy of Hamlet, the Prince of Denmark.* Some depicted very original interpretations, especially of the Ophelia character. In fact, all of the actresses portraying Ophelia in someway resembled the Ophelia now sitting next to me.

How can this be? There have been more than fifty versions of Hamlet since the 1900's.

When the last clip ended, I was not sure what to say. Was this perhaps an advertisement campaign for some new product that Ophelia wanted me to include somehow in my business? If so, why not include all the local business owners, not just me.

"I know that you must have many questions, possibly even more now, since you have seen the cinema. This is quite natural. What I am about to reveal is far beyond anything that you could possibly imagine. And, once you learn all of the details I am hoping it will be a life changing event," Ophelia said, taking a small sip of her tea.

Ophelia was certainly right about being confused What exactly was happening? I had so many questions that I was not quite sure which ones were the most relevant. I suppose the most obvious one is why me? Why has this quite idiosyncratic young lady sought me out to pitch her proposal? If, in fact it truly is some proposal.

Finally, after a short time of pleasantries about the countryside of England, and how different Denmark is from Great Britain, I asked the inevitable, obvious question, "Who are you really, Ophelia, and why are you here in St. Augustine?"

I thought that my question might be too direct, or even offensive, but, Ophelia continued to be as gracious as a well prepared, polished lady from any aristocratic family. She smiled pleasantly, as if she knew all the answers, but was only allowed to reveal each secret as the appropriate moment became necessary.

" My dear Sabriel. May I refer to you as dear? I realize that we have only spent a short time here enjoying our company, but you have known me for many years. You have been a true champion to my reputation, even questioning the validity of well respected scholars. I must thank you especially for that

I was rather taken back at Ophelia's response. Was she suggesting that SHE was the real, authentic, OPHELIA, made eternally famous by William Shakespeare? Surely she did not expect me to believe this. Almost as if she had privy to my personal thoughts, Ophelia once again continued with her narrative.

"Let me begin with my own personal metamorphosis. I will naturally abridge some of the details, or we may be here for days, and I fear that not even I could prepare enough tea to continue this party. I might have to fetch my friend Alice from her looking glass to continue."

Ophelia was trying to make this revelation appear light, but I knew instinctively that what she was about to tell me was much more serious. Maybe even challenging.

"Let us begin when Gertrude first requests an audience with me, in Act IV: Scene 5. She has heard from Horatio that my latest behavior appears to be quite disturbing , even insane since I learned of my father's death. Horatio suggests that Gertrude speak to me in an attempt to draw unwanted attention to me and the Crown of Denmark."

Ophelia daintily takes another sip of tea, and allows me to add any additional side notes about this event before proceeding.

I am now thoroughly engrossed and fascinated to hear this young girls story regardless of her motivations.

" Very well. Since we are now both observing that scene, the one that I also included in my introduction montage we just viewed, let me continue. In this original scene, Shakespeare has Gertrude prepare a drug for me that will numb my body and mind. Basically to stop me from drawing attention to the court. It is this drug that causes me to lose my balance in the lake and drown. Not suicide. Shakespeare revised that scene, not including the drug. In fact, as you often taught in your lecture classes, 'Ophelia was a much stronger character than Shakespeare realized. She would never have committed suicide due to her father's death or even Hamlet's own demise'."

She was right. Whoever this Ophelia was, she quoted me correctly. Perhaps she was a former student. That would explain why she looks familiar and her astute knowledge about the play *Hamlet*. Those lecture halls could hold a hundred students . It would be easy for Ophelia to fade into that large crowd, although at this moment sitting next to her and listening to her speak I could never imagine not noticing her.

But, what Ophelia had to say went beyond her expertise on the various interpretations of *Hamlet,* or even the Ophelia character.

Although it is not in my nature to invite a complete stranger to come home with me, I could not ignore that there was something extremely alluring about this young lady. I had to hear the rest of her story and how my role in this new production was to evolve.

High Tea with Ophelia was only the beginning. It would soon lead to many other fascinating characters. I certainly would never again complain that my life was boring.

Chapter Twenty Three

What's real and what's not? People we meet in books, Holden Caulfield, Captain Ahab, Huckleberry Finn, Harry Potter, Bilbo and Gandalf and Frodo—can become more memorable, and more important to us, than people with birth certificates and driver's licenses. Characters spawned in an author's imagination find a home inside us. They make our lives richer. They become our best friends. They never disappoint. And, they never die.

—Michael R French

SABRIEL and OPHELIA

❝This is exactly where I pictured, in my mind, that you would be living, Sabriel. I know how painful it must be to have lost Bradley after such a short time of marriage. But, let me assure you that what he shared with you during your time together will make everything in your future so much more relevant. And, my friend, you will never feel alone ever again," Ophelia said, removing her white brim hat and placing it on the antique coat rack.

That coat rack was one of the first items that I purchased from a local vendor when I bought this cottage. It has never been used before. It seems now like it was just waiting for the proper hat to make it useful.

Although Ophelia's remarks sounded as if we had been close friends forever, I was much too anxious to hear what she still had to tell me. Questioning how she seemed to know me and Bradley would merely muddy those waters.

"May I suggest an excellent glass of Sangria that I prepared using our own local San Sebastián Winery? It is quite refreshing," I said.

Ophelia was already sitting comfortably on one of the vintage Queen Ann chairs that Bradley purchased on a trip to England prior to meeting me. Ophelia looked as if she was imported from the early twentieth century. I would have taken a photo of this bewildering gentlewoman, but it could never capture the real effect that she expounds.

"That is a lovely idea, Sabriel. May I help you in the preparation?" Ophelia asked, in her very obvious British/Danish accent.

"There is no need for any preparation. I just remove it from the fridge and pour. One of the advantages of our modern world. We can delight in samples of the past centuries and always return to our own conveniences ."

Ophelia smiled, as if I had said something quite profound.

"That is definitely a fine introduction for me to continue with our story. Now that I have revealed my own transformation allow me to further explain the benefits of me visiting you and how this happens."

This was the first time that Ophelia clearly confessed that she truly was Ophelia, a literary character with many different facets.

"Very well. As you know, when plays are performed, preferably live on stage, the characters have literally moved from print to human form. And, I just want you to imagine Sabriel, that whenever you open a novel, you release those characters. They then take residence in your mind, most of the time. However, some of us have learned how to take this process one step further. We have found a way to become part of the human race for a short time. That time varies based on what our mission is. How long we remain, truly depends on why we are summoned." Ophelia stopped allowing me to absorb all that she just said.

It was quite extensively enlightening. If I understood her correctly, what Ophelia was disclosing is that she is the real life version. Not merely any actress portraying Ophelia, but Ophelia herself.

Could this really be true? If so, it would revolutionize our entire literary academic institution. And, if this is not real, what do I do with Ophelia? There is nothing that makes her appear crazy or dangerous, except her story.

"What you are asking me to believe Ophelia is that you have somehow escaped the constraints of the printed pages, found your way here to St. Augustine, and I am the one to benefit from your visit. In addition, you imply that there will soon be more arriving.

Although I consider myself an open minded person this just appears far too much for even me," I said, trying not to sound too skeptical.

"Naturally Sabriel, I don't expect you to accept all that I say now without evidence. I assure you that it will come soon. What I am asking you to understand is that because we remain in each persons psyche, our entire lives have altered the course of the world, championed for women's rights, equal rights, and civil rights. What you must realize is that many of us choose to leave the comfort and security of our pages to visit humans like you because we are dedicated to revealing the truth. We are the ones that make you toss in bed, or wake up in the middle of the night, trying to understand what motivates us. We also get no credit for those original ideas that inspire you to engage in some new exciting venture. Most of the time it is the authors that get all of the recognition, when it is us that have made them famous."

I was beginning to agree with Ophelia's logic. Although it was unorthodox, those were exactly the kind of ideas that educators hoped to inspire in their students. But, how was it possible?

"Have you ever wondered, Sabriel, why Shakespeare chose to portray me the way he does? After all, there are many other female characters in his plays that demonstrate much stronger personalities. Certainly you will agree that Juliet, in *Romeo and Juliet*, or Cordelia, in *King Lear,* demonstrate stronger tenacity than the weak Ophelia that most people remember. It was not until some very innovative changes to my character in the twentieth century did I begin to feel confident to join others to celebrate our independence."

I could see that Ophelia was beginning to be more animated as she recalled how she finally became this new version with the ability to think autonomously .

When I suggested that perhaps she was similar to an apparition or ghost, which I was fairly familiar with, because of all Bradley's research, Ophelia insisted that she was definitely not a supernatural being.

"Only humans are capable of being ghosts my lady. I have never been human therefore it is impossible for me to be a spirit. I am an exact reproduction of your imagination that has for the time being become very close to a human reproduction. Someone else may not have seen me as the Ophelia that you created, but they will still accept me if you do. You see, authors create the first image of a

134

character, but then they are no longer in control. You certainly must agree that while authors are writing, there comes a moment when the characters take over the story and they evolve at their own pace. Most authors will explain this process as purging. It is when they allow their characters to freely wander away from their subconscious. Without this happening the authors become self consumed and lose direction," Ophelia said.

This actually was not the first time that I had heard this interpretation. Many authors reveal that without allowing their characters some freedom of choice they would result in demons eating their brains. A rather nasty image.

"Very well Ophelia. Let us say that for lack of any other excuse I accept who you say you are Now what? I am still not sure why you are here, in St. Augustine. And, who are these other characters that I may expect to arrive," I asked conceding that Ophelia presented a convincing argument.

"Why I am here will be your decision. Without sounding too haughty, I really have many positive qualities. Just imagine what I can add to any of your book clubs. I am familiar with most of the literary characters, as well, as the authors. Don't you think that your patrons would benefit from such personal anecdotes? " Ophelia said.

This was something that I honestly never considered. During this discussion I was only focused on what Ophelia might want from me. When in fact she has made a very significant point. Once a month the **CARCOSA** offers an insightful examination of a well respected classical novel. Previous book clubs have been well received, and I enjoyed sharing my interpretations with fellow members. Although, some are returning scholars and, retired English teachers, there are also several whom simply enjoy reading and participating in a lively discussion.

This month our showcase novel is, *Wuthering Heights,* by Emily Brontë. I am curious if Ophelia even knows this novel? How would I even introduce her to this group? Certainly it might be a lively discussion.

"This might sound strange Ophelia, but have you ever met Emily Brontë? I mean, are you familiar with any of her body of works?" I said, not believing that we were having this conversation.

Ophelia stood up and moved toward the bookcase that included most of my favorite novels, biographies, historical epics, and even a few of Bradley's supernatural books that he used to write his treatise. She selected a first edition of *Through the Looking Glass, and What Alice Found There*. It was published in 1872 , in red cloth and a picture of the Red Queen on the front.

" I understand Sabriel that it will take you some time to accept who I am and what I know, but let me assure you that I have traveled widely and extensively through the literary world. This novel, by Charlie is one of my favorites. Not only did I know him personally, I was friends with Alice. Since you are obviously also fond of her, I may be able to convince her to at least to make a cameo appearance, if you like."

Ophelia handed me the book. Bradley bought this for me on my Birthday last year. It was one of my most prized possessions. But actually meeting Alice might be disappointing. I am not sure how she would adapt to my lifestyle.

"Oh, and yes, I am familiar with *Wuthering Heights*. Jane Eyre is a very complex, but a fascinating character. We were never close, but, there is a mutual respect. And, about the others that I mentioned, maybe I can explain this in a more simple way. The world of literature is an underground movement that few have access to. It is not as bizarre as the occult, but some people try to make a connection to the supernatural. Since Bradley was so close to discovering our group in his research, it only made sense that we would choose you to continue his work."

I was not sure how to respond. Ophelia was correct that at the end of Bradley's life I accompanied him to several sites, including here in St. Augustine, where he seemed to move closer to discovering how the supernatural has influenced much of the literature that we read. Unfortunately, his untimely passing prevented him from any final analysis. And, although I was included in his visits, and we discussed some of his discoveries, I certainly never presumed that I could carry out his legacy, especially if it included publishing his thesis.

"I am afraid Ophelia that you are giving me too much credit for my late husband's research. My concentration has always been on providing as many people as possible with the opportunity to enjoy literature, particularly many novels that have been read only in college. I now offer them a comfortable non threatening setting, some guidance in our discussions, where everyone participate with some very introspective points of view," I said, still waiting to hear who these other visitors might be.

"Perfect.Then we are, let's say, both on the same page. You of course are familiar with TS Eliot? Well, although many of his poems are some of the best expressions of humanity in literature, it is his *Old Possum Book of Practical Cats,* that was used for the most original musical, adapted on stage by Andrew Lloyd Webber, in 1981. I was at that premier at the West End of London . But, I won't bore you with those details. Nevertheless, we can use the idea of The Jelekyl Ball to illustrate why characters decide to make themselves available to humans. Just like the the cats came out to celebrate once a year, we do the same, sometimes, even more frequently if we believe our presence is needed. As far as who will be here, I really am not certain. But, I do know that it will be soon." Ophelia sounded excited, and optimistic about this new chapter she was creating.

So, here I am, sitting in my newly refurbished English themed cottage, with beautiful Ophelia, across from me looking exactly as I had always imagined.
Was I losing my mind? If so, I could not imagine a more exciting way for it to happen.
"I have not even asked you Ophelia, do you have a place to stay? I presume that while you appear in human form you also need the same necessities as we do?" I asked, not sure what to expect her response to be.

"A very pleasant elderly lady that operates a local Bed and Breakfast, I believe it is called *The Saragossa,* offered to let me stay a few nights at no charge. It is close enough for me to ride my bicycle to the **CARCOSA** whenever I need to," Ophelia said, confidently.

I was not sure why, but I felt obligated to offer Ophelia one of my guest rooms. If I was going to really accept that Ophelia was truly who she claims to be, then the very least that I could do is extend to her a safe place where we can learn more about each other.

"The Saragossa is a lovely home, and Martha is a gracious hostess, but since you and I are starting to bond I believe you will be much more comfortable here. That is, of course if you agree?"

I was hoping that having Ophelia close by would also allow me to observe how she relates to everyday activities.

137

"Oh, my Sabriel, that would be so marvelous. I assure you that I am quite 'low maintenance', I believe is the expression you humans use," Ophelia said with a genuine smile.

"Wonderful. Then it is settled. I will contact Martha and let her know your change of plans. Do you have any luggage that we need to address?" I said.

"Not really. I travel very lightly. Somehow it always works out for the best. I did leave my bicycle at *The Corazon,* but I can take a walk tomorrow morning to fetch it," Ophelia replied.

I did not know how Ophelia planned on staying for any length of time without even a change of clothing. But, if necessary we could stop by *The Way We Were* vintage dress shop. I am sure there would be plenty of appropriate attire to choose from.

Whatever was to happen from this moment on I was quite certain would be an improvement on how I was living. It was almost sacrilegious that all around me were these wonderful images of the past, and present fusing together and I could not appreciate it. Ophelia was a new breath of life, literally , that I needed.

Chapter Twenty Four

Wit, is a glorious treat, like caviar. Never spread it about like marmalade.

—Noel Coward

SABRIEL

Ophelia was a perfect fit with everyone at the **CARCOSA.** Anna thought that she was just what we needed to attract new customers to our book club. Chloe was fascinated with at all the stories that Ophelia shared, and Bailey would follow her around like she was his new best friend. Of course it didn't hurt that Ophelia always had treats in her pocket for him.

Nobody ever really asked why Ophelia was staying with me. Anna seemed a little surprise once I shared with her the living arrangements, but, once I explained that she would be helping us with the different events, it seemed to take away any doubts.

"Today we are starting the introduction to *Jane Eyre.* Do you have any ideas on what you would like to contribute?" I asked during our morning tea in the garden.

Ophelia would rise early, prepare some decadent pastry, and serve it with a variety of different tea that she would buy from *The Spice and Tea Exchange,* a wonderful specialty shop just a few miles away at Hypolita Street.

Today Ophelia prepared one of my favorite, black chocolate tea, with butter croissants.

"Well, I am presuming that you don't want me to share with the group my relationship with Jane Eyre and our afternoon tea discussions in England," Ophelia said, with an inquisitive smile.

"Honestly Ophelia, I don't think that anyone is ready for that much intimacy. But, if you can find a creative way to include some of those insights, it would be a great way to excite the group to read on," I said.

It has now been a few weeks since Ophelia arrived, and everyone who visits the bookstore is enchanted with her. Not only is Ophelia well educated about so many novels, even many of the most recent, she is also able to provide the customers with a vivid book review. I soon realized that many of my returning patrons would search out Ophelia to thank her for her recommendations or just sit and visit with her in the café.

"I thought that perhaps we could share some interesting background details about Charlotte's life without going into specific detail on the origin. How does that sound to you, Sabriel? Relatively safe, I would think," Ophelia said, one day.

I was curious to hear more about how she was going to actually deliver this message. Most readers who have not studied Charlotte Bronte do not really want a lecture on the author's life. What they really want is to be convinced that a novel written in 1848 has some relevance to their life today.

The fact that it was published by a first time author known as Currer Bell, not Charlotte Bronte, is an interesting footnote, but may not add to the readers' enjoyment of the novel. I knew, from past experiences that our readers really cared nothing about that background.

Nevertheless, Ophelia had such a wonderful rapport with so many customers, I made the decision to allow her to lead the introduction any way she chose , with the exception of trying to convince them who she really is.

At two'o clock exactly there were ten ladies comfortably sitting in the loft on love seats, overstuffed couches, comfy high back chairs, and even bean bag seats.

Ophelia arranged to have Anna set up a lovely tea set with enough mini sandwiches for everyone. I had no idea where all this came from, but by now I no longer was surprised.

" Good Afternoon, ladies of the **CARCOSA** Book Club. Many of you look familiar, but if I have not had the opportunity before to make your acquaintance, I am Ophelia. And, today I hope to get you excited about reading a wonderful novel by an interesting woman author, Charlotte Bronte. I would like to ask all of you to imagine that we have gone back in time. We are now sitting in Charlotte's cottage at Haworth, WestYorkshire, England. What Charlotte is going to reveal to each of you today is very personal and rarely shared."

As I watched from nearby, it was fascinating how Ophelia captured her audience. Like a skilled performer is able to captivate their audience, each person in this room was now transfixed into another dimension.

Pursuing the role of a very shy, yet confident ex governess, Charlotte Bronte, Ophelia spoke about her life and many of the misinterpretations of who she really was. Although Ophelia was presuming the role of Charlotte, much of what she was sharing also sounded quite personal.

"What all of you should keep in mind, while reading my novel, *Jane Eyre,* is that since William Shakespeare's time, to even now the present, women are either portrayed as innocent maidens or loathsome sinners who have no control over their own choices. Take Ophelia, from *Hamlet,* as an example. She embodies this virgin/villain dichotomy that my close friend Emma McGrory ,once noted in her observation. It is our obligation, as women in the twenty first century, to praise the works of independent writers before us."

It was obvious that these ladies were being entertained by every word that Ophelia spoke. And, even I was paying full attention.

"How many of you are aware that *Jane Eyre* is not going to be the traditional romance novel that many expect?"

No one raised there hand.

"Well then, let me simply introduce you to a few things that you can expect. First, it is an uneasy relationship with sex. Second, Jane Eyre is not a romantic heroine. Many will say it is sacrilegious to say this. After all Jane is obviously an obsessed teen age governess who is in love with her boss who is many years older. What I am suggesting is that you look beyond the obvious love triangle, and see a woman who fights for love, but at the end abdicates to her emotions. It is the path that takes Jane to that point that makes this novel exciting. I certainly look forward to hearing your opinions in a few weeks." Ophelia said, quite graciously.

After all of Ophelia's admirers finally left, I walked up to praise her for keeping these ladies excited when often they appear to have a very short attention span.

"I am very impressed Ophelia. You were just absolutely stunning. Everyone listening seemed to be enthralled by what they were hearing," I said, sincerely.

"This was fun. I enjoy speaking to anyone willing to listen to me. It must be just because of what has happened over so many years of visiting a variety of people from around the world," Ophelia said laughing.

"Whatever it might be, I certainly wish that I had some of that energy when I was teaching. I never taught *Jane Eyre,* but I read it often. She was my heroine and I could relate to her being an orphan," I said, not certain if I had ever mentioned this before.

"I was not aware of this. Most of what us characters know about our visitors, is their literary backgrounds. You, and Bradley were quite intriguing. When a heartbeat in one generation ends, it is revived in a new generation. There are several layers of film that holds together previous lives. Characters from classical novels are resuscitated when an author recasts them into another era with a different scenario. All of the characters that you will soon meet, including myself, have appeared in many different artistic expressions," Ophelia said.

Everything that I was hearing made sense but what I could not explain rationally was why me? Every time that I would ask that question, Ophelia assured me that I would know when the time was right. She honestly convinced me that even she was not privy to those details.

I did learn that Charlotte Bronte, and all of the sisters, were fascinated by the supernatural. It began with an admiration of Lord Byron's poetry, which I was aware included much mysticism. As part of the Bronte sisters art studies they admired the fantastical imagery of the painter John Martin. But, it was their housekeeper, Tabitha Aykroyd, that introduced the girls to legends, folklore, and fairytales.

When Charlotte's brother, Branwell was given a set of toy soldiers in 1826, Charlotte suggested that each of her siblings create their own island within Branwell's Confederacy. Branwell and Charlotte created the world of Angria. They wrote prose, poems, maps and included other imaginary worlds.

Charlotte's journal, *Glass Town Confederacy,* later demonstrated her ability to switch from imagery mentality to her own reality. It was this dreamworld of Angria that she was afraid would hold her back from her desire to write. But, in fact this fantasy does appear again in *Jane Eyre.*

I was certain that Ophelia would connect those dots during the book club's next meeting. With all the supernatural events still going on in St. Augustine, the ladies could easily relate.

"By the way, Ophelia, I have two tickets to *Blythe Spirit* , by Noel Coward at the Lincolnville Theatre tomorrow night. Would you be interested in attending?" I asked.

"Oh, that would be so splendid. I have been missing live theatre and this play is just so amusing. Thank you so much for considering me, Sabriel," Ophelia said, sounding excited.

"The Lincolnville never disappoints, and everyone is just so friendly. We will have a super time,"I said.

Ophelia was on her way out riding her bicycle to some unknown destination, and I was going up to my office to finish some invoices from the previous week.

In retrospect having Ophelia join my staff at the **CARCOSA,** and even sharing my house has made my life much more fulfilling. Although I am still a little anxious about when the next characters will arrive, it is not controlling my life. Ophelia has taught me to believe in Ceste la Vie.

Chapter Twenty Five

"You call yourself a free spirit, a "wild thing," and you're terrified that somebody's is going to stick you in a cage. Well baby, you're already in that cage. You built it yourself. And it's not bounded by the west in Tulip Texas , or in the east by Somali-land. It's wherever you go. Because no matter where you run, you just end up running into yourself."

—Truman Capote, *Breakfast at Tiffany's*

SABRIEL and OPHELIA

For days *Blythe Spirit* was all that Ophelia could talk about. She insisted on telling me that in 1941 while visiting Wales she met Noel at the local neighborhood market.

"I had no idea that he was a playwright. He seemed like a country gentleman searching the local merchant for a fresh filet of salmon to serve for dinner. I offered him a delicious recipe that was given to me by an Irish actress who portrayed me in an interesting improv of *Hamlet*. Noel and I then started to discuss how Shakespeare's plays are often misinterpreted. That conversation continued when I offered to make him dinner at his nearby cottage," Ophelia shared with me at breakfast one morning.

"I remember reading that Noel Coward slipped away from London to Wales so that he could write this new play. Did he share any of this with you during your visit?" I asked, fascinated how Ophelia was able to move in such grand literary circles.

"Well, naturally at the time I had no idea that this was his purpose. However, once I revealed to him who I really was, he never even doubted my story. Actually, he appeared very interested about all of my visits to other authors. Then he told me that he was working on a new script, that he said he was calling, *Blithe Spirit*. I was curious to learn more. Noel began to tell me that in his words it is a , "very gay, superficial comedy about a ghost," Ophelia said.

Noel Coward was not one of my favorite writers, but this play just seemed so well timed. Not only because St. Augustine is celebrated for its supernatural nature, but also because of Bradley's obsession with discovering as much as possible how the occult relates to so many famous literary works throughout history. And, then of course, out of nowhere, Ophelia shows up. Although she insists that as a literary character she knows nothing about ghosts, I still believe there must be some common ground.

In *Blithe Spirit* a novelist, Charles Condomine has arranged to host a séance with a well respected medium known as Madame Arcati. What Charles does not expect is that his first wife, Elvira, known as Elveera, unexpectedly surfaces after being dead for five years.

The fact that Elvira decides to visit him after so many years, and Ophelia is here with me now somehow does not seem coincidental. Thankfully in the play only Charles is able to see his dead wife, but everyone can definitely see and speak to Ophelia. If not, I might think that I was truly losing my mind.

The Lincolnville theatre, located on King Street, was once a local high school, and the entire neighborhood can be traced back to 1866 when it was known as the crossroads to history. It was a local place for exhibitions, and stories to be heard. Once the theatre was added, the St. Augustine community embraced the various productions that are now being offered.

Since it was an inviting September evening, Ophelia and I both agreed to walk to the theatre. Many local businesses began to slow down during this time. But, the **CARCOSA** depended mostly on the local community. The vacation season did not seem to effect our business. Because we are located on San Marcos Blvd. there was always plenty of walking tourists who stop in to pick up a good book to read while on the beach, or a fun souvenir of their visit. But, even in September when most of our tourists are here for just an afternoon from Jacksonville, or Orlando, the **CARCOSA** has a good business revenue.

Tonight, because of the pleasant Florida weather, there were also many residents out, taking a sunset stroll to the Plaza de la Constitution where they could stop to listen to a local band play traditional rock and roll in the kiosk. If it were not for our tickets to the play I would have been sitting on a blanket with my well disguised glass of wine enjoying this evening with the other residents.

"How old is the Lincolnville Theatre where we are going to see *Blithe Spirit*? " Ophelia asked.

She was always curious to learn about all of the local buildings in St. Augustine. I was not surprised in her interest. Most people are eager to know the charming history of this ancient city.

Although I had already shared with Ophelia the general information about the theatre, I added now that it was also an African American History Museum. It is housed in the theatre where in 1925, The Excelsior School building was the first black high school in St. John's County, until after desegregation, when it was used as office spaces.

"When was it finally converted to the theatre?" Ophelia asked, now listening attentively.

"When the city announced that they were considering demolition of the historic site, a group of former students, and community members rallied to save the old Excelsior. Thankfully they were successful. It is now known as The Lincolnville Museum and Cultural Center," I said.

"I am always fascinated by how modern everything is when I visit your America. But, here, in St. Augustine, I actually feel more comfortable, more at home with the architecture and how so many people have embraced their past. Thank you, for allowing me to stay and enjoy your world," Ophelia said.

I wasn't quite sure what she meant by "allowing" her to stay. As far as I could tell I really had no choice. This is not to say that I didn't appreciate Ophelia. She definitely is a wonderful asset to the **CARCOSA** literary family. Not only do our patrons love Ophelia, she is a favorite among the staff. And, of course there is nobody that can compete with her scones, croissants, and homemade current jams.

I knew that we were soon approaching the theatre. Close by is one of my favorite local breakfast restaurants, *The Blue Hen*. Prior to Ophelia arriving, Anna and I would make it a point to visit nearly every Sunday morning. Not only are the fresh biscuits heavenly, but they also serve the very best fried chicken I have ever tasted. This rave comes from a Georgia girl.

146

"The Blue Hen Restaurant, there on the right, was named after the owners offered a contest to the community to name their new restaurant . There once was quite a notorious Lincolnville bar here, known as *The Blue Goose.* That is another story. Until you arrived, *The Blue Hen,* was my favorite breakfast spot," I said, as we both decided to take a brief rest before approaching the theater.

"Whatever happened to that *Blue Goose Bar?"* Ophelia asked, inquisitively.

"I am not certain why it closed down, but the actual building where people used to visit in the 1950's is now a renovated modern cottage, close by. I believe it may be rented," I said.

"Quite interesting. It will be one of the places I explore on my bicycle in the next few days," Ophelia said.

When we arrived at the theatre there were a few cars parked in the lot, but I knew that there were no assigned seats. Once we showed our tickets and took the elevator upstairs, it was clear that the lobby was crowded with guests waiting for the doors to open.

I advised Ophelia to go directly to the center of the theatre and select whatever she decided were the best seats. Since the theatre only accommodates about one hundred seats, with no bad ones, there really was no reason to rush. But, Ophelia asked if we could sit in the front so that she would be able to see every expression on the actors faces.

"Most people sitting in the audience are interested in the action of live theatre. However the real details are in facial expressions and voices. This tells us so much about how the playwright and director wants the final effects to be presented." Ophelia sounded like an authentic play critic.

The seats Ophelia chose were in the very front of the stage. We could not be closer without being actually on stage. I honestly believe that Ophelia would be completely comfortable if she could move right up on that stage..

"This is so perfect, Sabriel. I especially like that there is no curtain. The simplicity of the set means that the actors will get all the attention. And, the intimacy of this theatre will help the characters achieve their theatrical goal."

I almost corrected Ophelia when she referred to the characters rather than actors. But, then it must be how she interprets her own role as a character, rather than an actor. Which actually does make it sound logical.

Once the lights dimmed, everyone became quiet with all attention on the stage. At times it was more interesting to watch Ophelia's reaction than to concentrate on the play. She seemed to be totally engrossed in all the action, following attentively each of the actors throughout the first act.

When the house lights came on, Ophelia sat up straight, still engrossed in the last scene when now that Ruth has died, she and Elvira are haunting Charles even more intensely.

Before I could ask how Ophelia enjoyed the first two acts, she started to tell me, with animated enthusiasm, how this theatre experience is truly exciting.

Then without any warning Ophelia suddenly just stopped in mid sentence. Her eyes lit up as if it were Christmas morning. As I turned to glance at what caused this dramatic change, I saw a slim young lady approach us, moving through the crowd of guests on their way to the lobby. She was wearing a chic black jumpsuit with hair the color of ebony flowing loosely to her waist. But, it was the tortoise shell oversized sunglasses, that she had on, in the dim lit theatre, that caught my attention.

Before I could say one word, Ophelia was embracing this stranger as if she was her lost sister, finally united. I was fairly confident that Ophelia never had a sister, even in any of the many modern interpretations that she liked to share with me.

"Oh, my goodness Sabriel…" Ophelia finally said, remembering that I was sitting next to her, "Let me introduce you to my best friend, Lulu Mae, but you of course might know her better as Holly," Ophelia said, still holding her friends hand.

It took at least thirty seconds for me to respond. Not really because I was being introduced to the very infamous Holly Golightly, standing before me in human form, but because it was like looking in a mirror twenty years ago.

Every where I went, people would insist that I looked like the interpretation of Holly in the film version with Audrey Hepburn . Although flattered for the compliments I saw myself much more like this image facing me now. This Holly was much more like the Natalie Wood version of Willie in *This Property is Condemned,* by Tennessee Williams, with traces of Daisy Clover, and Lolita.

148

"I am so pleased to meet you Sabriel. Ophelia always selects the most interesting people to visit. Once everyone else arrives this will truly be a celebration, " Holly said, taking the empty seat next to Ophelia.

"The pleasure is all mine, Holly. I really had no idea that you would be one of the Jelekyl Cats that Ophelia alluded to, but I am thrilled," I said, smiling at Ophelia.

Whatever similarities that I saw between Holly and myself, she never mentioned it. Perhaps later I would share with her that Bradley used to call me Holly, but at this moment I was still trying to accept that sitting next to me was Ophelia, from the play *Hamlet,* and, the oh so popular, Holly Golightly, from *Breakfast at Tiffany's.*

After the play I suggested that we all return to my house. It would give us an opportunity to talk in a private relaxed atmosphere. Any other option on a Saturday night would mean large crowds and loud music at the most popular night spots.

"You will simply love Sabriel's cottage, Holly. She has the most adorable secret garden that leads into the **CARCOSA** directly from her back gate. I will explain later all the details. I am just so thrilled that you decided to join us."

Ophelia and Holly were embracing each other as I followed behind them like a well trained puppy.

Once we were inside the house, Holly followed me to the patio. Seconds later, Ophelia somehow appeared with a pot of fresh hot tea and crumpets.

"You wouldn't have something just a little stronger than this, my love." Holly asked, politely.

"Let me offer you some local bubbly," I said, returning to the kitchen for some champagne that had been chilling for months. It was a housewarming gift from Alex when he finished all the renovations.

" Perfect. Now this is much more like a homecoming," Holly said, removing her heels, and curling up like a content cat on a comfy pillow.

Listening to my two exceptional guests was like watching an exclusive premiere event of a long awaited reunion. Although I know that neither of these ladies wanted to exclude me, there were just so much being revealed yet, I had no idea what it all meant. One thing that was very clear is that although these two characters were hundreds of years apart in literature, they appeared as close as sisters this evening.

I didn't even ask where Holly was planning to stay while visiting St. Augustine. I knew that she would be staying with us. Ophelia assured me that even though Holly appears to be more "high maintenance", she is very easy to accommodate.

"Holly and I will be roommates. There is plenty of space, and we have lived together before. It will be so much fun Sabriel. Just wait and see," Ophelia said, before I could make any other suggestions.

I was not sure how much "fun" all of these characters, appearing as guests in my home would be, but I was beginning to adjust. And, quite honestly how many people have the opportunity to spend exclusive time with the famous Ophelia, and now Holly Golightly?

Chapter Twenty Six

"For we wrestle not with flesh and blood, but against powers of this world. But—don't worry, here we meet in the castle of lost souls. In the land of the black Swan, The Prince of Darkness. Welcome little captive, to the waterfall of sweet dreams. Malory says it washes all our cares away, but I need—stronger stuff."
  Wade Lewis, *Inside Daisy Clover,* by Tennessee Williams

Holly Golightly
AKA: Connie Gustafson, and Lulamae Barnes

Truman Capote was a genius! The proof is me of course. Like many authors, I would even say most, the characters that evolve from their imagination into print is people they have known or would like to know. Whenever a person opens a novel, or watches a play, characters literally come alive. Although there are many interpretations of what a character might look like, we all tend to have our own unique style. Perhaps this may be due to so many human viewpoints that blended together creates who we really are.

Most of the time authors and playwrights, even some directors are given the credit for our popularity, and even our immortality. But, has anyone really thought about why Truman Capote decided to portray me this way? You notice I don't use the word create. This is because only God can create. Whatever we are, we all agree, that we are born from imagination.

Once we have been polished and ready for our final drafts, does anyone wonder what happens next? When humans are not reading about us, or watching us on the stage or cinema, as characters we continue to develop. Nobody has exclusive rights on who we are beyond the imagination. Once we start meeting other characters, who we have also studied , we realize that many of us have similar traits. This allows quite engaging discussions.

I do find it amusing that many people believe that once we are in the human realm, all we do is drink tea and socialize with one another. When actually, we are quite busy sorting out all the misconceptions of who we are, and what our motives are. At times this can be extraordinarily complicated to hear, but also quite amusing.

When Truman was deciding what would be my perfect name, he first thought that Connie Gustafson sounded more like the name of a child bride from this odd, unknown city Tulip, Texas. But, there was just something still not right. Maybe Connie was too sophisticated for an orphan child , who with her brother Fred, somehow ended up living with a widowed farmer with four children.

The details of these circumstance are revealed when the narrator notices a man in his "early fifties, with a hard, weathered face, and grey forlorn eyes" (BAT) examining my mailbox. Truman introduces at this point the very man that I was married to just before I turned fourteen.

Although Doc Golightly shares with the narrator at *Hamburg Haven,* that he has no idea why I would run off, he also blames the Hollywood magazines that I read for this irresponsible behavior. In some ways Doc is correct. When I would see all the models and actresses living a life of glamour, it was something that I strived for; it was something that I dreamed of.

Then one day, while I was taking a walk, on the road, that the Greyhound Bus stops at once a week, I used the grocery money Doc gave me and bought a one way ticket to New York. I regretted leaving Fred behind, but I also knew that Doc would care for him much better than the "mean no-count people" (BAT) that we escaped from.

Some people, readers and critics alike, have judged me as being consumed with fantasy; selfish, and even narcissistic. But, little is said about the fifty year old widow that took advantage of me at the age of thirteen. This was not any different than a slave owner who picks sex objects like those who picked cotton.

Was it really a surprise that when I had the opportunity to escape that I would? It also should not be any surprise that the reason that I picked the name Holly, is a derivative of Hollywood. Golightly was an added bonus. Together it is the perfect pairing. One that initiates so much discussion.

Another important point that I would like people to know is that I am not Audrey Hepburn. I am Holly...Holly Golightly, and some seem to forget how Truman describes me when the narrator recalls our first meeting.

"...the ragbag colors of her boy's hair, tawny streaks, strands of albino-blonde, and yellow...caught the hall light...she wore a cool, slim black dress, black sandals, and a pearl choker. For all her chic thinness , she had an almost breakfast-cereal air of health, a soap and lemon cleanness, a rough pink darkening in the cheeks. Her mouth was large, her nose upturned. A pair of dark glasses blotted out her eyes. It was a face beyond childhood, yet this side of belonging to a woman. I thought her anywhere between sixteen and thirty" (29 BAT).

Throughout the years I have managed to keep that description along with the Hollywood version of Audrey Hepburn, strolling down Fifth Avenue towards Tiffany having my early breakfast, looking very much like the models I once admired. People also expect me to look like this. What they don't expect is to learn how many people throughout the years have claimed to be the original prototype of Holly Golightly. Truman even called it "The Holly Golightly"sweepstakes.

This included many well known celebrities such as, Gloria Vanderbilt, Oona O'Neill, Carol Grace, and many more. I find this particularly ironic since I admired many of them in those magazines that I read, while married to Doc.

If there was any model for me, that Truman used it was more likely, Nina Capote, his mother. Both she and I have hick names. Mine Lulamae, and hers Lilie Mae Faulk. I was born in Texas, and she lived in Alabama. Both of us married older men as teenagers, and we were also abandoned by relatives . There are so many other stories but, none of them really reflect who I am today.

One very irritating aspect of being a character is that literary scholars enjoy dissecting you into small pieces and then trying to reassemble you into their own interpretations. Several years ago I met Zachary B. Wunrow who decided that he was going to write an article about how I was a fugitive from the feminine mystique. It did catch my attention, although I was not certain how much I understood.

153

Authors have always been my real Achilles Heal. Even in *Breakfast at Tiffany's* the handsome writer portrayed in the film version by George Peppard, was quite delightful. But, anyway back to this article, Zach, after days of talking with me came to this conclusion:

"Your identity, Holly , may be termed 'subversive', in the sense that you transcend the codified female position as "bearer of meaning", to "maker of meaning".

This did take me a very long time to try and understand. After all, as a character we always want to portray ourselves as our writers suggest, but also grow with interpretations.

What Zach was suggesting, among all of his fancy vocabulary, is that I was evolving into a new role model for millions of young girls and women who felt trapped. In the 1950's and even more so in the 1960's woman were being torn between, "the should" and "should nots" of gender roles offered by many more writers.

Many, including myself would agree, that I am far too quirky to ever be mistaken as a stereotype. I was not a "Lady", the term used during that era, and certainly far too independent to ever be a "housewife", as Doc hoped I would be. As a matter of fact, I was rebelling entirely against that stay at home female, portrayed by television sitcoms like *The Donna Reed Show*, or *Leave it to Beaver*.

No, my ideal women are the mysterious Jayne Mansfield's, Bridget Bardot's, Sophia Loren's, and of course Marilyn Monroe. My all night parties, sleeping in the nude, most of the day, and occasionally shoplifting just for excitement, seems much more appropriate. Even making changes to the acceptable domestic rules, like sipping coffee from a glass jar around noon, or while drinking champagne before breakfast, all seems normal to me.

In one very memorable scene with Paul, I tell him that, "it is lucky enough that you are not rich enough to marry." This is followed by a passionate kiss from me luring him into a perfectly acceptable non committed relationship. Now, of course this happens every day. But, during my conception by Truman, he needed to be quite careful that I was not viewed as too "loose", a term often used then.

It is not clear to me or many other critics, whether Truman actually even understood how my new feminism would be accepted. But, it is now clear, many decades later, that an eccentric young woman, not really glamorous under traditional standards, could be

154

intentionally challenging the institution of marriage. After all marriage was safe. Stepping outside those boarders could be quite dangerous.

But, then independence has never been something that comes easy. Even Truman could not let me find happiness in this new lifestyle. Nevertheless, I was able to escape from Lulamae Barnes, who married at the age of thirteen in Tulip, Texas and pursue my own self actualization. I was able to listen to my own inner voice that told me that I can do more than just be a wife and raise children.

Alone in New York allowed me to write my on identity. At times that was based on how others saw me. After all, it was necessary for me to see twenty six different men in the powder room, for two months, just to feed myself and pay rent. I have changed so much since those days. Once I chose to step outside of my novel into new worlds I realized how much I contributed and how much is still needed.

What I look forward to now, in St. Augustine is knowing Sabriel better and meeting the other members of our group. This will truly be a fascinating time to celebrate many strong women who have changed the world and are still dedicated to changing this life.

Chapter Twenty Seven

The whole series of my life appeared to me as a dream. I sometimes doubted if indeed it were all true, for it never presented itself to my mind with the force of reality.
Mary Shelley, *Frankenstein*

SABRIEL, OPHELIA, and HOLLY

T he following morning after Holly arrived was quite uneventful. Honestly, very disappointing. I expected her to show up to breakfast wearing that famous black dress, with her hair in a French twist, and holding that famous cigarette holder. Instead, sitting at my breakfast table, with long legs crisscrossed, was a very sylphlike girl, slender, and graceful. Her chestnut dark hair was in a ponytail, and on her forehead was a black satin sleeping mask, that matched her pajamas.

But, what really caught my attention was the cherry blossom silk kimono that she wore over her sleeping garb. It was as if I had stepped into the pages of *Breakfast of Tiffany's* rather than Holly stepping out.

"Good morning, Sabriel. I hope you don't mind me having a bowl of cereal with some of your frozen berries. This is just so delicious. The only time that I can really enjoy breakfast is when I step into your world. I know that this might sound very ironic since I come from the world of *Breakfast at Tiffany's,* but if you remember those were early mornings after being out all night. And, living in a city that never sleeps, well it makes a normal lifestyle quite impossible." Holly said, while eating her cereal.

I was speechless for a few seconds. What seemed last night to be quite natural, now in the morning sounded much different.

"Good morning, ladies! What a beautiful morning this is with my two special friends,"

Ophelia said, dressed impeccable as usual.

156

"Let me start the tea for you, Sabriel. I also have some fresh scones and raspberry jam, in the pantry," she said, moving quickly before I could stop her.

Then I decide to just sit down across from Holly, and let the rest take its course without any questions. Allowing these ladies to join me in my new life somehow seemed natural. It was difficult to explain. It made no logical sense, but it was working.

"I thought that I would show Holly around the city, today if you don't mind, Sabriel?" Ophelia said.

"Oh, I think that is a marvelous idea. You can use the jeep if you like. I am going to work in the office most of the day," I said, actually glad that I would not need to explain who Holly was to anyone.

"Thank you, but the bicycle is much better. We don't have to worry about parking issues and it gives us a closer encounter to the places that are so interesting to visit," Ophelia said.

I wasn't sure where Ophelia was planning on finding another bicycle. I never even knew where she found her bike. But, less than an hour later the ladies were gone.

Bailey enjoyed chasing the lizards in the patio and watching the birds perched in the massive oak tree, that was our natural umbrella on the patio. Meanwhile, I finished my tea while browsing through the St. Augustine local newspaper, *The Record.*

In New Orleans Bradley would read the local paper every morning. I would always tease him about how old fashioned that was. His response was always, that feeling the word in print allowed him to believe that there was still hope in the world that literacy would prevail. I would argue that the most current news was always on my phone app.

But, for some odd reason, since I arrived here, the current events in the world were less important to me than knowing how the pulse of my community was beating. Anna said that the real reason I subscribed to *The Record* was because of the charming reporter who wrote the glowing review of the **CARCOSA** when it opened.

"Are you suggesting Anna, that I am so swayed by a young handsome reporter that I would waste my money on a newspaper?" I said, defending my actions.

"Well, my dear friend, first let me point out that Eric Pacetti, is much more than a young reporter. That Pacetti heritage dates back to the eighteenth century when his Italian great great grandfather married a beautiful Minorcan lady. They have lived here since at least 1875. Anyway, I just wanted you to know that Eric is much more than a good looking man," Anna said.

"And, I might add, that he isn't that young. Eric graduated from high school with me and I am forty two. I think that would make him slightly older than you, Sabriel."

"It just must be the Fountain of Youth nearby that makes everyone look so young," I said, without wanting to further discuss my slight physical attraction to Eric Pacetti, whom I never would see again.

Currently, my problem was not Eric, but Holly, and whoever else might be soon arriving. Ophelia was now working well with the others. The ladies in the book club raved about how wonderful she was, and all the regulars that came in for storytelling or open mic poetry evening always enjoyed how Ophelia supported them. But, Holly I wasn't too sure.

"What do you think Bailey? Give me some advice about this predicament that I am in."

I said, looking deep into his brown eyes.

After all if characters can walk out of their novels, why shouldn't dogs talk?

Bailey, just walked over to where his leash was hanging, and said in his silent way, that it was time for us to leave.

"How was the play last night at The Lincolnville?" Anna asked, remembering .

I was trying to find a way to explain how Holly was going to be visiting for awhile.

"The play was very well done. It also had a good attendance. You, Chloe, and Alex should go see it before it closes," I said, still not knowing how to insert Holly into this conversation.

"Maybe. Alex has really been busy with restorations lately. Which is good for the business but he is so tired by the end of the day there is little that he wants to do even with Chloe," Anna said, offering me another cup of hot tea.

Bailey wandered off upstairs looking for Chloe, hoping for a ride to the beach and some seaside action.

"Ophelia and your cousin, Holly stopped in briefly to pick up some sandwiches and drinks for a picnic. I must say that Holly and you look more like sisters than cousins," Anna said, sitting down with me at the café table.

Cousins? When did Ophelia think of that? And, it would be nice if she had let me know. Well, whatever. Now that she has gone this route I guess I must follow. Hopefully Anna will not ask me too much, and not remember that I once lived in an orphanage in Atlanta.

"It must be a nice surprise having Holly visiting? How long does she plan to stay?" Anna asked, all the obvious questions.

"Yes. It was a surprise, especially showing up at the theatre. We really haven't discussed very much. She can stay of course as long as she wishes to. We have a lot of catching up to do,"I said, thankful that I didn't need to give too many details.

"Chloe, actually told her where you and Ophelia were. She came here first. I hope you don't mind that Chloe told her," Anna said.

"No, not at all. It was a nice homecoming surprise," I said, trying to sound convincing.

It must have worked, because there were no further questions as I proceeded toward the office. I was going to take this opportunity to read *Breakfast at Tiffany's* once again. I wanted to know as much as possible about Holly as I could. It also might give me some insight why she is here.

It had been many years since I read that short novella by Truman Capote. If I remember correctly one of my teachers in eighth grade. Miss Tipton, gave me a copy. I knew it was her own personal copy because it was signed by the author himself. Miss Tipton was a lovely spinster, or at least all of us thought she was a spinster. Always dressed very conservatively and proper. It was because of Miss Tipton that I chose to be a teacher. Of course at that time in the orphanage, I never would have believed that I would earn my doctorate and teach in a university.

Before, I moved to New Orleans, I sent Miss Tipton a short note thanking her for all of her encouragement and support when I was so young with no direction. I felt very sorry that over the years I never made any attempt to visit her personally. A few months later, I received a small box, that had been forwarded from my apartment in Atlanta to the new cottage that I was leasing in New Orleans. I could not imagine what it could be. As I unwrapped the butcher paper, inside the box, I recognized the book, *Breakfast at Tiffany's a short novel and three stories, by Truman Capote.* It was the same edition that Miss Tipton gave me many years earlier to read.

I looked for a note, or something that would explain why I was receiving this gift. Then I noticed that there was also another book beneath the original. It was *Music for Chameleons, by Truman Capote.* When I opened this book I noticed it was also signed, but this time it said,

To Sabriel Shelley
My dear friend
—Truman Capote

There was no date, so I had no idea when this was signed or where. But, the fact that Miss Tipton remembered me, a shy orphan girl, after so many years made me feel extremely special. I recognized the writing on the note with my name. Miss Tipton always had an elaborate cursive penmanship that appeared like something from the Victorian Age.

My dearest Sabriel,
These books are some of the few literary possessions that I have of any value. They are being sent to you because I know that you will be the best custodian of them. I am sorry that I was unable to attend any of your graduations throughout your academic successes. I have not been physically mobile for many years. I wish you the best future and wanted you to know that to me you were always a shining star.
—Madeline Tipton

There was also included with this note a memorial clipping from the local Atlanta paper informing the public that Miss Madeline Tipton passed away on August 12, 2015. What I noticed immediately is that she had no family. It said that,

"Miss Tipton was an orphan with no known relatives or husband. However, she leaves a community of loving students and faculty that grieve her passing. She will always be remembered."

It felt rather odd recalling all of this now , when once again I needed to read about the mystery of Holly Golightly. It was as if Miss Tipton was somehow still trying to show me how to adapt to this chaotic world. Oh, how I wish that she was here to meet Ophelia, and Holly. And, I was also reminded that now that Bradley has passed, Miss Tipton and I may have very similar obituaries.

160

Chapter Twenty Eight

The women laughed and wept; the crowd stamped their feet enthusiastically, for at that moment Quasimodo was really beautiful. He was handsome—this orphan, this founding, this outcast.
—Victor Hugo, *The Hunchback of Notre Dame*

SABRIEL

*B*ut, *in the spring a postcard came; it was scrubbed in pencil, and signed with a lipstick kiss: Brazil was beastly but, Buenos Aires was the best. Not Tiffany's but almost. Am joined at the hip with $enor. Love? Think so. Anyhoo am looking for somewhere to live.($enor has wife, and 7 brats) and will let you know address when I know it myself. Millie tendresse. But the address. If it ever existed, was never sent , which makes me sad, there was so much I wanted to write her; that I'd sold two stories , had read where the Trawlers were countersuing for divorce , was moving out of the brownstone because it was haunted. But, mostly what I wanted to tell her was about her cat.. I had kept my promise; I found him. It took weeks of after work roaming through those Harlem streets, and there were many false alarms, tiger-striped fur, that on inspection, were not him. But, one day , one cold sunshiny Sunday winter afternoon, it was. Flanked by plotted plants and framed by clean lace curtains he was seated in the window of a warm looking room; I wondered what his name was, for I was certain he had one now, certain he arrived somewhere he belonged . African hut or whatever, I hope Holly has to. (Breakfast at Tiffany's, by Truman Capote)*

I wanted to add a postscript to this chapter that said, no worries about Holly Golightly, she is living safely with me in St. Augustine, currently touring the city on bicycles , with her friend Ophelia.
But, why did I not recall how complex Holly truly is? I do remember that when I first read this story, what caught my attention was the

connection between Holly and me. We are both orphans. We both inspired to be more than this, but not really certain how to accomplish it. I of course had the advantage of realizing that if I was attracted to the glitter of Hollywood I would never move beyond my restrictions.

And, now all that reality has been challenged. What I do believe is possible, is some rational balance. I have been transfused with a new energy that allows me to view life from different lenses. Reading *Breakfast at Tiffany's* now encourages me to recognize what was always there but what I never SAW.

Taking advantage of being alone in the house, with Bailey contently curled up on his favorite couch, I stared out of my kitchen window watching the typical September thunderstorm empty buckets of water into my flourishing garden. It seemed that every afternoon at 3:00pm the tropical storms would last for about forty five minutes. Then, within a short amount of time, the sun would reappear with a rainbow close by. It was the perfect moment and setting for reflection.

When Holly appeared last night at the theatre I was both surprised and delighted. Ophelia never prepared me for her arrival. Perhaps she was as surprised. Nevertheless, because it was unexpected, and late by the time we arrived home, it gave me little opportunity to speak to Holly about her visit to St. Augustine. I suppose what I wanted to know was if she feels a kindred spirit with me as I do with her?

If it had not been for mentors like Miss Tipton I could easily have taken the same path as Holly. Neither of us can imagine being tied down to one person. Holly has Fred, her brother, but even he is not enough to keep her home with Doc.

Bradley realized that although I loved him and married him, he could never control me if I started to wander. Our short time together was always happy. But, for whatever, unknown reason, I never really imagined a "forever" life with Bradley, or anyone else. Even when he insisted on this
Twin-flames idea. We definitely had something rare, but when he died, the flame died with him.

This is why I understand that Holly never remains anywhere for any length of time. The longer you remain, the more difficult it is to be free when you must leave. And, that desire to leave will always be there.

We both want to experience the world on our own terms. Unfortunately for Holly, she is uneducated. Yet, she has enough natural instincts to understand that any average work that she is capable of doing will prevent her from any innovative future achievements. Her only choice is to use her exotic looks, with her acute intuition, acquired from studying the male persona, to survive in the New York Jungle where any signs of fragility will hang around your neck like an albatross. Holly prefers the pearls and diamonds that her suitors offer in exchange for her outer beauty. Those superficial suitors have no desire to learn about the inner beauty that Holly possesses.

I may have been able to avoid many of those pitfalls that Holly experiences, but this is only because I used Holly as my alter ego for so many years. Living behind those sunglasses allowed me to avoid many unpleasant visions. And, as Holly, I use my outer appearance, whenever possible, as a masquerade that conceals my weaknesses. Until I am able to focus on the admirable qualities that provide me with the aplomb needed to act out the advantages of my façade. This has worked for me most of my life. Now Ophelia discovered me here in St. Augustine. And, with Holly arriving things could become even more interesting.

"The weather out there is rather scary. For about one hour Holly and I were delayed at the Flagler College. A very nice elderly gentleman escorted us to the dining room. It was quite impressive. Did you know that it has seventy four Louis Comfort Tiffany windows? And, the light shining through those windows casts this beautiful glow over hand painted murals on the walls and ceiling. I just can't imagine having all my meals there every day. I hope that those students appreciate where they are eating daily," Ophelia said, drying off with a beach towel that I keep nearby just for these daily showers.

"My breakfast at Tiffany's could hardly be compared to sitting down surrounded by all of those windows. Although, I do prefer the diamonds, pearls, and emeralds at Fifth Avenue," Holly added, taking a seat at the window.

"We didn't miss the book club, did we? You know I don't wear a wrist watch or carry one of those popular cell phones everyone has," Ophelia said.

" No. No…of course not. I would have rescheduled if necessary. You have a few hours. But, I just think that if you want to join us Holly, it might be wise to be discreet," I said, almost immediately regretting how this sounded.

"No worries, Sabriel. Like you humans say, 'This isn't my first rodeo.' Ophelia reviewed with me how the *Jane Eyre* book club is going thus far. I will probably just let her continue. Maybe when the rest of us get here we will have a little round table discussion or something as entertaining," Holly said, not sounding too offended.

"Great. I am going to go over to the **CARCOSA** just to make certain that Anna doesn't need any help. You two can relax, take a shower, or nap if you need to. There is some fish and chips that Alex brought over from *Hurricane Patty's* a few hours ago, if you are hungry, feel free to eat what you want. *Mi Casa es su Casa,"* I said waving goodbye walking out the back door.

I obviously lost track of time, reading and reflecting on the past. It was now time to return to the present.

"I am so sorry, Anna that I just vanished today. How is everything going? Do you need a break,
lunch?" I said, sounding totally confused.

"Everything is fine. You are the one that needs a break every once and awhile. There are plenty of us here to take care of the normal routine. Pamela ordered some French pastries from *Le Macaron.* They will be delivered here by 6:00 pm for the book club. And, Abby has the coffee, tea, and condiments already sitting on the table with all the cups and paper plates," Anna said, smiling.

"Don't know what I ever would do without you, Anna. How can I ever show you my appreciation," I said.

Anna handed me a 5x7 colored flier with the words, **CHAUTAUQUA** in bold black letters.

"What is **CHAUTAUQUA** ?" I asked, reluctantly.

"I thought of all people, you would know what this is. **CHAUTAUQUA** was very popular during the 19th and 20th centuries. A traveling group of actors brought entertainment and culture to often remote rural communities. Although many of the original shows included lectures the most popular recent ones are dramatic narratives. Actors represent such authors as, Mark Twain, CS Lewis, or even Charlotte Bronte. On Saturday there will be Mary Shelley, Margaret Mitchell, and Louisa Mae Alcott," Anna said, as I reviewed the details.

Apparently **CHAUTAUQUA** was going to be performed in tents on stages at Francis Field. This will also be the location for food booths, craft shops, and local musicians. The charge for tickets in advance is $15, and an additional $10 to hear the speakers. The flier noted.

"I just thought that this would be a fun evening that we could all enjoy. I am sure that both Ophelia and Holly will be excited to see at least one of these performances," Anna added.

"You are probably right. Can we get enough people to cover for us? See if some of the college kids are willing to do split shifts. I will take care of the tickets, and let the girls know tonight. It should be a wonderful evening. Looking forward to it. Thanks, Anna."

By the time I finished all the emails on my computer, I noticed that the book club was already in progress. I took the elevator, located at the rear of the loft to avoid any disruption.

The ladies were listening attentively to Ophelia, while Holly, now dressed all in black, her signature color, wore a very chic ankle length pant suit with slightly balloon pants at the knee. Only someone as slim as Holly could pull this look off without looking like she was a clown at the circus.

In the corner, near the children's nook, I found a comfortable rocking chair where nobody could see me, and yet, it was easy to hear.

From my vantage point there were about ten ladies all listening tentatively to everything that Ophelia was saying. By this time everyone had read *Jane Eyre* which meant it should be a lively discussion.

"How many of you ladies, now that you have finished this novel, consider Jane a feminist character? Ophelia asked.

Nearly all the ladies raised their hands, with the exception of two older women sitting toward the back together. And, of course Holly.

"Wonderful! This will allow us to engage in a lively discussion. Those are the very best. And, by the way, I would like to introduce you to Sabriel 's cousin, Holly. She will be visiting a few weeks with us from New York."

165

All the ladies gave Holly a standing ovation welcoming her to the group. I was thankful that Ophelia continued with the idea that Holly and I were related, although I wasn't sure what I was going to say if anyone brought up that I was an orphan. That would be something that I would deal with later. No need to project problems when everything was moving along so nicely.

"Alright, then, let's discuss first why Jane is often referred to as one of the earliest feminist characters," Ophelia said.

She sounded very natural. As if she had lead these group discussions before. There was not even any notes for her to glance at. This reminded me of my own informal discussions with students when I was teaching in New Orleans.

"In feminist literature," Ophelia explained, "it is less important to identify any novel as entirely feminist. What is important to note is the feminist merits associated that influence our society then and now."

A young girl sitting comfortably in the front raised her hand politely. She reminded me of what I always thought the younger Jane Eyre would look like. In the Victorian era she would be considered simple. In today's world we might even call her "plain Jane". Regardless of her physical limitations this waif spoke very eloquently .

" May I say that when I read this novel I was only focusing on Jane's character development by Bronte, not how her heroin might change the feminine world as we know it now, or even at that time." The young girl then sat down. Waiting patiently for Ophelia to respond.

"That is a very keen insight, my dear. May I ask you to share your name with our group?" Ophelia asked.

"Yes, of course. My name is Savannah. I work here at the Colonial village as an authentic character during the weekends, and study theatre at Flagler College in the evening," she said to the group of ladies, who were all curious to hear more.

"Thank you Savannah. Maybe after our reading group you can talk about how you prepare for that reenactment and how it is different from the feminist movement today"

Ophelia said, bringing back the attention to the group. What neither Ophelia, nor I expected was Holly coming forward to speak.

"Well, may I suggest that we all put ourselves in Jane Eyre's world for a moment. Without understanding her we cannot make a fair judgement of who she is. And, I am not implying that any of us intentionally judge others, but, from my own personal experience I know that it is easy to misjudge a character," Holly said, now sitting comfortably on the bean chair explaining her analysis of Jane Eyre.

I held my breath when Holly said that she was once an orphan, like Jane. Thankfully she did not elaborate on how this effected her marriage at thirteen to a man old enough to be her father. More importantly is that Holly did offer to the group that Jane Eyre's deeply rooted moral beliefs is what makes her life choices sometimes more difficult.

And did anyone now wonder how we could be cousins, if Holly was an orphan. If they did, nobody said a word.

By sharing with the reading group their own personal experiences, without revealing exactly who they were, both Ophelia and Holly gained the respect and admiration of all those who attended.

After the last guest left, I appeared just in time to help my new friends clean up the leftovers.

"You ladies were very impressive. It is refreshing to listen to someone who is experienced, yet willing to accept other points of views," I said, truly captivated by their knowledge.

"This was so much fun. When I am captured in the pages of my book, I am limited by how my creator, Truman Capote, designed me. But, in fact, he was talented enough to leave many loose ends, and even various interpretations. Like Ophelia, I have expanded my characterization each time I visit your world," Holly said excited

"Well ladies I have another surprise for you. All of us, including Anna, Chloe, Alex, and maybe even Bailey, are going to the **Chautauqua** festival next Saturday," I said, showing the girls the flier.

"Oh my goodness. Have you ever visited one of these?" Ophelia asked, extremely joyful.

"No, I haven't. Today was the first time that I ever heard of this. But, from what Anna told me it should be very exciting. This flyer says that the **Chautauqua** is featuring Margaret Mitchell, and Mary Shelley. Two very interesting authors." I said.

"Are you related somehow to Mary Shelley, Sabriel?" Holly asked, genuinely curious.

I laughed, since this was not the first time I was asked this question. By the time that I was ten years old, books were my best friends. While others were reading *Pipi Longstockings* and Mary *Poppins,* I was attracted to the Romantic poets, and sometimes to the mysterious novels such as *Wuthering Heights, The Hound of the Baskervilles,* and, of course *Frankenstein.*

When I started college I pettioned the courts to change my last name to Shelley. Since I was an orphan without even a birth certificate when my grandmother died, my request was approved.

Sabriel Shelley just seemed to be a perfect pairing. Like just the right choice of wine with a good meal. It was another similarity that Holly and I shared. She also chose her name adopting Golightly for her moniker. I knew that once I was known as Dr. Shelley I finally was independent.

Chapter Twenty Nine

How mutable are our feelings, and how strange is that clinging love
we have of life even in the excess of misery.
—Frankenstein, by Mary Shelley

SABRIEL

O phelia and Holly were inseparable the next few days. Both
enjoyed working at the **CARCOSA,** spending the afternoon
at the beach, and walking the ancient streets of St.
Augustine. During the short time that Ophelia was here most of the
local businesses knew who she was. Well, at least they knew as
much as she allowed them to. Everything from spices and teas at the
charming shop on Hypolita, to the *Ancient Oil Gourmet* located, on
Kings Street.

A lovely blue willow china vase, that just somehow appeared one
day, now sits on the fireplace mantel, next to Bradley's urn. There is
always lavender, that Ophelia keeps fresh weekly. I can only assume
that she visits *Pelindaba Lavender Gift Shop,* on George Street
during her morning walks. Every morning that I see those flowers I
am reminded that I must visit *Cassadaga,* and make plans to put
Bradley's ashes to rest.

"Do you know the names of the Lions that welcome you on the
bridge?" Holly said one morning.

"Darling Holly, I am certain that the majority of tourists and
locals have no idea that those Lions even have names," I said, during
breakfast.

"Well, now you will learn something new," Holly said.

"Ophelia is really the one to thank. One afternoon she took me on
this lovely boat called *The Osprey.* Since she somehow became
friends with the captain of the boat, he took us around the bay where
the dolphins play. This is where I learned that these lovely lions
were sculptured by an Italian named F. Romanelli, for the city.

These original two lions were named, Firma and Faithful, the same words on the World War I flag monument across the street," Holly said, pausing for me to react.

"Oh, I do think that Anna did tell me this once, but certainly not with so many details," I said, reaching for the fresh blackberry preserves, that also appeared magically.

"But, then the story of the two newer lions at the other end of the bridge was a gift from a couple who fell in love, right here in St. Augustine. In 2015 Pax and Peli, who represent Peace and Happiness were introduced. You know, I don't really believe in true love, because I have never felt this. But, these lions I believe will bring you luck, Sabriel. And, when I return to my pages, and you see these two lions, I hope you will remember me," Holly said, looking directly into my eyes.

I reached across the table, held both of her hands, like she was the daughter I never had and said,

"Holly, I have held you near my heart longer than you could ever understand. I need no lions to remember who you are," I said, for the first time admitting how much she has influenced me.

"Is everyone ready for the great **Chautauqua** Festival today?" Ophelia said, entering the kitchen.

"I certainly am," Holly said, raising her hand.

"What time, do all these festivities begin?" I asked, trying to logistically plan my day.

"Anna said that we should all meet at the front gate by noon, since this is a very popular event, at St. Augustine. To avoid parking problems, Holly, and I will take our bikes, and Anna says you can ride with her, Chloe, and Alex," Ophelia said, confidently.

Since it seemed that all the plans were already made, I finished my last cup of tea, and walked through the garden to the **CARCOSA.** Greeting me at my Secret Garden Gate that leads to the **CARCOSA** patio, are two marble stone lions that look exactly like the ones on the bridge. Like all of the other mysterious gifts, I simply graciously accept how fortunate my life is at this moment.

Just as Anna predicted, the **Chautaqua** Festival was a success. Alex agreed to let us out at the gate where Holly and Ophelia were already waiting, talking to some friends that they must have recently met.

When they saw us approaching, Ophelia ran towards me and anxiously grabbed my hand, leading me to the front of the line. She reminded me of a child attending her first carnival.

"Let's go in, Sabriel. Alex will find us. We can wait for him next to the beer garden. He can't miss us," Ophelia said.

Everyone agreed, and as Ophelia predicted, within ten minutes Alex met us, with a frosty mug of ale.

"Hey, babe, do you want to meet us at the **Chautauqua** Tent? I think the performance lasts about an hour. Then we can check out all the other craft booths," Chloe said.

Alex decided to stay with some of his friends at the Beer Garden, and meet up with us later.

Although Mary Shelley wasn't scheduled to appear until 3:00pm, the ushers let us in as long as we sat in the unassigned seats at the back. On stage was an actress performing as Margaret Mitchell, author of *Gone With the Wind*. As many other people, in my generation, living in Atlanta, Georgia as a young child, we all knew about this novel. We also all wanted to be like Scarlett O'Hara. But, to be honest, it was the movie starring Vivian Leigh, as Scarllet, and Clarke Gable as Rhett Butler, that we're our role models.

Quite honestly, none of us, including me, knew much about Margaret Mitchell.

On stage, sitting at the desk was a small framed, petit woman with short brown hair coiffed in a traditional bob. Anywhere else, the lady would appear average, but as we all listened attentively it soon became apparent that the Margaret Mitchell we were observing spoke with authority.

She shared with the audience that she was just a normal southern belle born in 1900 to a wealthy political family. Her father was an attorney, but her mother was actually a suffragette. It was her maternal great grandfather, Philip Fitzgerald who emigrated from Ireland and owned slaves on his plantation, that became later the model for *Gone With the Wind*.

All of these details that I was listening to were interesting, but not until Margaret started talking about Scarlett did everything become truly fascinating. In 1928 on a Remington portable number three typewriter, her second husband John Marsh insisted that she write the story that was stored in her head. This actress narrating was very impressive. At one point I leaned over to Ophelia to ask if she might be the real Margaret Mitchell, and not just an actress.

"I have told you before, Sabriel that people reappear as ghosts, not like us characters," she whispered, turning her attention once again on the stage performance.

Finally, when "Margaret" told us that she at last began working exclusively on her civil war epic novel she named her original heroine Pansey O'Hara. It was only days before publication that she changed the name to Scarlett.

"Most people don't know this, but after spending so many years writing this novel, when my publisher insisted that I change Pansey's name to Scarlett, I replied,

"Sir, we could call her Garbage O'Hara as far as I care. I just want this to be over with," Margaret said. Some in the audience laughed, while others appeared shocked.

"Another interesting fact that many of you may not know or even appreciate, is that *Gone With the Wind* consumed ten years of my life. When I shared the news, with a friend that I was considering writing a novel, although it was already completed, she made the nasty remark that, 'imagine you ever writing a novel". That was what made me send my manuscript to a Macmillan editor the following day."

At the conclusion of Margaret's performance, she announced that there would be a fifteen minute break befor the next author, Mary Shelley would begin. Most of the audience left while we moved closer to the stage. That was when Ophelia almost ran across the theatre to embrace someone that I could not see from the angle where I was sitting. But, as Ophelia started to walk back, with her friend, I immediately knew who she was.

The raven black hair, styled perfectly so that it flows loosely past her shoulders beneath the straw hat was the first clue. Then as she approached, we all became speechless. Standing before us wearing a lovely southern belle gown, with the tiniest waist I have ever seen, was this perfect replica of who we all knew was Scarlett O'Hara. Like Holly, it was difficult to guess how old this lady was. Her green eyes, was what attracted me to her at this very moment.

"I am pleased to introduce you, to my friend Scarlett. She is anxious to learn more about St. Augustine, and all of you," Ophelia said, quite casually.

Scarlett extended her hand, politely to me, Anna, and Chloe, without saying a word. And, we of course were speechless. Even Holly never said a word.

After the initial shock that I was sitting next to Scarlett O'Hara, although Ophelia never mentioned her last name, I asked Scarlett if she was visiting from Savannah. Since Bradley and I were there not long ago, I hoped that we could start a friendly conversation before Mary Shelley appeared.

"My dearest Sabriel, I am visiting from numerous places in the south, including Savannah. There will be time to share all of that with you during my stay. I am so looking forward to hearing Mary Shelley speak. And, thank you so very much for inviting me to your home," Scarlett said in a very strong southern accent.

I looked at Ophelia for some answers, but before she could say another word, the lights dimmed and the stage lights were on a very petit, lovely woman standing near the stage.

Anna took my hand, realizing that I was clearly confused, and whispered," Everything will be fine. Scarlett is probably looking for work with the local character agency."

I acknowledged, nodding my head that she was probably correct, knowing better. I did have two more guest rooms, but it was beginning to feel like a boarding house. At this moment, with Mary Shelley speaking, I was just hoping that Frankenstein would not also appear asking to stay with us.

"In this living history dramatic interpretation you, the audience will learn why Mary Shelley was inspired to write her famous novel, Frankenstein, and perhaps even reveal some unknown facts about the author. Without any further delays, I am privileged to introduce to you, Mary Shelley," the master of ceremony said. The audience applauded as Mary Shelley stood up from the desk, and walked closer to the skirt of the stage.

"I am so very pleased to be here tonight in the ancient city of St. Augustine, which is older than I am!"

The audience laughed, but did not want to disturb the show with anymore distractions.

"Many of you know that my husband, Percy Byshee Shelley, is the famous romantic poet. When *Frankenstein* was published, there were critics that could not believe that I, a woman had the creative skill to write such a profound story. They must not have known, or forgotten that I was the daughter of philosophers and writers William Godwin and Mary Wollstonecraft.

What began in a Switzerland chateau with friends on a snowy day developed into a novel. This is when Percy insisted that I pursue the short 'ghost' story into a complete novel. But, none of this is why I am here today. Today I want to share with you some of my truly private reasons for creating the 'creature' who was given no name intentionally."

Mary Shelley moved quite gracefully back to a rocking chair with the spot light following her. I was mesmerized. Whoever this storyteller was, outside of this arena was not important. At this very moment I could feel the spirit of Mary Shelley in the room.

For the next forty minutes, without a musical background, or special effects Mary Shelley captured the attention of her audience. When she read from her diary the following excerpt every woman, a mother or not, had tears in their eyes.

I was eighteen years old when I began writing Frankenstein, or The Modern Prometheus. Two years earlier I lost my first child, at sixteen years old. In this very novel for ten days, I would write 'nurse the baby'. Then on the eleventh night, I woke up to give it suck. It appeared to be sleeping so quietly that I would not wake it. Then in the morning, I found it dead. My nameless child was dead. With grief came fear that my milk was poisoned. Yet, my breasts continued to fill, with no baby to feed. I would dream that my child would awaken again, but of course it did not. For many years, after that, and the death of other children, and Percy, I was convinced that I was at fault as I was when my mother died giving birth to me. Finally, Frankenstein would be my child; my literary child would show to the world who I was; who I am!

Later I said, when Frankenstein staged in London in 1823, and one critic called it 'This anonymous andromeda' that this nameless mode of naming the unnamable is rather good.

After all, just as Frankenstein creates the creature from various thrown away limbs, I am also an assemblage of parts. A feminist mother that I never knew. A reknowned philosopher admired by many. A gifted husband who died much too early. And, of course my many buried children and my one living son.

So many scholars have critiqued, criticized, and even suggested that my husband wrote most of this novel. None of this is important.

What is important is that every generation take responsibility for their creation. And, ask who is the creator?

At the end of the presentation, Sophia Adams, who personified Mary Shelley received a standing ovation. Ophelia, Holly, and Scarlett decided to remain longer to speak with the storyteller. Anna, Chloe, and I visited the few craft booths that remained open.

When Alex arrived at the front gate to take us home, I decided to walk by myself. It was a beautiful fall evening, and there was a lot on my mind.

Hearing about Margaret Mitchell, and Mary Shelley was beginning to stir some hidden places in my psyche. And, now there is Scarlett. I really am not sure how she fits in with Ophelia's overal plan, but I am certain it will soon become quite transparent. At least I hope so.

Chapter Thirty

"Dear Scarlett! You aren't helpless. Anyone as selfish and determined as you are is never helpless."
—Scarlett O'Hara , *Gone With the Wind*

SCARLETT O'HARA

One of the most difficult choices for me, is to step out of my beloved *Gone With the Wind,.*This is because there have been so many different reactions to who I really am. Similar to Holly Golightly, I am always seen as Vivian Leigh, which is very limiting. I am quite confident that before Margaret sold the rights to David Selznick, in 1936, for $50,000, no one who read this novel before, imagined that I looked like that actress.

It isn't that I don't like Vivian Leigh, after all she was confined to a script editor that chose to make many changes. In a novel that is over one thousand pages, you can just imagine how many editings took place. Enough that it took Margaret ten years to complete the sixty three chapters of her historical, romantic novel.

Early drafts even indicate that Margaret first refered to my plantation as *Fourtney Hall.* This was modeled after several Antebellum establishments nearby. But, it was the *Clayton County* plantation, where her maternal grandmother lived, Anna Fitzgerald Stevenson, that she used. It was also this lady, that Margaret chose to be my mother in the novel. She was the daughter of an Irish immigrant, who like many Plantation owners depended on their black slaves to be wealthy.

This idea, of slavery, I have heard most people now condemn. But, this does not change the novel that I reside in. At first , I tried to defend myself. After all it is the time era I lived in. I knew nothing else. And, Margaret wanted to depict accurately the historical background where I lived. My visit here to St. Augustine in the twenty first century is really not about me, and that will be difficult for me to remember. But, this is why I have other supporting characters to help me.

Gone With the Wind, if anyone ever had any doubts, is really all about me! At one time Margaret even considered using, a line from my own dialogue, *Tomorrow is Another Day,* as the title. Thankfully she came across this poem by Ernest Dowson, *Non Sum Qualis Eram Bonar sub Regno Cynarae*

"I have forgot much Cynara!
Gone with the wind,
Flung roses, roses riotously
With the throng,
Dancing, to put the pale, lost
Lilies out of mind"

To me it really doesn't matter what the title is. I am the real reason why anyone reads her book. I provide the entertainment. I provide the analysis for my actions. And, I provide so many different views of feminism that it makes my head spin sometimes.

I really do not know how much Sabriel understand who I am. She is an extremely lucky human that I would take time to spend with her. Why the others are here, is not really very clear. Ophelia is a respectable character, but why Holly Golightly? I mean, *Breakfast at Tiffany's?* It is not even a novel. It barely qualifies to be a novella. How can a real character develop into anything reliable in those few pages? Well, I suppose eventually I will be told why she is here.

What I want everyone to remember is that I am a very prominent lady who lives in a wealthy community, even after that nasty Civil War when I lost *Tara.* My aristocratic descendants were well respected in Savannah, Georgia for many years.

Most of my admirers notice first my jet black hair, green eyes, and pale skin. Something that I will need to be careful with here in the Florida sun. Of course, it is my tiny waist that allows me to wear clothes that accentuate my perfect body. And, yet with all my beauty I could not attract the one man that I wanted, Ashley Wilkes. Instead, that annoying Rhett Butler keeps showing up in my life.

Even after I agreed to marry Rhett, and give him a child, at the end of the novel he leaves me. But, it is I that have the final words. I intend to share all this knowledge with Sabriel. She definitely needs some advice about men. It has been already a few months since Bradley passed and yet no serious beaus. We will work on that problem along with several others that Ophelia briefed me on.

Some have called me strong and vain, but without the insight needed to make good choices. This might be true, when I was younger, but I assure you it is no longer a valid observation. Everyone asks what happens to Rhett at the end of the novel. But, no one ever asks what happens to me, Scarlett. Well, I am here to tell everyone that Scarlett is a survivor; she has learned how to take control of her own life.

Many people who have met me, outside of the novel now agree that I am not the iconic example of a southern belle. Rather, I am a very independent thinking female. Some people have expressed that I was a fierce supporter of the Confederacy, and ultimately slavery. This is not really true. My loyalty is only to me. When I realized that the south lost this war, my loyalty also changed. And, as far as my negro slaves, how was I to know that they weren't happy at Tara? I was far too busy entertaining my many suitors. It was not something that I ever thought about.

Now, my cousin Melanie Hamilton, was truly a good person. She is my antithesis. I hated that she married, Ashley, but I loved her for her sincere, authentic love for everyone, including me. Melanie succumbed to the restrictions placed on us by family, community, and of course our husbands. I chose to rebel, and continue to live. Melanie behaved, and died.

These four cardinal values that all women were bound to follow are, piety, purity, submissiveness, and domesticity. What I discovered in my travels is that these cult restrictions on women continued into the twentieth century. And traces of these outdated norms still reseurface even in this decade, today. I am here to remind Sabriel to enjoy life on her terms.

During my time in the novel, *Gone With the Wind,* I was so much more than a southern belle. Being a caring daughter, wife, caregiver, nurse, all seem to be duties of a proper maiden. But, the only time that I adhered to these obligations was when it was forced upon me or benefited my situation.

Many people will be surprised to know that the Civil War actually liberated me from many of the restrictions that the south imposed on women like me. Naturally, the war also exposed me to extreme changes. Fleeing Atlanta with Melanie and her baby, nearly all on my own, with only a passing assistance from Rhett, on his way to fight with the Confederacy, challenged my entire being to stay strong. Could any other Southern Belle accomplish this? I think not!

When I returned to Tara and saw the destruction around me, including my parents, I pour myself a drink, and tell my father,

"I know no lady drinks spirits, but today I'm no lady, Pa. There is work to do tonight."

And, work I did. Everyone knows by now that I did whatever was needed to keep Tara, including working the fiields. But, when I married Frank Kennedy to get the money I needed for the taxes on Tara, many conservatives thought I crossed the line of decency. What those people do not give me credit for is that I work as hard as any of those men. In retrospect I should be credited for beginning to erase the boundaries between genders. Instead, many critics focus only on my personal flaws.

Although nobody ever asks me, I believe that Margaret Mitchell created me in her own image. The image that she wanted to be. I try to continue to share this with other females that I meet. Those of us who have stepped from the pages of our books are dedicated to showing Sabriel Shelley what her life can be.

I find it more than ironic that Margaret chose the title from a poem that refers to a girls name, Cynara, which means thistly plant. I am Scarlett a thorny plant that must be handled with care.

Sabriel is a prickly pear.The two of us should become great friends.

Chapter Thirty One

I'm not a romantic, but even I concede that the heart does not exist solely for the purpose to pump blood.

—*Downton Abbey*

SABRIEL and ERIC

I did not expect to see anyone I knew walking home from *The Chautauqua* . After all the festival was still going on quite lively, with plenty of wine and other spirits offered at the beer garden until midnight. It was a perfect night to lounge around on picnic blankets, with your favorite sweetheart, and listen to a nice mix of Rod Stewart, *Fleetwood Mac,* or classic jazz. Several live performing bands were on stage singing all the old favorites.

Everywhere throughout St. Augustine, even in the local cafes, off the popular streets, there was music being played. If not by musicians, there was always a streaming music channel with rock 'n roll from the 60's, or the sounds of saxophones, reminiscing well known tunes that set a mellow mood. The diversity of this town is what surprises, and energizes me everyday.

"Sabriel? Sabriel Shelley? Is that you competing for a 5K? "

I heard a man's voice that was just slightly familiar. When I stopped and turned around, Eric reached for my wrist. When he realized what he had done he released my arm.

"I am so sorry if I startled you. It was just I wanted to get your attention before you ran so far ahead of me that it was too late," Eric said trying to catch his breath.

Once I realized who it was, I apologized for my rude reaction.

"Although I never really was afraid of walking the streets of St. Augustine, it still makes me nervous when I pass the *Huguenot Cemetery* on Cordova Street. I guesss that my mind was just imagining all kinds of strange encounters when I heard your voice,"

I said, actually thankful now that I had someone I knew to share the walk with.

In the moonlight Eric looked particularly like the actor George Peppard. If that name does not sound familiar, George was a well known actor in the 1960's. Really even before my time. But, when I saw *Breakfast at Tiffany's,* shortly after reading the novel, I fell madly in love. Not really with the actor, but his role as Paul Varjak, a young writer struggling to be recognized as an author in New York.

I must have watched that movie one hundred times. Each time hoping that Holly Golightly would change her mind, and live happily ever after with Paul. When it always ended the same, I cried for hours. Finally I just stopped watching, and decided that I would be Holly. I would rewrite the ending to my own story. And, when Bradley came into my life, I thought that my story was now complete. And, then it all fell apart.

"Are you okay, Sabriel? I just thought that it might be nice to walk together since we are going the same direction," Eric said, quietly.

"Yes, I'm fine. So sorry for spacing out. Of course I am pleased to have company. Were you at *The* **Chautauqua** tonight? I didn't see you there?" I said, while we continued to walk.

"I was there to write a feature story about Margaret Mitchell, and Mary Shelley. Those two actresses portrayed the writers so effectively that I almost expected to see Frankenstein and Scarlett O'Hara appear in the audience."

If only Eric knew? But, it was not going to be me to reveal how crazy my life has evolved. I would not even know where to begin this absurd story. Who would ever believe that I now have living in my house three famous characters from well known literary novels? And, by the way, there may be more arriving any day.

"I think that the *Tini Martini Bar,* at the *Casablanca Inn* is still open. Can I buy you a night cap?" Eric said, stopping a few steps in front of the hotel.

"I'm not sure if that is a good idea. It is getting rather late for me, and I have to open the **CARCOSA** tomorrow morning, since my entire staff is still at the Faire," I said, politely.

"We both need to get up early. I need to get this story edited for the Sunday edition. But, it is only 11:00pm. One drink would be a nice way to end this lovely evening," Eric said, now opening the front door to the Inn.

"Okay, one drink, and one drink only," I said, reluctantly.

Eric suggested that we sit on the verandah that faces the Matanzas Bay. Although this bar was only a short distance from my house, it was my first time here. The menu was incredible. I had no idea that there were these many choices.

"How am I supposed to choose from this menu? " I said, smiling totally confused.

"No worries. I will order for you. Do you trust me?" Eric said. His grey eyes looked directly at me for the first time.

Trust you? Yes. Do you trust me? That's the real question. Don't really think that one drink is going to make us best friends. I will always be friendly, but although you are graceful, charming, and more beautiful than a man deserves to be, I will not walk into your polished life.

"Well, lets just say that I trust you enough to order me a drink," I said, continuing to stare at him until the waiter walked up to take our order.

"The lady will have *Kiss on the Lips,* and I will have the *Classic English Martini,"* Eric said, confidently, as if he was an expert. As, I am sure he is.

"That was an interesting choice," I said.

"It was the ingredients in the Martini that I thought you might enjoy, although the name was also quite appealing," he said, once again in control.

I decided to ignore the temptation to respond, and volleyed my next question into his court.

"Anna mentioned to me that you have quite an interesting legacy here in St. Augustine. Have you lived here your entire life, Eric," I asked, sounding as if I was interviewing him.

" It was nice of Anna to share with you some of my background, although I never really talk about it very much. It is the present that keeps me occupied most of the time. That is why I decided to be a journalist. Current events, even here in St. Augustine, can be quite stimulating," Eric said, cleverly avoiding my question.

Before I could rephrase, and ask once again, our drinks arrived.

"Let's celebrate a new friendship, and many more evenings like this in the near future," Eric lifted his class for the toast. I of course felt obligated to follow, although I wasn't exactly sure what he was implying.

"How many years did you live in NOLA? It must have been such an exciting place with all its history surrounding you," Eric asked.

Once again, Eric found a way to use his skills to bring the attention on me. I wasn't sure how much he already knew about me or how he found out that I lived in New Orleans, but I was careful to only reveal the minimum. This was beginning to feel now more like a chess game than a tennis match.

"New Orleans offers many different facets to those who are lucky to live there. It is also surrounded by poverty. Many people who visit come to be entertained rather than to appreciate all of the true beauty it has to offer. Have you ever had the opportunity to see New Orleans?" I asked.

It was his move now, and I felt fairly confident that my chess piece was in a safe area.

"As a matter of fact, I was in New Orleans several years ago. I was a freelance journalist at the time. I was there for The New Orleans Jazz and Heritage Festival in May 2016. The festival started in 1970 when it was originated by the New Orleans Hotel and Motel Associaton. The history behind how this festival was organized was quite extensive. It also included many well known performers, like Mahalia Jackson, Duke Ellington, Fats Domino, that would invite local bands to play with them. Although, those performances were earlier than my time I was able to interview many others that shared with me their personal experiences. Two years later I finally completed a few short stories and self published the book."

"I am very impressed. My husband…I mean my late husband wrote several historical books. At the time of his death he was writing a study on how the supernatural influences literature in the mojo triangle of New Orleans, Savannah, and St. Augustine. Unfortunately he was never able to complete his work," I said, revealing more than I had intended.

"Dr. Bradley was a well respected writer. I have read his books, and had the opportunity to meet him when I was writing the jazz pieces. When I heard of his passing I was truly saddened. Have you ever considered completing his manuscript, Sabriel?" Eric asked.

Now I was in a real quagmire. I revealed far too much about myself. And, why didn't Eric ever mention earlier to me that he knew Bradley? I was beginning to feel like I was in checkmate, or at the very least check. My next response would determine this outcome.

"What is the title of your book, Eric? You know that the **CARCOSA** has an entire section for Indie Authors. I would be happy to promote it. The Lincolnville has a yearly jazz festival of its own which is much smaller than those in New Orleans, but nevertheless quite entertaining," I said, standing up preparing to leave.

Before Eric could respond, I added,

"Thank you so much for the walk and the late evening drink. I will be looking forward to reading your book. Don't forget to bring me a few copies next time you are downtown."

Thankfully the *Tini Martini Bar,* truly is tiny. I was able to be out the door and downstairs before Eric could even pay the bill.

How could I have agreed to have this simple drink ? Maybe because it appeared like safe territory. Anyway, it's over now. Hopefully all my guests are sleeping, and I don't need to explain where I was or who I was with.

I decided to go through the front door, rather than the garden, just in case anyone was sitting in the patio. As soon as I turned the lock I was in the living room. Bailey greeted me with kisses and his tail wagging.

"Is there anyone else home?" I whispered to Bailey,

He looked at me confused, smelling my pants hoping to discover where I had been. Once Bailey understood that I was going to my bedroom he followed behind. That made me fairly confident that the girls were home sleeping. Bailey never goes to bed until everyone is accounted for.

Once in my bed, Bailey jumped up and took his designated place next to me. When Bradley was alive, Bailey always found a space next to both of us. Since his death, Bailey has been the only male in my bed, and feeling him next to me always brings me comfort.

The next morning, it was the sound of a television that woke me up. Bailey was no longer sleeping next to me, and somehow opened the door to let himself out. But, who was watching television? Since Ophelia arrived several weeks ago, she never once showed any interest in watching anything on television . So why now? I decided to find out.

Sitting on the sofa was Ophelia, and Scarlett already dressed in the same distressed jeans and terry cloth sweaters with hoods. The only distinction is that Ophelia's sweater was a lavender purple, and Scarlett's was a magnolia peach. Nobody would ever guess who these two were in there modern attire.

On the floor, staring methodically at the action on television, was Holly. Now she did resemble my image of her character. Wearing tight white linen ankle pants, with a watercolor cotton long sleeve button front blouse, hair in a pulled back ponytail, legs crossed like a Indian on the wood floor she looked sixteen.

"Why have I never heard of this movie before? It is absolutely splendid. I am just in love with everything about *Downton Abbey.* Aren't all of you also?" Holly said, without taking her eyes off of the screen.

"Most likely, Holly, you haven't been called out into the human world as often as Ophelia and I have. After all, darling, how can you expect to have the same status as Ophelia , who was created by the greatest playwright in the world, or myself, the most desired woman in the world?" Scarlett replied, arrogantly.

Before Holly could respond, Ophelia spoke up.

"The reason that you both enjoy this series is because, Holly you are very similar to Sybil, the rebel daughter who runs away with the radical Irish chauffeur. And, you, dear Scarlett certainly can relate to the oldest daughter, Mary. Both of you are so pompous, that all the men stand in line to be your suitors," Ophelia said, trying to be the mediator.

That is when I knew it was time to make my presence known.

"And, you Ophelia remind me of the brilliant grandmother, Violet, that always knows what to do," I said entering the room, still dressed in my pajamas.

Everyone turned around at me, not knowing how long I was standing there. It was Scarlett who spoke first.

"Good morning Sabriel. You just missed a very handsome beau who stopped by with some wonderful southern biscuits, gravy, and peach butter. Since your servents must not work today, I put everything in the kitchen. "

I was not quite sure what Scarlett meant about some beau, or servants, but Ophelia filled in all the blank spaces.

"The gentleman that Scarlett is referring to is Eric Pacetti. He asked me to give you those boxes of biscuits from *The Blue Hen,* that are in the kitchen, and also this book."

Everyone in the city knows that the *Blue Hen* makes the freshest homemade biscuits anywhere. The first time that I stopped in for breakfast, I saw a mail carrier picking up an order of biscuits to go, and two military men in fatigues sitting at the counter. Once I tried them myself I knew what everyone was talking about. But why did Eric bring these to me? And, there were enough here to serve all of us. Delivering it here, rather than the **CARCOSA** is also questionable. Not many people know exactly where I live. But, then again Eric is reporter.

I looked at the book that Ophelia handed me. *The Influence of Jazz on Life and Culture in New Orleans, by Eric Pacetti.* I did suggest last night that he bring his novel to the bookstore and I would showcase it in the Indie section. But, now that I was holding it in my hands, I decided to read it first. Perhaps it would give me some insight into who this Eric Pacetti was.

Since Eric seemed to know much about me, I also decided that I would do some research about him. Anna would be my first resource. The next time that Mr. Pacetti and I would meet the chess game would have a different result. Playing games is something I try to avoid, since I am such a bad loser.

Chapter Thirty Two

Man is least himself when he talks in his own person. Give him a mask and he will give you the truth.

—Oscar Wilde

SABRIEL and SCARLETT

Two weeks past and everything seemed normal. Well, as normal as it can be when you have literary characters who have taken residence in your head, and your home

When I asked Ophelia if there were going to be any further surprise guests in the near future, I could never get a definite answer. All she would remind me of is that characters only appear on human territory when or if they are needed.

It is true that, at least this far, Ophelia, Holly, and Scarlett are all women that I admire or want to learn more about. But, as a literature professor there are many characters that I am fond of, but I don't have enough room in my house, or my mind for all of them at the same time.

Then there is also the question of what do I do with these characters daily. I have a business to run, and I cannot spend my days being a tour guide or plan my agenda around the activities of my guests. In a few weeks the holiday season begins with Halloween, and there is no sign of any characters leaving.

Ophelia continues to lead the book groups. Currently they are reading, *Their Eyes are Watching God,* by Zora Neale Hurston who lived in St. Augustine for a short time There is a small memorial park dedicated to her on the corner of Ponce de Leon Boulevard and King Street.

Holly became interested in the relationship that Zora had with another local author, Marjorie Kinnan Rawlings. She is the author of *The Yearling.*

Even Scarlett decided to learn more about Zora. A black woman author was something that Scarlett never believed possible. But, listening to the ladies enthusiasm made her realize that her limited viewpoints were only due to the racial society she lived in.

One afternoon Holly told me that Scarlett had seen *The Scarlett O'Hara Restaurant and Bar,* located on the corner of Hypolita Street. She became so excited that there was this very popular establishment named after her.

"She insisted that Ophelia and I go in with her, promising that we would just look around and have some sweet Georgia tea. Her main reason was to make certain that everything was authentic.

"After all ladies, if it was your name out there on a marquee wouldn't you want to know it was legitimate?" Scarlett said.

So, we agreed, but Ophelia made Scarlett promise that she would behave and not embarrass us.

Apparently, once inside, the building was quite rustic. It was once a house built in 1870. Rumors have it, that the owner was murdered in the bathtub. Like many other buildings in St. Augustine the man's ghost is a regular visitor.

What attracted Scarlett was the *Gone With the Wind* memorabilia and menu. The food was all authentic southern, but it was the several images of her and Rhett that made Scarlett smile.

"I didn't want to say anything to spoil Scarlett's day but those pictures were not of her, they were of Vivian Leigh, who portrayed her on the screen. I wanted to tell her that nobody even knew what she really looks like, since everybody has their own imagination. But, Scarlett can be such a nasty bitch, that I decided to avoid the conflict," Holly said

Unfortunately, it did not end there. Scarlett , somehow using that southern charm convinced the manager to let her be the hostess. She could circulate the dining room and bar entertaining the customers with "true" tales from *Gone With the Wind.* The manager agreed, and even provided her with a costume.

The next day the manager got much more than he expected. Everything went well until a young black couple came in. They were seated near the stage where the band was about to play.

When Scarlett approached the table she pulled up a chair and started telling the couple that they looked just like her slaves at *Tara.*

Obviously this was not acceptable to the guests, who immediately left after complained to the manager about the racist comments.

Scarlett could not understand his grievances. In her mind she was being honest, authentic, and definitely real. When Ophelia tried to explain to Scarlett, she became defensive and hurt. Holly said that she has been locked up in her room now all day. Once I heard this, I left the **CARCOSA** and went home immediately. Not sure what I could say to improve the situation, because Scarlett was definitely out of line, but maybe if I could give her a crash course on twenty first century etiquette behavior it might resonate.

Upstairs, I knocked politely. Although it was still my home, Scarlett was a guest like any other visitor, and deserved her privacy.

A few moments later, Scarlett slightly opened the door. When she saw it was me she threw the door open and gave me a huge hug, and said, "Oh Miss Sabriel, I am so sorry…I never wanted to embarrass you. Ophelia tried to explain to me why everyone was so upset. I came here to help you, not to cause you any trouble."

I lead Scarlett to the bed, where we both sat down. Her eyes were red and swollen from hours of crying. It was not the time to address why she was here, although I am still trying to find out that answer. Now, it was more important to make Scarlett feel welcome.

"Please trust me Scarlett there is nothing that you can do to ruin my reputation in this city. Everyone says and does something that they are sorry for later. What is important is to learn from those experiences. Now you are limited by the life you lead in your novel, *Gone With the Wind.* I am not sure how many other opportunities you have had to leave the security of that novel, but I can tell you that even in the Twenty-first century there are people that cannot accept the idea that we are all equal. This means that the color of our skin does not determine who we are, or how we are treated. Now, I will tell you, that what you said was improper, but many people in this country still think like you, even today," I said.

Scarlett had stopped crying. She was listening attentively, but still looked confused. Finally she said, "If the blacks are now part of the white community, then why is there still a problem ?"

I wasn't prepared how to answer that question. Many other people keep asking that same question. But, I did say,

" We do the best we can Scarlett. The more often that you are able to interact with the black community the more natural it becomes.

189

Now, I want you to put all of this aside, and prepare for the holidays. Do you know what Halloween is?" I asked, changing the subject.

"Yes, I have heard about this event. It does sound like a very fun activity. Do you think that I can also participate? I have no idea what to do, but maybe Ophelia can help," Scarlett said, sounding normal once again.

"Holly is the one who will be able to give you more advise. She is closer to this decade. I am sure she would be glad to help," I said, glad that we were moving forward.

Scarlett had this odd look on her face. It was as if she was trying to determine how to respond without being ungrateful.

"Miss Sabriel, I would much prefer your assistance. Holly truly hates me. She thinks that I have no true qualities. It reminds me much of what I have heard others write about me. I have been referred to as someone who is always self conceited, selfish, pompous. But, nobody realizes how difficult it was for me to go from riches to rags and survive. Holly has no respect for me, and I have much contempt for her," Scarlett said.

I knew of course that there was no way to change these negative feelings in one conversation, but I really did not want drama while both these ladies were residing with me. And, I am certain that they were not invited here for that purpose. I could discuss this issue with Ophelia who appears to be the leader, but that might appear like I could not handle a simple disagreement. Certainly this minor personality contrast can be corrected.

"There is nothing that I can do about those negative analysis, Scarlett, but while you are here, with Ophelia, and Holly we will all enjoy each other's company. Therefore, any personal disagreements will all be held inside. The holiday season will bring out the best in all of us," I said, raising from the bed. I was confident that there would be peace once more.

Now it was time to research Eric Pacetti. I sent him a pleasant text message thanking him for the *Blue Hen* gift, and novel. There was no further communication. After reading his book, I asked Anna to call him.

"Are you sure you don't want to call him yourself, Sabriel?" Anna said, smiling coyly.

"I know what you want to do Anna, but we are just friends. He is a nice gentleman, but that is all. Just call him and ask if we can send someone over to *The Revord* to pick up about ten of his books. We can showcase them on the Indie book table," I said, trying to sound casual.

"Okay. But, you can definitely be friends with Eric without thinking that it has to be romantic. Just because he is intelligent, handsome, and fun to be with doesn't mean that you need to fall for him," Anna said, obviously thinking she was being clever.

I just walked to my office without responding. If he was interested in me, Eric would have responded to my text. I wasn't even sure that he didn't have a girlfriend. Whatever the reason for him avoiding me, I was going to keep our relationship on a business level.

Anna did mention that he had an interesting family background well known in St. Augustine. I decided to use the internet to do some research. What I discovered was that the Pacetti name derives from the Latin word "pax" which means peace. This name was first associated with Negusanti Pacetti who was friendly with Emperor Federico I. Both settled in Bologna.

There were so many famous men from Venice to Rome during the sixteenth century. First there was Luca, a mathematician well known in Venice. Later Iacopo was a well respected painter. And, Aspilio, was appointed musical director of King Sigismund II, at the Royal Chapel of Warsaw, Poland. Definitely an impressive resume.

But, it was Anna that said that Eric had local ties to the community. And, I do remember driving past Pacetti Bay Middle School once, after I met Eric at the **CARCOSA** grand opening celebration. I believe it was then that I asked Anna if there was any significance associated between the two names. At first, Anna just gave me some general background. It wasn't until she learned that we had drinks after the **Chautauqua** she revealed more about Eric.

What I learned was that the Pacetti name that everyone associates with in St.Augustine is not related to Eric. When he was growing up here, many people assumed that Eric came from a wealthy family. He never shared any details with anyone. It was not until he graduated from high school and left for New York to attend Columbia University, on a full paid scholarship, did anyone know that Eric was homeless, and lived in foster care.

Nobody knows all the details, but Anna remembered hearing that at seven years old, Eric was found eating from a garbage can outside of the *Columbia Restaurant* parking lot, by one of the waiters. He took Eric to the St. Francis Housing Crisis Center.

After a few weeks a foster family agreed to keep Eric. It was not clear why or how he ended up living on the streets of St. Augustine. None of the regular homeless people recognized Eric or knew where he came from. But, once he was in school Eric quietly began to excel in every subject.

By the time Eric was in high school he participated on the swim team, became editor of the newspaper, and the yearbook. In addition he became a member of the debate team, student government, and theatre. It was not until the school announced that Eric was graduating Magna cum lauda, did anyone realize how smart he really was.

Although Eric dated, he never had a serious relationship. When he came back to St. Augustine to work as a reporter, everyone was surprised. According to Anna, no one ever expected to see him again. Somebody later said that he heard that Eric chose the last name Pacetti when he saw that name on a sign for St. Augustine Beach mayor. He liked the name because it sounded important.

Eric was right. The Minorcans in this area are combinations of different nationalities including Pacetti. It is well documented that many of these people came from the Mediterranean in 1768 as indentured slaves. Once the Spanish took over the city again, they became interwoven with history as evidenced by the street names, businesses, and bridges.

Although Eric was not a known descendant of the Pacetti family, it certainly gave him the desire to keep that name proud. Anna, assured me that I didn't need to worry about Eric wanting any commitments.

She said, quite seriously that,

"It is not in his genes. Everyone knows that Eric enjoys being a part of this community. That's why he returned here from New York. But, let me tell you, Sabriel, Eric has had many opportunities to be with some beautiful young ladies, but he is quite happy being a bachelor. So feel free to be friends. He is safe!"

This sounded like an interesting story. But, there were too many missing details. The real question is do I want to know what they are?

Chapter Thirty Four

Like a moth attracted to fire
Yesterday's memories are
Laced with lethal visions that
Invade our dreams,
Invade our lives,
Invade our piece of mind.

—Gabriella Girard, *Destiny Revisited*

SABRIEL meets GABRIELLA

October in St. Augustine is not only the beginning of a tropical fall season it is also the preparation for a spooky Halloween. In a town where Ghost trams are popular all year, now the entire downtown begins to prepare for ghouls to walk the cobblestone streets.

Anna, Chloe, and Savannah were busy decorating the **CARCOSA** as soon as I turned the page on the calendar. We all decided to dress in appropriate Halloween attire to promote the holiday spirit. This included adding a children's spooky storytelling on Tuesday evenings.

Chloe, dressed as the *Good Witch.* This was a very popular Hallmark and television show about the mysterious Cassandra Nightingale that appears at a haunted house in a created suburban town of Middleton.

After the ghostly storytelling, Chloe included a video party of the *Good Witch,* that was very popular. We served pumpkin cookies, and apple cider while the kids were watching the program.

I was the only one hesitant to dress up, although as the owner of the **CARCOSA** I knew that I had no choice. It was just that Halloween was not my favorite holiday. In fact it frightened me. Even when I was married to Bradley, living in New Orleans, another ghostly city that celebrated for weeks the dead, it made me very nervous. Maybe it was because Bradley was so very consumed about the occult when he was researching it for his manuscript. I knew that there was another world beyond ours. I even now have living characters to prove this. But, the macabre was much different. Celebrating the dead and inviting them to appear are two very different events.

Anna, however, came up with the perfect suggestion. Since the Flagler College is often called Hogswart, since the buildings are so similar, I would be Hermione, from *Harry Potter.*

This was something that I could actually accept.

I wore a white button down shirt with a red and gold striped tie, and black leggings. The black robe with a hood had a *Gryffinfor* patch. Then to truly make it authentic I included the *Gryffinfor* scarf and knee high socks. Anna found me a magic wand that a friend bought her from *Universal Studio.*

"Well, Anna, what do you think? Please tell me if I look ridiculous," I asked, facing the long mirror in my bedroom.

"Ridiculous? Absolutely not, Sabriel! You look better than Emma Watson. I think that you should wear that costume all year. It is HOT!" Anna said.

"Thank you for all of the compliments, but I am glad to only have to play this part for a short time," I responded.

Now my character guests were all thrilled with this Halloween month. It meant that they could all be themselves, including wearing their favorite attire. But what they liked most is that they could tell people who they were .

"Now girls, for this entire month you will be able to role play who you really are. It gives us the opportunity to truly be free spirits. Just be careful not to over play with those that you meet. Have fun, but always remember that we are Sabriel's guest."

I overheard Ophelia say one morning to Holly and Scarlett. Even with Ophelia's warning I was still worried how the community would accept them. Especially after Scarlett's confrontation at the restaurant last month.

"Darling you worry far too much. I can assure you my sweet Sabriel, that we will all be well behaved characters. Now we thought that it would be nice to have lunch at the park near the marina and lighthouse. Would you like to join us?" Ophelia asked.

"Thank you for reassuring me about all my apprehensions. Lunch sounds delightful. Do you want to take the bikes on the Jeep carrier. That way we can all go together. I will bring Bailey also. He needs some exercise," I said, looking for his leash

"That sounds great! I will go see if the girls are ready. We will meet you outside," Ophelia answered.

Within minutes everything was in place. Including the three bikes that were already on the bike rack by the time I came out.

As Ophelia predicted it was a lovely afternoon for a fall picnic. There were few people at the park, which allowed me to let Bailey roam freely. St. Augustine is a dog friendly environment with many people taking their dogs to even restaurants. But, they also expect you to keep them on leash and not leave their excrement behind. Today the only other couple at the picnic table also let their dog off leash. Bailey enjoyed the company.

Ophelia took Scarlett on a tour of the Lighthouse. Holly, Bailey and I took a short walk after lunch. As we walked down the dirt roads with the marvelous lush trees providing a tunnel that blocked the sun rays, Holly found a street with her name on it.

"Can we do some exploring Sabriel? I would like to find what is at the end of this street," Holly asked.

I was curious also. So, Holly in front, with Bailey and I close behind, walked to the end of the street, which lead us directly into the Marina. It was a beautiful view of the Lighthouse from one vantage point to the open sea on the other side. There were several motor boats enjoying the warm October weather.

Just about the time that I was going to suggest that we start back, Bailey broke loose and went straight to a large rock protruding from the water. Holly ran after him.

Once she reached him I could tell from a distance that Holly was embracing someone, while Bailey was jumping up and down barking.

After a few minutes Holly took her sweater off and wrapped it around the stranger. It was difficult to see if this was a child, small man, or another animal.

As they were approaching closer, I could tell that it was definitely a young woman. She had her head down looking at the ground being led entirely by Holly and Bailey.

Finally they reached me and Holly said,

195

"Sabriel, we must do something. This is Gabriella. She is lost and desperate. I do not even know if she has a last name. Maybe Ophelia will know what to do with her?"

I gently raised the lady's bent head. Her emerald green eyes were glassy, lost. We were likely the same age.

"You don't need to worry about anything. We are going to take care of you. Can you tell us where you are from," I asked, very quietly not to scare her.

Then, she noticed the lighthouse and pointed at it. Her voice still shaken she said,

"I was sitting on the sand at Tybee Beach and the Lighthouse…Jake's and my Lighthouse…this is all I remember seeing from the ocean. How did I get here? I mean, where am I? I have to get back to the hotel now. Tomorrow is Molly's wake. I need to give the eulogy. Please…please help me. I must be there on time."

"We will help you the best that we can, but somehow you are here now, at St. Augustine. Last year, my husband and I visited Savannah, Georgia and we rented a quaint cottage at Tybee Island. But, don't worry, I have a friend that I am sure can help you," I said, really hoping that I was right.

Thankfully the confused lady trusted Holly and I to take her to my house. Bailey sat in the back seat with her, feeling very protective. All of us were very quiet. Holly offered our new guest a soda, but she refused. Instead she tilted her head next to the window and closed her eyes.

When I pulled into the driveway, the bicycles were on the porch. Ophelia and Scarlett must have taken the bike route home. I led the young lady into the house, and called Ophelia from the stairs.

As soon as she saw this stranger holding my hand, Ophelia immediately knew what to do. She took her other hand, without saying a word and left Holly and I downstairs .

"Don't you worry, Sabriel. Ophelia is truly an old soul. She may look young but don't let that fool you. Ophelia will know exactly what to do," Holly said, sitting next to me.

I turned on the television, just as a distraction. But, it was Holly that always watched whatever was on, always fascinated by the people talking to her.

About one hour later, Ophelia came down alone. She handed me a book with a picture of a lighthouse on the cover. I remembered buying this novel when I was in Savannah with Bradley.

"Is this the Tybee Lighthouse that she was taking about," I asked.

"Yes. But, I know nothing about this novel. I will read it tonight. Anyway, the mystery lady's name is Gabriella Girard. She lives in this novel, *Destiny Revisited.* I am really not sure yet why she is here, but maybe after I read it I will understand more. She is sleeping in the third bedroom. I don't dare put her with Scarlett, even though they are both from Georgia. I will let you know more tomorrow," Ophelia said, walking back upstairs.

I left Holly mesmerized in front of the television, while I moved into my bedroom for some solitude. There are now four very different characters living in my house with no sign of leaving soon. Just as I was going to take a nap my text message notified me. It was from Eric asking me about the Halloween Party at the *Corazon Theatre.*

It was just too much for me to take at this moment. Scarlett's famous line at the end of *Gone With the Wind,* seemed most appropriate at this time, "After all tomorrow is another day!"

Chapter Thirty Five

"Letting go means to come to the realization that some people are a part of your history, but not a part of your Destiny."
—Steve Maraboli

GABRIELLA GIRARD

Savannah, Georgia in 1963 was like living in the Charles Dickens novel, *The Tale of Two Cities*. My two cities were represented by a high school where I never felt accepted, and the other was my "undercover" world with Jake Chevalier where I always felt loved and safe.

But, my life is just like Dickens begins his tale by saying, "It was the best of times, it was the worst of times, it was the age of wisdom, it was the age of foolishness, it was the epoch of belief, it was the incredulity, it was the season of Light, it was the season of Darkness, it was the spring of hope, it was the winter of despair, we had everything, before us, we had nothing before us, we were all going direct to heaven, we were all going direct the other way—in short, the period was so far like the present period, that some of the noisiest authoritied insisted on it being received , for good, or for evil, in the superlative degree of comparison only."

My name is Gabriella Girard. My story is not as well known as Ophelia's, or Holly Golightly, or certainly, not Scarlett O'Hara. But, in many ways I am a product of each. Just as we have all arrived here in St. Augustine to be a part of Sabriel's world, all of these characters and so many more were an intricate part of my own world.

Literature, all forms, including, scripts and movies offered me an escape from a threatening universe that I never felt I belonged. When I met, Jake Chevalier I was only thirteen years old. He opened my heart and eyes to the real possibility that I could escape the restraints of my safe imagination.

Jake became my real, Lancelot. And, I was able to share with him the secrets that James Joyce, T.S.Eliot, and William Faulkner taught me. That is, until the Vietnam War marched into our lives destroying any chance for a future.

My very best, and only friend, Molly saved me from total self destruction. It was because of her that I rose from the ashes of grief, like the mythological Phoenix, and recaptured my life, at Georgetown University.

While I was earning my degree in literature with plans to be a university professor, Molly attended the Savannah College of Art and Design. Eventually, Molly moved to Paris, France and opened her own art studio. She was living her dream, when one evening, a terrorist ended it when a bomb exploded while Molly was sipping wine on the Champs-Elysees.

At the time I found that her sudden death, although tragic, was in many ways much more kind than that Vietnam bomb that changed my life the day that Jake lost his leg. By the time that this happened to Molly, my own life was no longer worth living.

The day that I left Savannah, Georgia for Georgetown University, I never planned to return. I was almost able to keep that promise to myself, until I learned that Molly's last request was to return to Savannah for her final resting place.

What else could I do? There were so many skeletons in my past walking those streets in Savannah, including Caden Cassidy, another chapter in my sordid life. I could see no way of escaping this ordeal.

What I was able to control was how long I would remain in Savannah. Rather than spend any time longer than necessary, I decided to stay at Tybee Beach. If you want to really learn about why the Lighthouse and Tybee Beach was where I returned, may I suggest that you read *Destiny Revisited*. It is my story, but I have been told by many that it is theirs as well.

Besides, this is not the place or the time to recruit more readers for my novel. As, Ophelia explained to me yesterday, we are all here on a mission to assist Sabriel from making any more mistakes with her life. I am not certain what my contribution will be, but once Sabriel reads *Destiny Revisited* perhaps it will become more evident.

What I do find quite interesting is that at least three of us at this moment are from the south, and more precisely, Georgia. Is that merely a coincidence? I think not. Anyway, we shall soon discover what we all have in common.

One of the advantages that I have, over the others, including the very wise, Ophelia, is that I have read all of their books and have studied their characters very extensively. Whereas, none of them know me, yet.

I understand that this encounter is not a competition, but if we are all going to be here with the primary purpose to enlighten others, including Sabriel, there must be a degree of respect. How will Sabriel, or any of the other characters be willing to accept the advice that I offer if they have no idea who I am?

Next time that I speak to Ophelia, hopefully after she has completed reading, *Destiny Revisited*, I will suggest that all the characters read my story. After all, one advantage that I already have is that I am a contemporary character, one that has lived in the same century, even decade as Sabriel. The other is that none of the other characters have a sequel written about them by their original author. This makes me authentic.

I do realize that there was a written sequel to *Gone With the Wind*, but the author is Alexandra Ripley, and her version was adapted as a television series. Even, Janet Maslin of *The New York Times* said it was a "stunningly uneventful 823 page holding action." And, the author, Donald McCaig of *Rhett Butler's People*, wrote that Margaret Mitchell's estate was "thoroughly embarrassed," by *Scarlett*.

On the other hand, both *Destiny Revisited*, and *Destiny Revealed*, written both by my own author, received awards.

Although Indie authors do not receive recognition that they deserve, I am pleased to hear that Sabriel, in her book establishment, **CARCOSA** has included a place for these authors whom are just as talented, maybe even more so, than writers published by well established marketing moguls.

For whatever reason, I am honored to have been included in this group of characters . It is the first time that I have walked out of my pages of comfort, but I do look forward to my visit at St. Augustine. Now that I have been told that I am welcome to stay in this lovely cottage with Sabriel and the others, I must remember to follow all of the rules. This includes no references to my sequel. Ophelia has made it very clear that what I have to offer is within the pages of *Destiny Revisited* only.

I am not worried about this. So much happens in my life during that time, that I am certain it will be enough for my own contribution.

One thing does worry me. Ophelia said that I arrived just in time for Halloween. Apparently there will be a costume party at a local theatre on October 31. This brings back extremely bad memories. On that evening I was kidnapped by two men and raped, nearly killed. If it was not for my dear friend Sterling Powers who was able to track my location, I would surely not be here today.

Ophelia will read about that event, and I hope understand why I would prefer not to attend. Perhaps she will have some suggestions on what I should do. Unlike the other characters that are able to take advantage and dress as they are known by the public, I do not have that freedom. Nobody knows who Gabriella Girard really is. Sometimes, I don't even know who I am myself.

Participating at the **CARCOSA** in every other way actually sounds quite fun. It has been a long time since I led any literary discussions, but it would be easy to prepare. Maybe, during the Christmas season I can suggest to Sabriel that we offer *The Christmas Carol,* by Charles Dickins. It was always a favorite of mine. And, I would be happy to dress up like a Victorian Caroler, in exchange for passing on Halloween.

It is very odd that I lived so close to Savannah when I was younger and never came to St. Augustine. Maybe this was because in the 60's and 70's during the Vietnam War and racial inequalitypeople chose to stay close to home. And, after that my life was constantly in turmoil, between my responsibilities to the Blair family, and my extramarital affair with Sterling Powers there left little time for anything else.

Being near the ocean once again will allow me to breathe fresh air into some very stale lungs. Losing Molly was just too much for me to handle. When Holly and Sabriel found me sitting on that rock in the Marina I am not sure if I was considering ending my life, or if someone had already saved me from attempting to take my life. Whatever it was, I am thankful to now be in a better place.

Even finding an appropriate Halloween costume for the party in a few weeks might not be that bad. After all, this isn't about me. It is about Sabriel. It is her story; it his her life.

Chapter Thirty Six

Where there is no imagination, there is no horror.
—Arthur Conan Doyle

SABRIEL and GABRIELLA

Gabriella, "Gabby" Gerard was truly a delightful addition to my growing family of characters. Maybe it was because we were both from Georgia, although, I believe it was more than that. We just have so much in common. Although, Gabby was born in 1949, which would make her older than me, she could be the mother I never knew. Yet, there was something more. It was her free spirit, that I connected with and admired.

Just as Ophelia suggested, I read *Destiny Revisited* in two days. Much of what I read was almost a warning of the direction that my life was taking. I knew that making the wrong choices would lead me to many regretful decisions, but being able to witness Gabby's mistakes were much easier to identify than recognizing my own.

There were also several other similarities. We were both from the south. We were both literature majors. I was able to receive my doctorate degree, and I am certain that Gabriella would have also, had she not been distracted by the wealthy Alex Blair. There was also the way that Gabriella would fade in and out of literary scenes. I knew exactly how that felt. It was something that I have always needed to control.

Then, of course, there is *Alice in Wonderland*. Both of us admired how this character is able to somehow challenge rules and still survive.

One important difference between Gabriella and I is her undying love for Jake Chavalier. I have never really experienced this. Not even with Bradley. It isn't that I didn't love my husband, or that I didn't mourn his passing, but it is just that I accepted it and moved forward. That should be a good quality, don't you think?

203

Maybe. But, at this time I do feel guilty. As if I should miss him more. Especially since the reason that I am here in St. Augustine, enjoying my life, is only because he made this all possible.

I sometimes try to imagine how our lives would be different if Bradley and I had grown old together. Would we still remain close? Or move apart in different directions as many older couples do? Maybe the powers that determines our lives know better than we do about relationships.

Like the other character guests, Gabriella enjoys spending time at the **CARCOSA.** In some ways it is much easier for her. She enjoys reading many of the contemporary novels, particularly those in the Indie section. After reading the novels, Gabriella writes book reviews. We then print the reviews on a **CARCOSA** newsletter that is sent to our customers..

Gabriella is also more present in the bookstore than any of the other characters. It is as if she fells more comfortable here than exploring the ancient city..

Although, one afternoon, Holly convinced Gabriella to go with her to *The Lighthouse.* At first she hesitated, but Holly convinced her that she would truly enjoy walking through the grounds. Holly also agreed that they would not go inside the lighthouse avoiding the 219 steps to the observation tower.

I never shared with Holly that the *Tybee Lighthouse,* near Savannah, held some lifetime memories for Gabriella. It was not my call to share this with anyone. If Gabby wanted to tell her story she would.

One unexpected discovery for Gabby was *Down The Rabbit Hole Antiques,* located near the Lighthouse, on San Marcos Avenue. When she noticed it Gabriella begged Holly to stop there. The moment she walked in that store, Gabby knew she was in her special place.

"Oh Sabriel! Have you ever visited *The Rabbit Hole?* It is extraordinary. There are just so many vintage items, that I could have spent the entire afternoon sorting through all of these treasures," Gabby said, walking in with three shopping bags.

"I am certainly pleased that you are doing your part to support our local business owners," I said, anxious to see what Gabby found.

The first item she reached for was a fine replica of an elegant Renaissance gown.

"Isn't this just absolutely adorable? It is almost exactly like the Juliet costume that I wore years ago at Georgetown when I attended my first fraternity party. That was truly a lifetime ago," Gabby said, anxious to model it for me.

I did have to admit that Gabriella still looked very desirable even at her age.. The empire waisted dress with cream colored lace at the sleeves and neckline appeared very similar to the one wore by Olivia Hussey in the 1968 movie *Romeo and Juliet* directed by Franco Zeffirelli.

"And, check this out Sabriel. A rhinestone tiara and a sequined mask! I have found my Halloween costume. You don't think Ophelia will be offended," Gabby asked, worried.

"Of course not." I added, "why would you ever think Ophelia would mind that you chose to be Juliet? She will understand your reasons better than anyone else," I said reassuringly.

"I am so thankful to Ophelia, and of course you, Sabriel for making me feel welcome here. When I heard about this Halloween Party it made me feel nervous. But, now Ophelia and I can go together as 'sisters' from different Shakespeare plays," Gabby said, adding, "I'm going to tell her right now."

She ran upstairs anxious to share her news.

The Halloween Costume Party at the *Corazon* was in three days. I made arrangements to close the **CARCOSA** early allowing everyone to have plenty of time to dress accordingly. Although I was the least enthusiastic of us all, even I was looking forward to seeing all the imaginative costumes. What I was not looking forward to was mingling with many people I have never met. Anna, who is always gregarious, laughed at my hesitation.

"This is the least threatening method of meeting new people. Just think about it, Sabriel. Everyone is on equal ground. We are all wearing masks, or make up, that protects us from anyone moving too close or too fast. If you find someone that you connect with, then later you can decide if you feel comfortable enough to remove your mask. By the way, when was the last time you and Eric spoke? Talking about hiding behind a mask," Anna said, as we were closing the bookstore.

"I am not sure when I last spoke to Eric. We have both been busy. I planned on asking him if he would like Gabby to do a book review for him, but it just keeps slipping my mind," I said, avoiding any details.

The truth was,that I did think of Eric more than I wanted to admit. Since our evening walk after the *Chautauqua* festival I planned on asking him to lunch as a way to thank him for his thoughtful gift the following morning. I just felt awkward doing so. And then of course, Scarlett and Gabby arrived. I wasn't sure how to explain these surprise guests that just keep appearing without notice.

"Well you do know that Eric will be at the Halloween Party, right? I expect that he will be there with a photographer, in costume. If I were you I would make plans to meet with him before or after the event," Anna suggested, locking the front door to the CARCOSA.

"I am sure that he will be busy all night. He won't have time to socialize with me," I said, moving toward the back gate to my patio.

"Just call him Sabriel. It is the friendly thing to do. As a reporter, trust me, he will find some time for you. Besides, it is good free advertisement for the **CARCOSA**." Anna said, waving goodbye.

Finally I did take Anna's advice and called Eric. He was very pleasant, and I think surprised that it was me calling.

"I am so glad you reached out, Sabriel. Halloween is a major event in St. Augustine. With the exception of *Nights of Lights,* this is the next most popular holiday. With all the Flagler College students, and locals out celebrating it really is a fun evening," Eric said.

"That is what Anna told me. I thought that we might meet for a burger, or something before everything gets crazy on the streets, unless that doesn't work for you?" I said, allowing him a way out.

"I would like that. Why don't I pick you up about 5:00pm. *The Corazon,* always has appetizers available at the bar, and then maybe once I get all the photo shots and interviews that I need, we can slip away," he said, sounding eager.

Is this considered a date?

I suggested meeting Eric at The *The Corazon,* but Eric reminded me that parking would be impossible. Since he has a press pass, he has priority parking that would be reserved. I agreed, since there would also be the photographer with us, I determined it was not really going to be a date, merely a convenient interlude.

At 5:00pm sharp, Eric was at my front door. When I opened it, dressed in my Hermoines costume, there was Eric, dressed like Harry Potter. We both laughed at how our costumes seemed to be planned ahead of time. I do have to admit, even with his sandy blonde hair, Eric still looked like Harry .Potter.

It did cross my mind that Anna might have had something to do with this coincidence, although there was really no proof at this moment.

"Where is the photographer?" I asked, realizing that there was no room for anyone but us in Eric's BMW convertible.

"Oh, you mean Michael? He has the company van. It is much easier if we drive separately, since Michael spends more time roaming the city on his own with his photo crew than I do interviewing," Eric said.

He opened the passenger door and I slipped inside, now not really sure how this evening was going to move forward.

It really wasn't Eric's fault that I merely assumed that we would be a part of the news team. That was all my own presumption.

"Eric to Sabriel? Are we on the same radar wave?" Eric asked.

"Oh, yes of course. I was just preoccupied with how many people might be out tonight. Halloween, throughout the country has become so much more than a children's trick and treat evening," I said, trying to get back on track.

"Children turn into adults, and they either always enjoyed Halloween, or hated it and now feel more comfortable participating. What about you? What is your take? Love it or Leave it?" Eric asked.

It was several months since I needed to share any of my life with another person, particularly a man who I was spending the evening with for the first time. It took me a few seconds to carefully respond.

"I suppose that I am more in the middle ground when it comes to this holiday. Not sure why it is so popular everywhere. I can only imagine that people enjoy changing who they really are once a year without any consequences," I said, quite satisfied that I was able to respond without too much conviction.

"That is quite astute, Sabriel. Also very safe."

Eric looked at me as if he knew exactly why I answered so discreetly.

Before we could continue our conversation, Eric was parking behind *The Corazon Theatre.* He was also right about how many people were already downtown. Everyone that we saw was already in costume, taking advantage of their evening early to enjoy the most that they could.

We entered through the back door to the theatre, and just as Eric predicted there were trays of appetizers available with punch bowls spouting dry ice, creating an image of spooky fog throughout the dark hallway.

Inside each of the three theatres there were different libations that guests could enjoy. In the first theatre, there was a montage of Hollywood classic horror movies from *Dracula* to the latest *It* release. The one with that obnoxious clown.

Eric suggested that I might prefer the second arena, where local storytellers were preparing to perform their most frightening tales. Some were planning to read passages from stories like, Edgar Allen Poe's *The Raven,* or some less we'll know stories like, *Sredni Vashtar,* by H. H Munro.

"The third theatre is going to be a Halloween Trivia competition. I just thought you might enjoy hearing the story interpretations better than watching the classic films," Eric said, politely pulling out my chair.

At the round table there were also other guests already seated. One person, I was not sure, male or female, wore a Chewbacca outfit that I recognized from *Star Wars.* Next to Chewbacca was Sheriff Woody from *Toy Story.* Then there was Jessica Rabbit, from *Who Framed Roger Rabbit,* I presumed Woody's date. I thought they was a rather odd couple, but definitely clever.

The two witches sitting next to me were dressed alike. I later learned that they were married and lived in the very intriguing town of Cassadaga. This is the spiritual camp about ninety miles from St. Augustine, that I am supposed to visit with Bradley's ashes. It is known as the "Psychic Capital of the World", as Bradley used to call it.

The witch sitting closest to me placed a business card in my hand.

"When you are ready, come and visit us. We would love to tell you more about the spiritual world, and help you with Bradley's ashes," Wanda, the witch said.

Although surprised that Wanda even knew who I was, this was not the time or place to pursue this discussion. Rather, than to dwell on this comment, I focused on all of the elaborate costumes definitely impressed at the wide variety. I was so engrossed that I never even realized that Eric had left.

It was about that time when a lovely lady, that looked exactly like Glinda the good witch of the North from *The Wizard of Oz,* whispered to me that Eric would return as soon as possible, and that I should enjoy the program until his return.

If I was still considering this a traditional date, there was no need for any doubts. My "date" was gone. I presumed he was doing what he said, and interviewing the ghosts, and ghouls roaming the street, but for some reason I thought I would be joining him.

Eric was correct. The storytellers were outstanding. Although the **CARCOSA** also offers this event as part of our program, it is designed more for younger children. This performance was delightful and entertaining.

At the conclusion, I noticed a film crew behind us. The local news from Jacksonville and the *St. Augustine Record* were both here. Many of the guests, including myself, were asked to take phot shoots with the performers. Michael, I read his name on his press badge, took a picture of me next to the Raven who read Poe's poems.

By the time the photo shoot had ended, Eric had returned as mysteriously as when he left.

"Oh, perfect Eric! Let's get a picture of Harry Potter with Hermoines," Micheal said.

Before I could agree or object, Michael had taken at least ten shots with Eric's arm around my back, and our heads next to each other.

"I now know why celebrities hate the paparazzi," I said, after the photo shoot.

"Please forgive me for abandoning you. I was so busy with all the people dressed in costume that I had no idea that it would take this long. I promise to make it up to you," Eric said.

"You have nothing to apologize for. I knew you were here working. And, these storytellers were so much fun. If you need to be somewhere I can call Anna. She is somewhere around here," I said, trying to make him feel better.

"Oh no, Hermoines, we still have a few hours left before the bewitching hour. I owe you a burger remember?" Eric said.

"I am not even sure if we can get into any place nearby," I replied..

"I know the perfect place. Just trust me," Eric said, leading me out the back door we came in.

Once out of downtown I realized we were moving toward Vedra Beach. When Eric turned onto Yacht Club Drive I was thoroughly confused.

"I don't think that *Fish King Grill* is open this late, even on Halloween," I said when Eric pulled into the paking lot.

"You, my lady, must have more confidence in the magic of Harry Potter," Eric said, parking next to the boat dock.

I was still not certain what was going on, but, once out of the car, Eric took my hand, and led me down a ramp to a small motorboat.

"Are we going to take this boat to hamburger heaven?" I asked, not believing that we really were going to go on the water.

"You ask too many questions," Eric said, touching my nose gently with his pointed finger.

On the motorboat, Eric maneuvered his way through several multi million dollar yachts until he stopped in front of a fairly large boat.

"Welcome to *The Paper Chase!*" Eric said, helping me out of the motorboat.

"Is this your boat, Eric?" I asked, totally surprised.

"Well, yes. It belongs to me and my pal here, Harry Potter," he said removing his black cape and striped tie.

I wasn't sure how to respond . How could a local journalist afford a luxury boat like this And what other mysteries does this man have? Ironically, I wasn't afraid of him, I was in awe.

"So, how do you like your burger? " Eric asked, already starting the grill.

All I remember about the remainder of that evening was finishing a second bottle of San Sebastián Vinters Red, and waking below to the cabin berth by myself.

Chapter Thirty Seven

You only have one Twinflame . One soul that can bring you back to your true authentic self. One soul who truly loves every part of you. You are eternally connected and unlike other connections it's the only love that can never be eroded by time or difficulties.
Anonymous

ERIC'S STORY

I was seven years old when I was born. Well, at least that is when I was able to start remembering who I was.

Before that time the only thing that I recall is a woman with long white hair. We were on a bus traveling across many cities for several days until one afternoon the bus stopped at a station and everyone got off. The white haired lady took my hand and walked with me to a large park with many people. She made me sit down on a park bench, and gave me half of her turkey sandwich that she took from a knapsack.

When I was finished, she removed a small orange blanket with many small animals printed on it. I was told to lie down under the massive oak tree and take a nap. I always did what I was told with no questions. In the past when I asked questions that white haired lady would scream at me. Soon I knew never to question whatever she did.

The loud sound of thunder was what woke me. Startled, I stood up looking for that white haired woman. She was gone. But, the sky lit up with a rainbow of lights that sparkled so bright that my eyes were burning. It sounded like gunshots, but nobody was running. Everyone was looking up at the sky.

I was not sure what I should do. Maybe run? But to where? Stay under the tree on my blanket? But, for how long? That was when a young girl, maybe twenty, it was hard for me to know for sure, took my hand.

"Are you by yourself?" She asked, softly.

I was not scared. Actually, I was relieved that someone, anyone, noticed that I was here.

I said nothing, but shook my head affirmatively.

"I will take you somewhere safe, until the morning. Then we will find out where your parents are," the soft lady said, as she led me away from the crowds.

What happened after that is really a blur. For years I replayed that day in my head, trying to pause and remember who I was then. But, it all resembles a collage. I am never sure of the sequence, and all the faces are erased.

What I do recall is sleeping on a soiled mattress on the ground in a camp with a fire. People were talking loudly. Some heating cans of beans, or hash over the camp fire. The soft lady brought me some biscuits with beans, in a small paper cup, that had a picture of a young girl with red braids on it. I didn't care that the beans were cold. My stomach was empty.

In the morning, when I awoke, the soft girl was lying next to me with her neck bleeding. She was not breathing. The mattress was soaked in a crimson color.

"Get up boy! You belong to me now. Do whatever I say, and we will be best friends. Try to leave me, and you will end up just like that pile of shit next to you," the man who smelled, told me.

I am not sure how or when I arrived at St. Augustine, but I do remember an older woman whose name was Sonia, took care of me when I came back from panhandling with the smelly man. Sonia was the one who taught me how to read, write, and learn mathematics. That was the only recreation that I had, and she made it a game.

"Eric. You are a beautiful boy, smart, and kind. This is not your destiny. One day you will be a fine young man. When you meet your twin flame then, …then you will feel true peace in your life,"Sonia said one day.

Later I heard someone say that Sonia was a teacher in Cuba. When her family was killed by mauraders she fled to Miami by boat. With no money, and nobody to help her she became a member of the homeless community.

Like most of us, we were greatful to be here in St. Augustine. The large tourist traffic assured us that we would all have some money to eat and drink. Whenever the money was scarce, there was always

Dining With Dignity. I was told that it was a community ministry that serves dinner every evening at 6:00pm at the corner of Bridge and Granada Street.

Whenever I was with Sonia, she would take me there as much as possible, and to *Home Again St. John's* on Sunday, Wednesday, and Fridays. There was a meal provided indoors. But, what I liked the most was that I could take a shower. And, once a month I was given a change of clothing.

The only problem with all of these services was transportation. Some of the teens, and younger adults were provided with bicycles allowing them to become mobile. This also encouraged them to find at least part time employment.

Later, when I was rescued from this homeless environment, after two years, I understood why people living on the streets always stayed in St. Augustine. It was the safest alternative.

When I was found in the parking lot at *The Columbia Restaurant,* I was disoriented, starving, and scared. Sonia was no longer with me . She was my protector. I knew that she would never leave me without a good reason. But, here I was alone.

Thankfully, a kind lady who was getting off work from the restaurant saw me crouched down, hiding behind a giant trash can. At first, I ran towards a van when I saw her. But, then I looked again and she reminded me of one of those angels that were outside of *Cathedral Basilica of St. Augustine* during the Christmas season.

The light in the parking lot shined on this stranger's head like a halo. All dressed in white, with blonde flaxen hair, the angel said, " Don't be frightened. I am going to take you to someone who will care for you. Do you trust me?"

I never knew what trust meant. But, strangers always came and went without warning. For some odd reason this Angel was different.

St. Francis House was more than my refuge. Mrs. Kelley, the orphanage caretaker, refused to recycle me into the system. Later, when I was in high school, living with my foster family, she told me that during our first meeting, that she could not believe how educated I was for never attending school.

When my intelligence test results came back she told me that I scored 132; only 2% of the population score that high.

I had no idea what all of this meant. When Mrs. Kelley informed me that she had found the perfect foster family I asked her if they would be my twin flame.

Mrs. Kelley was speechless.

"What do you know about twin flames, Eric?" she asked, cautiously.

" Not much, really. Sonia told me that once I found my twin flame I would have eternal happiness. But, I don't even know where to start looking," I said, confused.

It was not until I discovered *Cassadaga,* a small community of spiritual leaders that I knew what a twin flame was. I was seventeen years old, my senior year at Sebastián High School, when a group of us thought that it would be fun to take a drive to *Cassadaga* and have our future told by an expert.

When it was my turn, the Psyche asked to talk to me privately. It was then that I learned what a twin flame is and how to find it.

First, I was cautioned that

Twinflames are not soulmates. Perhaps the greatest distinction is that soulmates have different souls. It is also possible for us to meet many soulmates throughout our lives, whereas Twinflames are one soul that decided long ago to split into one. Because of this distinct phenomenon, they are one soul that share all the energy together.

So, what does this truly mean? And, how do we ever know if we have a Twinflame? I was told that there is a sudden familiarity that you feel, different from any other person from your past. When you imagine that this person is going to be a significant force in your life, a person that can alter your future course of life, then maybe you are on track, but there is so much more.

You must be aware that this revelation may not occur until much later in the relationship. One of the most difficult obstacles to overcome is childhood, many different pasts, and even generations of family prejudices that might restrict you from moving forward.

What I was hearing was even more confusing than previously. But, there were some guidelines. Twinflames may have been separated when they were younger, even if they did not know one another. Other contacts may be similar also, leading them back to one another. Fear is the biggest obstacle. It will prevent them to move forward because it is the unknown.

214

Some have warned that it is difficult to be with your twinflame at first. Especially if they are not ready. Since you share one soul, it is like looking at, and feeling yourself through the eyes of another. This can be both rewarding and daunting. If you work together then you continue to grow stronger, eliminate major flaws, and contribute to improving society. If you fail, there is a chance that you will forever feel self conscious or even unworthy.

After learning all of this from the Psyche, I really felt no different. It was not like my life was now going to be devoted to finding my Twinflame, if even possible. No, after graduation I was going to Columbia University, become a writer, and finally start to enjoy life.

Everything went as planned. That is until I graduated from college. On that day, my foster parents, Ted and Barbara Wilkinson, were with me to celebrate, and to my surprise, Mrs. Kelley. As in high school, I also graduated Magna cum laud, first in my class at Columbia.

I won't bore you with the speech that I gave at my graduation, but it did allude to Don Quixote's windmills.

After all the introductions from the faculty, and obligatory thank yous to favorite professors, my family, Mrs. Kelley, and I continued the festivities at the *Flora Bar,* located in the Upper Eastside basement of the Met Breuer museum. It was definitely a splurge. A pricey event, but I had been working part time as an editor for a small publishing company all year. It was my way to show appreciation to the only three important people in my life.

When I showed Mrs. Kelley my diploma, she asked the same question many people had, but never asked, "Eric, is your last name really Pacetti, like the well known family who lives at St. Augustine?"

I thought for a moment. It would be fun to make them all believe that I was some long lost relative, but I decided against that. Instead, I revealed the truth.

"No, I am afraid not. When I lived on the streets I once saw the name Pacetti, on a sign. I thought that one day my name was going to be like this great man's name. Later I also learned that a middle school was named Pacetti Bay. That is when I decided to take that name and strive for the same recognition," I said, waiting for a response.

215

"Well today Eric you definitely achieved your goal. Congratulations at always being a brilliant, hardworking, and decent young man. Now, I was asked to hand deliver this folder to you," Mrs. Kelley said, smiling.

I had no idea what this could possibly be. When I opened it, everyone seemed as curious as I was. Inside was a document that said I would be receiving a deposit of $50,000 each year until I passed away. The typed note also said:

"In addition, to your allowance, there is a 45 foot motor yacht that is for you to use, sell, or upgrade as you see fit. Thomas Brown, your attorney, will answer any questions which I am certain there are many. Enjoy your life, Eric. Continue writing and searching for that Twinflame."

—Your very proud Benefactor

There it was, that reference to Twinflame once again. I was able, for years to move that thought outside of my mind, but now it was back. More importantly, who is this mysterious benefactor? Nobody seemed to know, including Mrs. Kelley. At least nobody was telling me.

For several years after graduation from Columbia, I traveled the world, and made a decent living doing freelance writing. I chose not to use any of the money that continued to be deposited as promised. When I did finally decide to return to New York, Mr. Brown informed me that my yacht would be ready with a crew to cruise the inter coastal route as soon as I wanted.

Was this another joke? I had not even seen or thought about this boat for many years. Now I was asked if I wanted to go across the Atlantic? Like exactly where across the Atlantic? I was quite happy returning to New York. It was the perfect place to get lost and find yourself at the same time. Why would I ever want to leave?

This was about the same time I received a phone call from a friend of mine who was on the swim team with me many years ago in high school. He was still living in St. Augustine, married, with three children. There was a position open at *The St. Augustine Record,* for a freelance writer, to report on local issues, but also to include any creative stories I might want.

At first I thought this request very odd. I had not seen or spoken to Ben since graduation in 1997. That was twenty years ago. I intentionally chose to ignore the invitation that I received to attend our twenty year high school reunion. The truth was, I never wanted to return to St. Augustine. There was nobody that I cared to see. Mrs. Kelley moved to Cincinnati to care for her aging parents, and my foster family passed away in a car accident in Daytona five years ago. Besides all of these obvious reasons, I could not imagine why my attorney thought I wanted to go joyriding in a yacht that I had never seen.

That was when from nowhere, that Twinflame phenomena returned. What if this was what I still needed to achieve, and I passed it by? The Pyche from *Cassadaga,* told me that to reach the level of happiness that I deserved, I needed to face my inner fears. The problem with this idea is that I did not know of any inner fears. But, it was that damn Twinflame idea that kept my interest.

My childhood was a blur, but then many people have poor memories of that time. For me, it may have been exactly the motivation needed to become self sufficienct. Let's be real now. I am an orphan child, with a secret benefactor that provides me with $50,000 a year for life, and a yacht at my disposal. What do I have to complain about? Unless, I am the character Pip from *Great Expectations, by* Charles Dickens.

Relationships. That is my albatross. It isn't that I don't want to have an intimate relationship it is just that it never lasts. So maybe if for no other reason, I should give this Twinflame theory a shot. I can always return to New York, and at least for now, will avoid that disturbing snow.

"Okay, Thomas, what is the earliest that the yacht will be ready?" I asked.

"It should be ready next week. I just need to confirm the crew. Do you want to sail on the yacht, or meet them there?" Thomas said.

"Oh, I'm definitely going to be on that yacht. I want to learn as much as possible about driving this boat," I said.

"You also need to name your yacht. It is bad luck to leave the dock without one. Any ideas?" Thomas asked.

Without hesitation I said, *"Paper Chase."*

"That was fast. You must have been thinking about the yacht more than you thought" Thomas said.

217

I wasn't even sure where that came from, but I knew it was right. Wherever I was chasing papers seemed like my destiny.

And, like Thomas promised we left the dock on October 1. Four days later we were pulling up to the slip reserved for *Paper Chase.* This was going to be my new home. At least for awhile. But, I was very careful not to let anyone know, particularly Ben, that I owned a yacht, or anything else about my life.

After living here for a year now, I have no regrets. I did eventually after, the holiday season, my first year at St. Augustine, purchase a condo near the yacht. It just gave me more flexibility. And, if I changed my mind, and decided to return to New York, the condo would be a good investment, according to Thomas.

And, then, I got a call from one of my few friends from high school, Anna Hanna. She told me about this fascinating lady, Sabriel Shelley who was opening a unique bookstore on San Marcos Avenue. Anna suggested that I interview her for the paper. I decided, why not?

Sabriel Shelley from our first encounter sent electric waves throughout my body. I knew better than to presume that she felt the same. But, just as the *Cassadaga* psychic warned, Sabriel was resisting. For whatever reason, every time I moved closer, Sabriel stepped several feet back. That is, until tonight. Tonight was perfect. She allowed herself to move toward me.

If it wasn't for that second bottle of wine, I would have let her feel my lips on hers. She would then know there is nothing to fear. But, now, watching her sleep peacefully I know the reason we are here together. Now I need to convince Sabriel.

Chapter Thirty Eight

There are all kinds of love in this world but never the same love twice.

—F. Scott Fitzgerald

SABRIEL and ERIC

When I woke up on the bed in Eric's boat I was disoriented. For a few minutes before I got up, I couldn't even remember why I was here, let alone where I was.

My cell phone said 11:00am. That's impossible! What happened last night, and where was Eric?

My head felt like a huge melon that someone used a hatchet to open. Somehow I was wearing a pair of sweatpants and a T-shirt just like the one I have at home. It is a souvenir from a Pink Floyd concert, just like the one I wore when I met Bradley at the faculty meeting at New Orleans.

But, where was Eric? I finally managed to allow my bare feet to touch the floor and stand up. When I walked to the bathroom, there was a new toothbrush, never opened, and tooth paste. I wonderd how many other ladies have found themselves in this predicament? I couldn't even think about this now. I needed to find out exactly what happened last night and where my clothes are.

"Good morning, sunshine. Drink this special "night after" solution. Guaranteed to rid you of all your aches and pains," Eric said, when I came on deck.

"What exactly is this drink supposed to make me forget?" I asked, taking a sip.

"Nothing, I hope. It was a beautiful evening and, it is now a wonderful Florida morning," he said, refusing to be specific.

Eric then placed a plate with eggs Benedict in front of me not saying anything else.

I took a bite. It was delicious. If it wasn't for the fact that we were on the water I would have thought that Eric had gone out earlier and picked this up at the *Odd Birds Café* located in the Marina.

"Okay. You win. Please tell me what happened last night and how I ended up sleeping here." I said.

"Well it is not as exciting as I would have hoped," Eric said, staring at me with those gorgeous George Peppard eyes. Those eyes always reminded me of Paul, in *Breakfast At Tiffany's*.

"What exactly is that supposed to mean?" I asked between bites.

"It means nothing happened. You know like sexually? By the second bottle of wine you passed out. I should have fed you first. But you know what they say about feeding Gremlins after midnight?" Eric elaborated.

"*The Gremlins* movie is about the only frightening movie I can tolerate. Anything else freaks me out. I think that is why Halloween has never been fun for me," I said, relieved that we were changing the topic.

" I can totally agree. But, I do like Halloween, since I never really dressed up as a child during that time. I was the one passing out the treats,"Eric said.

"Why? I mean, I lived in an orphanage until I went to college, but we did have Halloween parties," I said, surprised that I was sharing this with him.

"Really? I lived with foster families until college, right here in St. Augustine. What year did you graduate high school?" Eric, asked.

"1997. I feel so old. Especially now with the characters..." I caught my self. "I mean young girls visiting ."

"I know what you mean. I graduated the same year. Did you go directly to college?" He asked me.

Before I realized, I was telling him my entire life story as if we were rekindling an old friendship. I also learned that the Pink Floyd shirt I was wearing came from the same show I went to at Atlanta twenty years ago.

Then suddenly I bolted up realizing that nobody knew where I was. I never told Anna that I was going out after the Halloween event. I could just imagine the St. John's Sheriff's Department searching the city for us.

"It's fine, Sabriel. I phoned Anna last night and explained everything. All your guests arrived home safely last night. Oh, and

220

she brought a change of clothing for you just in case you didn't want to wear your costume again this morning."

"How was she able to get these to me from the dock?" I asked.

"She sent them over discreetly in this backpack using the water taxi," Eric said, handing me my bag.

"Great! Now everyone knows I slept here with you," I said.

Eric leaned over so that our faces were inches apart, and said, "Only if you tell them Sabriel."

He then kissed the tip of my nose. It felt like a feather was carcassesing me.

From that day on everything changed between Eric and I. It was not a whirlwind romance. I am not even sure if you could call it a romance. We enjoyed each other's company. Spending time together, sharing our days, our worries, even our fears seemed so natural. Even my marriage to Bradley never felt like this.

The one topic I did avoid was the characters. It wasn't that I didn't trust him, because if anyone could relate to this unique arrangement it was Eric. He not only was brilliant when we discussed literature, he enjoyed all the same authors and novels that I admired.

People in the community were beginning to recognize us as a couple. But even with all of this, all we ever did was occasionally kiss. Neither of us pushed the sexual issue. It was as if we really didn't need it. Although, it also meant to me that we were not truly committed.

When I shared this with Anna she agreed that we needed to take the next step.

"Even you admitted to me Sabriel that until Bradley, sex meant little to you. Maybe you are afraid that Eric cannot compare to Bradley. But, I will tell you again that Eric never was intimate with any girls that I knew when he was in high school. Some even thought he might be gay since he was so good looking, and without a serious girlfriend," Anna said.

"Well, I can guarantee that Eric Pacetti is not gay. There is something between us that is much stronger. I know that we both want to be sexual, but something beyond our control is preventing it from happening," I said.

"As long as you are both alright with this arrangement maybe it will happen when you least expect it," Anna offered.

221

Anna was not the only one with advice. Holly, also saw the similarities between Eric, and Paul in the movie version of *Breakast at Tiffany's.* Then Holly pointed out that she and I were both orphans. *Who told he that?*

"It is much more difficult for those of us who have been abandoned, to ever trust that anyone will stay with us forever," Holly insisted one early morning..

The other characters were all busy with special projects at the **CARCOSA.** I did agree with Holly. But, I never considered myself abandoned. When my grandmother passed, there was no one else to care for me. Was it a good childhood? Definitely not. But, it also was not a tragic one. Even Eric's childhood, which I would definitely say was tragic, turned out well at the end.

"But, Holly, Bradley and I were in love. We had a good life. We expected to grow old together. Then his untimely death changed everything," I said.

What I did not tell Holly, is that my relationship right now with Eric, is just so much more intense, so much more special, that I am afraid to accept that it is real. If I was writing a romance novel, Eric would have all the qualities that I admire in a man.

"Do you think that Eric may be a character from some unknown novel that has decided to join our little party here in St. Augustine?" I asked Holly, jokingly.

"I hope not, for your sake, Sabriel. Although it may seem that we are staying forever, our time is nearing to an end. And, it would be very unfortunate if your story would end like mine did with Paul," Holly shared.

This opened up the conversation to ask why exactly all the characters were here. But, at the moment I wanted to take advantage to find out why Holly let Paul go at the end of *Breakfast at Tiffany's.* It was something that always bothered me. Not so much that Holly left Paul, but why did she leave him.

"Would you mind telling me why you left New York for Buenes Aires. I know that you thought that you would marry that millionaire, I forgot his name, but was there another reason? And, do you ever regret that decision?" I asked.

"My, my, those are a lot of personal questions. But, since it is all part of the reason that I am here, I suppose I will tell you as much as I can," Holly said.

I started to make a new pot of tea, when Holly stopped me and said, " Actually a bottle of champagne is much more appropriate. I do believe there is a bottle chilling in the fridge," Holly said.

And, just as she promised, there it was. It didn't really matter to either of us that it was only 9:00am. After a minor inconvenience of uncorking the bottle, I poured us some of the bubbly and began to listen.

It was like listening to a private narrative of someone's life who is famous and talking to you uninterrupted. What Holly said was insightful.

Reflecting on how I came to my final decision to walk away from Paul really appears spontaneous, and it was. You must agree that we all have that one time in our lives, sometimes more than once, when an opportunity appears and without fully recognizing the alternatives, you make the choice. Ultimately this is what happened to me. But, now that I am outside of my pages of comfort, you know those places? Even humans experience those moments .You call it a "comfort zone", whatever that means, leads you to take the wrong path. I might remind you that the novella is considerably different than the movie version. But, because both are interesting interpretations I will use both to elaborate."

I had to keep reminding myself that this conversation, with the "real character", Holly Golightly, is actually happening, right here in the privacy of my own living room. Naturally no sane person would ever believe me. And, I can't even take the advantage of writing a scholarly dissertation, since it is only based on Holly's first person narrative.

Without interrupting, I refreshed our glasses with more libations. And, continued to listen attentively to Holly's story.

My relationship with the author Paul Varjack begins as a friendship that I am in control of. Keep this in mind. Being in control of my own life, or at least my misconception that I am in control, made it easy to let Paul into my world. And, what a world it was! Just the type that any thriving author would love.

I was a free spirit. Ageless. Spontaneous. Sometimes even careless, but that is what it takes to survive in New York when you are too young to know better. I wrote my own script. No longer was I a hillbilly from nowhere. Here I am the glamorous, gregarious,

Holly Golightly that always calls the shots. Like my cat, with no name. I have no right to name the cat because we don't belong to each other. We merely enjoy the time we spend together and then move on with no regrets; no sorrow; no goodbyes.

So why did I let Paul go? Because he didn't belong to me. And, why did I agree to Argentina with Jose? Because, like Cat, it gave me another escape route where I am unknown and can establish a new identity.

I like to say that the jewelry displayed in the showcase windows at Tiffany's is who I am. There the beauty of expensive diamonds are admired, but only when bought can they be appreciated. Why should I consider myself any less worthy than a Tiffany purchase? Honestly, Paul could not afford me.

There is no regrets for my choices. My life is left unfinished, just as the author Truman Capote wanted it to be. He leaves it to the reader to determine what happens to me, and that is why in the novella Paul is not named. He is only referred to as the narrator, like Cat.

But, you Sabriel...you are not a character. We are all here to remind you of this. When our time here on earth has ended, we return to our pages. We continue to live for eternity in those pages. Take advantage now with the new knowledge that we share with you. Apply what you can to your own circumstances. After all isn't that what real literature is all about?

This time with Holly Golightly was beyond whatever I could have imagined. Not only did it provide a new light on who she is, but who I am and who I want to be. Without ever mentioning Eric by name, the allusion to him was real. Not only does he physically appear as the actor in the movie version of *Breakfast at Tiffany's,* George Peppard, but he is also a writer. We both share a deep appreciation of the arts.

With all this that Holly just spoke about, now I need to digest how it applies to me, and Eric. What Holly also revealed, is that all of the characters are here to give me their own advice.

Would the remaining three have sessions like Holly and I have? If not, what can I expect?

Once again, I was reminded that all would be revealed when needed.

"What I am able to gift you with this morning will provide you with the foundation for the remaining four characters. Be prepared for different types of scenarios, each filled with wisdom, Sabriel," Holly toasted raising her champagne flute.

Four more characters? Currently there is only a total of four characters, and Holly just gave me her revelation. This must mean that there will still be one more guest joining our group. I better get the last guest room ready. Knowing Scarlett much better now, it is clear that she will not share her room with any fellow character.

Chapter Thirty Nine

Daisy was young, and her artificial world was redolent of orchids and pleasant cheerful snobbery and orchestras that set the rhythm of the year, summing up saddness and suggestiveness of life in new tones.

—F. Scott Fitzgerald

SABRIEL and ERIC

After my visit with Holly, I decided that it would be a good idea to re-evaluate everything that I knew about each of the characters now living with me. There had to be some common bond that tied us altogether.

I started with a very practical theoretical ven diagram often used during my lectures. By visualizing all of my known evidence I was hoping to establish a logical conclusion. However, what I soon realized was only Ophelia and Holly shared with me any relevant data about their character personas. At least those that are not already documented.

Using these two characters, I was able to find a few similarities that were related to my own life. All of us were orphans, or at the least only having one parent. That would tend to make us, using Holly's premis more susiptible to being overly cautious about any relationships. But, in Ophelia's situation, Hamlet was her only true love. Although, in the modern interpretation Ophelia was in control of the actions, or at least more so than in Shakespeare's play.

Independence. That is definitely a defining characteristic that Ophelia, Holly, and I share. But, to what degree is that independence controlling our choices? And, when is being independent a curse more than a gift? Could that be something that the other characters can shed light on?

"Knock, Knock," Eric said, slightly propping his head through the door.

"May I come in?" he asked, cautiously.

"Certainly. Come into my dungeon of iniquity," I said, realizing that Eric has never seen my working office.

"Sounds very inviting. What type of immoral or lavicious plans do you create in your cauldron? Should I be afraid?" Eric asked, taking a seat across from me.

"Well, since we are both Muggles studying witchcraft, right here at Hogwarts, I don't think that you have to worry about a thing, Harry Potter," I said, reaching for the wand I kept after Halloween.

"This is very true. We both seem to have some hidden powers, which makes this friendship just "spicey" enough to keep returning for more," Eric said.

His eyes this time seemed to see through my inner self. The first time that happened, I wanted to turn away immediately, it was so intense. But, I didn't. Now I was certain that we were both on the same wavelength.

"Seriously, Sabriel, what are you doing with all those novels on your desk?" Eric changed direction now.

Over the past weeks, we became much more comfortable with each other very quickly. This even included a four day secret trip to Jamaica on the *Paper Chase*. Nobody knew about this, except Ophelia. I felt she needed to know if anything strange happened with the other characters. Eric and I were both becoming very comfortable and trusting. But, even now there was no sexual intimacy.

Whenever I stayed the night with Eric, we would sleep together on the boat. And, literally sleep. It was our own private island of retreat. Only Ophelia knew where to find me, although I was sure that at least Anna knew where I was, if not all of my guests. But, I just could not bring myself to tell Eric about my characters. Besides the obvious fact that the entire situation sounds ludicrous, I was not sure myself how to explain why they were here.

"Running **CARCOSA** does require many hours of management, you know. And, since it is primarily a book store, occasionally I like to refresh myself with some of the well known classics" I said, closing *Gone With the Wind,* before he had anymore questions.

"Perfect. Then you might want to take a look at all of F. Scott Fitzgerald's novels since he is arriving at *The Lightner Museum* on Friday for a lecture series of the *Roaring Twenties.* The exhibition will also include some first editions, art work depicting various characters from his novels, and popular jazz music will be included," Eric said, showing me a handful of tickets.

"My, are we taking everyone with us?" I asked.

"The museum offered me as many as I wanted for opening night. I thought that it would be nice to include your guests and Anna, if you like?" Eric handed me five tickets.

"I will keep yours just to make certain that you don't dump me," Eric said, winking and standing up.

"Oh, and by the way, you may want to take some pictures of the gowns on display, since this years New Year's Eve Gala event is going to be the 1920's theme, in honor of us celebrating the 2020 New Year. Everyone will be in costume. It should be a spectacular event," Eric said, leaving before I could stop him.

How was I going to explain to Eric that I no longer celebrate New Year's Eve. Nobody, since I moved to St. Augustine, knows any specific details about Bradley and my life. They definitely don't know that New Year's Eve was our wedding day. The first day of the rest of our lives together. How can I ever celebrate with others this day again? The past few months all that I have wanted was to wake up the next morning and feel Bradley's arms wrapped around me. And this year, I am going to forget all of that because Eric wants to play dress up? It will never happen.

Thankfully, it is not something that I need to think about today. Like Scarlett, I will deal with that issue on another day. For now, going to *The Lightner Museum,* sounds like a great way to escape momentarily from reality.

"Oh my goodness, Sabriel, what a marvelous gift! I just know that everyone will be so excited about going out on the town to see this fantastic exhibition. Can you maybe tell us all a little bit about the history of *The Lightner?"* Gabriella asked. She was the first one that I told.

"Absolutely. Do you know where everyone is now?" I asked.

"I do believe that Ophelia is teaching everyone, including Scarlett, about the flower garden that she planted. I of course already know what all those rosemaries, pansies, daises, rues, and violets symbolize. I included them in my wedding with Alex Blair," Gabby said.

"Oh yes, you are right! That was such a clever idea. It really added an interesting foreshadowing to your future," I said, remembered being impressed.

Gabriella looked pleased that I recalled that detail from her novel, *Destiny Revisited*. Before she got up to leave I asked her to please let the others know that I have a surprise to share with them after dinner. We will then have a little impromptu storytelling evening.

As I predicted, everyone was thrilled, and eager to hear about *The Lightner Museum*.

"Okay. Now that you know about my surprise let me just give you a little historical background where we will be going. That beautiful building directly across from Flagler College where Ophelia, you and Holly toured last month, is now known as *The Lightner Museum.*. But, in the 1890's it was known by everyone who visited as *The Castle of Happy Returns*. This is because it was a hotel built by Henry Flagler that included an inside swimming pool. At the time it was the largest in the world. But, that alone was not what made it so special. It also offered its guests, a grand ballroom, sulfur baths, a steam room, massage parlor, bowling alley, archery ranges, tennis courts, and even a bicycle academy. When we arrive, Friday night to hear the introduction from the guest curator, you will be sitting directly over where the pool used to be," I said.

Scarlett raised her hand, anxious to ask a question. I felt as if I was teaching an elementary class.

"Since this event is going to be celebrating the 1920's as a prelude to the new year 2020, are we allowed to wear our period costumes. I have just the perfect ball gown for such a magnificent jamboree," Scarlett said, excited.

"Sorry Scarlett, but no. That is unless you own a flapper dress," I said.

Ophelia then added, "Be patient ladies. At the New Year's Eve Party, that will soon be here, you may dress in masquerade if you wish, even if it does not reflect the 1920's."

I was once again surprised that Ophelia knew more about what was going on in this town than I did, although I shouldn't be. Lately there were many other issues preoccupying my mind.

Once the other characters left, Ophelia pulled me aside.

"Is there a problem that maybe I can help you with? When I mentioned the New Year's Eve Party you looked ashen," she said.

"No, not really. It is something that I will need to work out on my own. Everything will be fine, once I resolve some past disruptions," I said, not wanting to think about Bradley at this moment.

"Alright then, Sabriel, but I do want you to fully understand that inside of you lives all of us. We are like mosaic pieces that once placed in the picture frame illustrate who you really are. Our Mission here is to remind you, that being an orphan as a child, does not dictate the woman that you are today. Having breakfast at Tiffany's on Fifth Avenue in New York City at 5:00am in the morning, or being a political pawn in the royal world of Denmark, is only one tile in that mosaic. And, there is inner strength even to fight your battles, like Scarlett does. When Gabriella, is sitting on a rock soaking wet, watching the ocean moving serenely around her, it is moonbeams reflecting off of her light house where she finds strength. And, very soon the final actor to our story will arrive to illustrate how the power of money cannot prevent, at least a glimpse, of reliving joy from the past," Ophelia said.

"I do want to thank all of you for stepping out of your pages. At first, I will admit that it was odd. But, now it seems so natural. Will you give me any further clues about this final character and her arrival?" I asked, knowing that there would be none.

"Let me just say, that you will recognize her immediately during the reveal." This was all Ophelia would say.

Everyone in my small circle of friends was overly excited on the day of the *Roaring Twenty's Exhibition.* Since Eric insisted that I arrive with him early to *The Lightner,* for him to preview the event, I left Anna in charge of chaperoning the characters. Between her and Ophelia I felt that they would be well cared for.

The front row of the exhibition hall, known as the *Alcazar,* where the pool originally was located,
had a reserved sign on all the seats. Although there were tickets sold, seats were not reserved. It was always a mad rush to find the best available, unless you knew someone, like Eric, who always was treated with VIP accommodations.

"Do you know how lucky you are to be arriving with me tonight to this sold out venue," Eric said, teasing.

"Actually, Mr. Pacetti, I hope that you appreciate that without the beautiful ladies that I arrange to follow you, nobody in this town would ever admire your suave demeanor," I skillfully rebutted.

"And, you my lady are the most gorgeous of all," he said, walking away once I was seated.

"He looked at me (her) the way all women want to be looked at by a man."

I wasn't really sure why that quote from *Gatsby* jumped into my mind. Maybe because I am here surrounded by memorabilia from F.Scott Fitzgerald? Or, maybe because Eric, dressed in his elegant tuxedo reminded me, for just a split second, how happy he makes me feel.

After a brief introduction to where all of the paintings, books, photographs, and letters could be found, the jazz began to play, releasing the *Roaring Twenty World,* surrounding us and inviting us in. Everyone, except Eric and I went separate ways.

"Should we move to the top floor and work our way back down?" I suggested.

"Yes. After viewing this preview I think that your suggestion will assure us of seeing it all," Eric agreed.

On every level, there was a variety of appetizers available, as well as flowing champagne. What did not go unnoticed, at least by any of us scholars, was the very obvious contrast between the glamour of Long Island aristocracy, and the rural poverty of the American bread winners. For example, there were elegant beaded gowns, on headless mannequins, juxtaposed to posters of everyday workers toiling in factories promoting pay raises.

This underlying theme continued to surface with a variety of Martin Lewis's New York prints of young ladies arriving at parties in the latest twenties fashions, followed by photographs and prints by notable photo journalists like Thomas Hart Benton, and Dorothea Lange.

Then of course on the second floor was all *The Great Gatsby* objects, including several paintings depicting Daisy Buchanan. Both Eric and I stopped simultaneously, and noticed that a copy of Fitgerald's iconic novel was turned to the page where Daisy is being described by her cousin, Nick Carroway, also the narrator.

I looked up at my cousin, who began to ask me questions , in her low, thrilling voice. It was the kind of voice the ear follows up and down, as if her speech is an arrangement of notes that will never be played again. Her face was sad and lovely, with bright things in it,

231

bright eyes, and a bright passionate mouth—but, there was an excitement in her voice that men who cared for her, could not forget; a singing cumpulsion, a whispered, "Listen," a promise that she has done gay, exciting things just a while since, and they were gay, exciting things hovering in the next hour. (1.33)

It was just as Eric and I finished reading the passage, and looked up together, that both of us felt the presence of someone next to us.

"I am so sorry to seem rude. But, you see that passage is about me, and I am always so impressed how Nick is able to do justice to who I really am. So many others are only able to see the outside without understanding how complex I truly am…Oh, please forgive me again, let me formally introduce myself. I am Daisy Fay Buchanan," the intruder proclaimed.

Eric said nothing. I extended my right hand, and said, "Dr. Sabriel Shelley. Welcome Daisy to St. Augustine."

The last character has arrived.

232

Chapter Forty

Human beings are born solitarily, but everywhere they are in chains—daisy chains of ineractivity. Social actions are makeshift forms, often courageous, sometimes ridiculous, always strange.

—Andy Worhol

DAISY FAY BUCHANAN

The Fay family of Louisville, Kentucky can trace their family roots back to the Mayflower. I am proud of my heritage. I am Daisy Fay Buchannan . When I married Tom Buchannan anyone and everyone who had any blue blood, attended our wedding. We are, what people like to say, are the established wealthy. Money inherited from generations of respected, powerful people.

Regardless of what people think of me now, after Jay Gatsby's body was found shot to death in his pool, there really was a time when money was not important to me. Or at the very least, not as important as it is now.

Many people who have read, *The Great Gatsby,* believe that it is a story about a dreamer named James Getz. Well, at least that was what Jay's name was the summer we fell in love. But, the real truth is, and anybody with any intelligence knows, that this story is all mine. Without Daisy as the catalyst there is no *Great Gatsby.*

Yet, even now there are so many misconceptions about who I am. That is one reason why I stepped out of my novel, to legitimize my reputation . The other reason, of course is to support Sabriel. Now, she has some real issues to resolve. And, they are issues that will effect the rest of her life. We, the characters, are all hoping that once she hears what we know will help her, and will be enough to lead her in the right direction.

Oh, my...how I would have loved to have had an intervention of wise women to prevent me from all the mistakes that I made. But, my life as a character, like all of us, is limited to our author. In this case, F.Scott Fitzgerald was determined to make, not only a statement about the wealthy in his era, but also the personal tragedies that result from what, Nick Carroway, our narrator would say, are, "…careless people, who (they) smash up things and creatures and then retreat(ed) back into their money or their vast carelessness or whatever it was that kept them together, and let other people clean up the mess they had made."

I forgive Nick for those comments about me and my husband Tom. After all, Nick was the only real friend that Jay had. When that insane cheap woman ran out into the street while I was driving, it was impossible to avoid hitting her. I was sure that she died instantly. No pain. You must understand that there was no reason to stop after I hit her. That would not change the situation. And, Jay understood this. That is why he chose to take the blame himself.

None of us could have known that this possessed woman, living over a garage in an area known as *Valley of Ashes* , could have destroyed our lives so selfishly.

Any way, I don't want to think about that unfortunate circumstance now. What I want to tell you is all about me, and who Fitzgerald modeled me after. Then you can draw your own conclusions.

Many people who read *The Great Gatsby* when it was released, assumed that I was very much like Fitzgerald's wife Zelda, since she rejected him, like I did Jay because he was not wealthy. But, in truth Zelda was not the first to refuse his proposals.

Ginevra King, a wealthy Chicago debutant, and F. Scott were immediately attracted to one another. If it had not been for Ginevra's desire to retain her social status, she would have been Fitgerald's wife. Fortunately for me, that heartbreaking experience was channeled into creating who I am, Daisy.

The one thing about me that I would like the readers to acknowledge is that much of their interpretations is limited by Nick's descriptions. And, to be fair, although we are somehow cousins, he knows nothing about my life or my hardships.

For, example, it is Nick that makes the very ugly assertion about my voice, being the most outstanding part of who I am. It is not until much later does anyone even notice my "dark shining hair." As a matter of fact, all the film versions ignore the color of my hair, always depicting me as a blonde. But, as you can obviously see now, that interpretation is incorrect.

Now, my decision to marry Tom Buchanan, shortly after Jay is sent overseas to World War I, was really not my choice. Could I have changed my mind? Maybe, but it would have been a disgraceful mark on my family. I cannot emphasize enough how restricted women in society were during the 1920's.

Yes, my best friend Jordan is much more independent. She is a professional golfer, enjoys being chased by men, almost shamefully. In many ways I wish that I had her personality. But, I chose to follow the traditional role, even when I learned how unfaithful Tom has been to me.

But, don't be too fast to say that Jordan represents the typical wild lifestyle of the modern flapper. She is no more liberated than I am. Tom controls the wealth, and it is abundant, while Jordan's wealthy aunt restricts how extreme Jordan can move in this very fast moving world dominated by sex, alcohol, and the Mob.

So, let's get back to me and Jay Gatsby. The real question everyone always wants to know is, did I ever really love him? Yes. As much as I could; not as much as he thought he loved me, but more realistically.

When I was told that Gatsby actually returned for me it was more than I could have ever expected. And, when I saw him, and his house, and the glamour that followed him, it was, exhilarating. Here was truly a man that desired me, not like my abusive husband that parades me around like a trophy.

But, I was wrong about Jay. He came back to prove that he had not lost me. This is not the same as loving me. Even when Jay reaches this epiphany and says that "...my voice is full of money...That was it. I never understood before. It was full of money—that was the inexhaustible charm , that rose and fell in it, the jingle of it, the cymbals song of it...High in a white palace, the king's daughter, the golden girl (7. 105-06)," even then he still wants me to admit that I only loved him, and never Tom.

If people who read *The Great Gatsby* fail to see that Jay's love for me is his obsession with reaching a status by any means possible, they will also not recognize that this is not love.

I am anxious to meet with Gabriella Girard , who I only heard of from Ophelia. Her character follows some of those same attractions to wealth that Jay did. I also understand that she and her very wealthy husband, Alex Blair, were married in Louisville, in the same church as Tom and I. From what I have been told, Gabby and I have a lot in common with cheating husbands.

Ophelia originally suggested that I share a room with Scarlett, but I think that Gabby and I together might be able to help Sabriel more when the time comes.

Like all of my fellow characters, I am looking forward to spending the holiday season in St. Augustine. The New Year's Eve Celebration theme, *The Roaring 2020* will bring back many memories of Jay's wild extravaganzas.

Although my visit here is shorter than the others, there is a lot to accomplish. Explaining the importance of discovering your Twin Flame is a lifetime journey that most never accomplish. We cannot allow Eric and Sabriel to be apart any longer. Our revelations must be accurate and time sensitive.

Now that I have arrived, we are able to complete our mission .

Chapter Forty One

Fortunately, some are born with spiritual immune systems that sooner or later give rejection to the illusory worldview grafted upon them from birth to social conditioning . They begin sensing that something is amiss, and start looking for answers. Inner knowledge and anomalous outer experiences show them a side of reality others are oblivious to, and so begins their journey of awakening,

—Henri Bergson

SABRIEL and her CHARACTERS

When Daisy appeared at *The Lightner Museum,* standing among all of the *The Great Gatsby* memorabilia, it was truly surrealistic. I wasn't exactly sure how Eric would respond, but naturally, always the gentleman, he was very polite. I think that he might have believed that Daisy's presence was theatrical. A planned event by the organizers to add some authenticity to their exhibit.

Of course, this all changed when Daisy moved in with me and the other characters. I knew that I had to explain to Eric why this happened, but nothing seemed very logical. It was already rather crowded in my four bedroom cottage. So much so, that I was actually pleased to spend most of my evenings with Eric, whenever I could.

It was actually Ophelia that suggested I tell Eric that Daisy was friends with Gabriella from Savannah. She would be here until after the holidays, and all the festivities have ended.

"That sounds plausible, but how am I to explain that she has the same name as the character from *The Great Gatsby,* and the clothes she was wearing? And, by the way, Gabriella and Daisy have never met before," I said, not convinced that Eric would ever believe this story.

"They may not have formally met, but I assure you that Gabriella knows Daisy. You have read *Destiny Revisited,* correct me if I am wrong?" Ophelia said.

"Yes, I have. It was the novel that I bought at that quaint bookstore in Savannah, the same day Bradley proposed to me," I said, recalling all the cats with literary names that lived there.

"Then you must remember that Gabriella married Alex Blair at the Seelbach Hotel Louisville, Kentucky, with the same pomp and circumstance as Daisy Buchanan. As a matter of fact, Gabby is as reluctant to marry Alex, as Daisy is Tom. It is one of the earlier scenes where Fitzgerald actually shows that Daisy has some true emotions. Do you recall that scene, Sabriel?" Ophelia asked me.

Naturally I did. Having taught that novel many times to my first year college freshman class that image of Daisy is crucial in analyzing her character.

"Let me help you recall that exact moment when Daisy decides to marry Tom. It is the evening before her marriage and Jordan finds her hysterically crying, holding a letter from Gatsby in one hand and in the other a string of pearls given to her as a wedding gift, from Tom worth $350,000. Daisy is only eighteen years old, living the life that her parents expect her to follow. Would she have made a different choice if Gatsby was there, with her at that moment? Does she really ever love Gatsby? What do you think the answer is Sabriel?" Ophelia asked.

"I am not sure. But, maybe now I will have the opportunity to ask her in person," I said, still not certain how to explain Daisy to a Eric.

I was surprised when Eric never asked me specifically about Daisy. But, also thankful.

Thanksgiving was spent during the morning serving turkey dinner, with all the extra dishes, mashed potatoes, gravy, stuffing, green beans, and pumpkin pie. *Dining With Dignity,* is a fellowship organization that Eric belongs to. I decided this year to join him in distributing the food.

Later that afternoon, we all went to Anna's house, on the Matanzas inlet for our Thanksgiving feast with the characters, her family and friends, and of course Eric joined us.

Everything went very normal. I was especially pleased that Scarlett didn't complain about the casual picnic on the grass, or the African American guests that were present.

Even Daisy was able to mingle with everyone without mentioning where she was from, specifically her novel. When Anna asked Alex to take a panorama picture of us all, I was not sure that any of the characters would appear.. After all, they aren't human. But, they did, and Ophelia reminded me that while on earth they all have human qualities, unlike spirits that are not photogenic .

The holiday season was now in full motion. After Eric and I returned from our Jamaica rendezvous that weekend, everyone was busy, preparing for whatever celebration that they chose. One very common tradition, regardless of religious belief is the *Nights of Lights,* in St. Augustine. It officially begins on the Saturday before Thanksgiving, and lasts through the month of January.

White lights are draped around all of the buildings of approximately twenty blocks. Since, I arrived in February this is my first year of experiencing how this ancient city comes alive with a burst of energy everywhere you walk.

But, the most exciting event is the Regatta of Lights. Eric decorated his boat with a giant balloon of Rudolph .The theme was The *The Island of Misfit Toys.* It originated from the very popular children's Christmas movie *Rudolph the Rednosed Reindeer and the Island of Misfit toys.*

For some reason I felt right at home. All of the characters also participated in costume. Holly was a rag doll. Scarlett, naturally was a porcelain Southern Belle doll, with her magnificent Christmas velvet dress and matching parasol. Gabriella chose to be a blue bird with fins, instead of wings. Daisy decided to represent a cowgirl riding an ostrich, which I thought very odd. Then Ophelia decided that she would be the spotted elephant.

After much deliberation, Eric insisted that I be the sugarplum fairy. I argued that she isn't a misfit. And he said,

"Of course she is a misfit on this Island. She is the only normal, beautiful creature. The Sugarplum Fairy has the power to save us all," Eric explained.

"But, it is Santa, not the Sugarplum Fairy that saves the misfits," I said, correcting him.

"Not, on my boat! On my boat the Sugarplum Fairy is the one with the magic wand."

And, then he handed me a sparkling, rhinestone scepter.

239

How could I argue with Yukon Cornelius, the captain of this vessel.

That evening truly was magical. From the magnificent sail boats to small trawlers, and yachts to shrimp boats, the Matanzas bay was shining throughout the parade path. Spectators waited on the Bridge of Lions, and along the bayfront sea wall, cheering for their favorite boats.

At the end of the evening, we all gathered at the dock to drink hot chocolate, mulled mead, or Irish Coffee. Other boats docked close by. Everyone was bragging that their boats were the brightest and fastest. But, nobody could argue that *The Paper Chase,* with all the misfit toys was the most original. No other boat had a crew of ladies dressed as toys. I wanted to add, that no boat could have the variety of authentic characters as Eric's boat that night. But, I thought it best to just be happy with the recognition we received, and of course First Prize for Best Theme Boat.

"So now what, Captain," I asked, once everyone left and we were alone.

I thought that maybe tonight with all of the excitement it would finally be the evening we would break this platonic spell that seems to be lingering everywhere.

Eric moved closer, and with only the stars in the sky now shining, lifted me up in his arms and carried me downstairs to the bedroom. We lay there nude, fondling, each other, every part of our bodies that we both knew well by now. But, then, after the most passionate kiss that I have ever felt, Eric said gently,

"Are you ready for this? Are you really ready for what all this will mean? I need to know, Sabriel. I need to know that you won't wake up tomorrow morning and feel nothing," Eric said, waiting patiently for me to respond.

I was just so taken by what he was asking that I wasn't sure what he meant.

Was I ready? Ready for what? How was I to know how I would feel with him after sex, if we never experienced it together?. What is it that he expects from me? Yes, I am ready to be physically with him. Yes, I want him. What else should matter right now?

Then it suddenly occurred to me. If I am unable to answer these questions, then I am not ready!

How will I know? Will I ever know?

Chapter Forty Two

Happiness is not something you postpone for the future; it is something you design for the present.

—Jim Rohn

SABRIEL

After the Regatta evening, I decided to spend more time at home with my characters. It would also give me some time to re-evaluate what I would do next involving, Eric and I.

Months ago I started a chart in my office trying to determine why the characters chose to visit me. If I could at least find some common denominators then perhaps their visit here would not be in vain.

My conclusions were inconclusive, yet there were some interesting insights. Ophelia, Holly, and I were all orphans. At the very least we had no female role models. Although Ophelia had her father, Polonius, and brother, Laertes, she was taken in by the royal court at a very young age. And, Holly...well, we all know how her experience at the orphanage turned out. She ran away to be a child bride. Anything was better, than the orphanage, even life with Doc Golightly. Until it was time to run away again.

There were other, similarities that appeared to be even more important. All of the characters fell in love, and it was not a happy ending. Including my marriage, that ended when Bradley died even before our first anniversary.

But, how did everyone else react to their loss?

Ophelia, in her own story, left the castle, gave birth to her and Hamlet's child, and moved on in life. We really are not told about the end of Holly's story. But, it is suggested that she learned to survive, without the narrator, known as Paul the author, (in the movie adaptation).

I certainly relate to Holly. She and Paul have a strong platonic relationship that they cannot move beyond. How would Holly's life be better if she agreed to stay with Paul? I don't believe Holly can even advise me on this.

Then there is Scarlett and Daisy. Two very self centered women, who cannot accept that someone can love them regardless of their flaws, even if it is for a short time. Is it better to have some love, even for a short time, than none at all?

Gabriella Gerard was the one character that I seemed to be attracted to the most. She and I were not close to the same age, but, we were both born in the south, and we're searching for the perfect relationship. What Gabby had, that I did not, was an unconditional love with Jake. Perhaps even more important is that their love was mutual. How can that even be possible? And, isn't it better never to feel that emotion than to experience it and then lose it forever?

I was almost so engrossed in these thoughts that the knocking on my door went unnoticed for several moments.

"Are you alright, Sabriel?" Ophelia asked, pushing the door just slightly open.

"Yes...yes! Come in. I am sorry that I didn't hear you earlier," I said.

"I just wanted to let you know that the characters, and I have reserved *The Raintree Restaurant,* for Christmas Eve supper. We met some actors from *The Limelight Theatre,* and they are going to be there all in Dickens Christmas attire. We all wanted to show our appreciation to you, for allowing us to stay here all these months," Ophelia said.

It was a nice gesture, but I was not sure that I wanted to be committed to anything on Christmas Eve. It was still three weeks away. On the other hand, with the way everything was progressing, or rather not progressing with Eric, this may be the perfect answer.

"That sounds lovely, Ophelia, but, none of you need to thank me. I am truly enjoying all of you, even Scarlett and Daisy who are sometimes challenging," I said.

"We all love this time of the year, and celebrating with those you love during the holidays makes this season even more memorable," Ophelia said, taking my hand.

"Has Anna told you already about the New Year's Eve Gala at *The Vault* this year? It will be the end to such a fantastic year, and the beginning of a new one for us all," Ophelia said.

"You know how I feel about New Year's Eve, Ophelia. It was my wedding day, only a year ago. It was the most romantic, magical evening in my life, and then it ended when Bradley died," I said, sadly.

Ophelia looked at me kindly for a moment, but then asked me a very poignant question.

"But, Sabriel was your love for Bradley magical? Was he able to touch the chasm of your heart and soul? Did Bradley fulfill every last desire that you thought he should? I am not suggesting that Bradley was not your soul mate. He may have been. From what you have expressed to me, the two of you shared an extraordinary bond. One that you now feel you will never share with another. But, you must understand that regardless how strong that bond was, it is now gone," Ophelia said, looking directly at my eyes, waiting for a reaction.

I was not certain what to say. It is true that I loved Bradley with my entire heart, and yet, it never seemed enough. There was something missing, but then life is never perfect. We learn to be happy with what we are given.

"I understand what you are saying, Ophelia, but how do I resolve those issues when I have no guidelines?" I asked, genuinely wanting answers.

"This is exactly why we are all here, Sabriel. We are your answers. You have always known what to do. Literature unlocked all the secrets that you were seeking. Through all the pages that you read, studied, and taught to others, our lives as characters have been your guiding force. If it is easier for you, think of us as your fairy godmothers. Although we may not be able to wave wands to magically provide you with silver slippers, and a pumpkin carriage, what you will learn from us will be even more rewarding," Ophelia said.

That conversation convinced me to try to move away from my past and meet the future head on. I still was not ready for a relationship with Eric, if that was even still possible after the Regatta fiasco, but I would attend the New Year's Eve festivities.

Just as Ophelia promised, our Christmas Eve dinner at *The Raintree*, was fantastic. Everything from the amazing dinner, to the entertaining Victorian Dickens characters. They added just the right amount of cheerful holiday songs and conversation.

Ophelia insisted on inviting Eric, since she knew he had no family. I did not object, but our first meeting in the past five weeks was very awkward. More so for me than Eric. He was of course his gregarious self. I did admire how much all the characters loved him.

By my request, I asked Ophelia to avoid seating me next to Eric. Unfortunately, I did not insist that we not sit across from each other. And, there we were.

As the evening continued to move naturally, I no longer felt it necessary to avoid contact with Eric. Once again our conversation moved on as always, pleasantly, and comfortably. Neither of us mentioned how long it was since our last meeting or the Regatta.

After dinner, we all drove to the Memorial Lutheran Church for midnight services. I drove my own car, and Eric never asked me to go with him, instead. I was not sure if I would have accepted that invitation, so I was thankful not to be put in that position.

At the end of the service, we wished each other a Merry Blessed Christmas, and parted once again for home. Eric and I exchanged a friendly embrace, but nothing more. It was late and we were all ready to end a wonderful evening of fellowship.

In the morning everyone was up early.. Bailey decided that he would sleep next to me, which was quite unusual since all the characters arrived. Most evenings he was curled up on the fluffy dog bed in the center of the living room. It was as if he felt this was the most strategic area to assure that we were all safe.

Holly, Gabriella, and Scarlett were responsible for the lovely decorated Christmas tree that displayed a variety of unusual ornaments, representing not only St. Augustine, and the seaside, but also miniature books with the titles of all the novels that represented each character. It was really quite lovely. What was missing is gifts.

Ophelia reminded me that none of the characters could return with anything but memories when it was time to leave. Therefore, no gifts would be exchanged. However, after our morning tea and scones, we all moved back to the living room, where Ophelia said,

"Each of us have wrapped you, Sabriel , one gift from us that we hope you will enjoy, as much as we have enjoyed preparing it."

"I know that you said we could not exchange gifts, because of your unusual circumstances, but I also found something I hope that you will all enjoy," I said, handing each of my characters their own gift wrapped box of truffles from our local candy store, *Whetsone.*

Each character became so excited once they saw it was a gift that they could actually eat. It was only Scarlett who said that she could not afford so many calories.

"You must understand, Sabriel how important it is for me to keep my waist slim, but I am grateful for the gift," Scarlett said.

"If you don't want your truffles Scarlett, may I have them? Chocolate is my favorite, and I don't care if I get as fat as a balloon," Holly asked.

"No, you absolutely cannot have my gift. I will find some way to enjoy them without gaining weight. Even if I have to jog ten miles afterward," Scarlett said, placing a truffle in her mouth.

It was now time to open the gift that Ophelia said the characters had prepared. The package was rather heavy and elegantly wrapped. It was almost a shame to open. But, once I did, I discovered a large leather bound tome. In Gold letters on the cover it read,

The Twin Flame Mirror

There was no author listed, but when I opened the book, and turned to the first page, it was signed by: *Ophelia, Holly Golightly, Gabriella Girard, Scarlett O'Hara, Daisy Buchanan*

When I continued to turn the pages, they were all blank.

"I don't, understand. There is nothing written on these pages," I said, confused.

"That is correct. Once you understand the power of the *Twin Flames* the pages will appear. You ask, and the answers are all there. These are the pages of your new life, Sabriel. A life that will bring you an abundance of joy that you could never imagine," Ophelia said.

I was still not sure what she meant by this, but I knew it was up to me to find out exactly how this book would change my life. What I did know is that without books my life would have been worthless. Not only was I able to escape through the pages that rescued me

Chapter Forty Three

Many speak to her, but she is looking for the one who knows her soul's language.

—Nikki Rowe

SABRIEL and ERIC

Christmas was finally over. Eric did stop by, that afternoon, on his way to serve dinner to the homeless. We exchanged Christmas gifts, and laughed when we discovered that we both bought each other limited editions of our favorite writers. Eric's gift was a signed copy of TS Eliot, *The Wasteland,* which I could only imagine cost him a fortune. Especially when he told me that he also insured it for one million dollars.

What was odd about this gift, is that I never told Eric that TS Eliot was my favorite poet. Somehow it must have been mentioned without me remembering.

My gift was much less valuable, yet as much appreciated. It was a signed copy of *Lush Life, a Biography of Billy Strayhorn.*

Billy Strayhorn was an American jazz composer that influenced Duke Ellington's compositions greatly. More so, Eric admired him for his tenacity during a time in history of racial injustices.

After a short, but very pleasant visit, we said goodbye, but agreed to meet up at *The Vault* on New Year's Eve. Daisy was going to take me shopping at a nearby vintage boutique so that I would be dressed appropriately for the party.

There was no one more thrilled than Daisy to attend this 1920's extravaganza. And, from the way everyone was reacting, it would definitely be the party of the decade.

Naturally there were many venues preparing for this event, but the most glamorous was by invitation only to *The Vault.* Most of us had no idea what all the hype was about. But, leave it to Anna, who is a native born resident of St. Augustine, to educate us on why *The Vault* is so exclusive.

"In 1927 The Treasure Building opened in St. Augustine as the central bank. It was later renovated to accommodate private affairs like ours. You will be amazed at the inside ballroom. There are eight towering columns and the architectural details are so exquisite that it successfully reflects the stunning glamour and romance that the 1920's are well known for.

But, the real focal point is the Vault Bar that reflects the speak easy atmosphere that everyone expects from such a replica. There is actually room for over two hundred guests, that will arrive at the two-story Grand Foyer where photographers will snap our pictures for posterity. Have I properly excited you? Everyone will be watching the crystal ball be released in New York's Time Square together, and I imagine they will even serve a breakfast buffet for those of us who plan to stay all night," Anna said, at last.

It did sound like a perfect evening. But, I had no date as of now. That is until Eric called.

"I know that the past few weeks that we have been on pause has been difficult since we keep meeting at different events, but, Sabriel, can we just forget about that evening after the Regatta? I miss you, and I may sound pompous but I know that you miss me. Now we are going to be at the same New Year's Eve Party at *The Vault* , will you please be my

date?" Eric asked. His voice sounded anxious.

I really wished that I had paid more attention to that Twin Flames book that the characters gave me. Even the blank pages might give me some answers. But, I could not deny that Eric was right. I did miss him.

"Yes. I will go with you. Are you doing any work tomorrow night, like interviews? Or is this just a real date?" I asked, casually.

"I'm all yours for the evening. No work. Is 8:00 alright to pick you up?" Eric asked.

"That's a good time. I believe the girls are going with Anna, Chloe, and Alex, so yes, eight works for me," I said .

When we said our friendly goodbyes, I walked directly over to the box that still had my **Twinflame Mirror** book inside. When I took it out, and sat down on the recliner to look it over, there was something dramatically different. The page following the dedication signed by all the characters , was now filled with notes where there was nothing written before.

I began to read the page titled *Symposium.* Immediately I recognized that this was the title of a work by Plato. But, what did it have to do with Twinflames? I continued to read.

Plato wrote that the human was split apart into two halves, one representing the masculine and one the feminine essence. Ever since this occurred one half searches for the other. This twin flame objective is to liberate all the restrictions of love.

Not everyone will have the opportunity to meet their second half or even recognize that half when they meet. But, once it is accomplished neither independent life will ever be the same. You must not regard the Twinflame as only your romantic partner, because that is incorrect. What happens is much greater than anyone can describe. What is agreed upon is that it pushes both of you beyond the limits of your imagination. Some people explain the feeling as a fast track to evolving without having any time to even catch their breath.

But, not only do you delve into each other's evolution, you also now set off deep wounds that you may have not even recognized before. It is your Twinflame that will allow the healing to begin.

There will be times that you may feel like your mind is in a daze, without the ability to control what you feel or think. As unnatural as this may seem, it is very normal. During this time you will want to always be together, but this only leads you to pull apart, say goodbye, and be miserable. This occurs because you have learned to be alone and survived. But, now there is another half of you that needs you to be complete. What results is a fire dance that burns both partners until each learns how to cope as one.

The objective is to cultivate a liberated love that has no conditions. This may require pain as your partner starts to trigger emotions that you have hidden deep inside. It requires you to accept that your Twinflame is far from perfect with many shortcomings, and yet you love everything about them. It is only then that you realize that being without them is far more painful than being with them.

It was difficult to comprehend all that I read and even more difficult to understand why I was chosen to read it. But, when I turned to the next page for more answers, there were none. The remainder of the pages were once again blank.

For now, it was all that I could deal with anyway. The next day, New Year's Eve would really test how far I could move ahead. I trusted and agreed everything that Ophelia advised me about how to approach my fears. But, soon it would be real.

As I expected, all of the characters, in their elegant twenties attire looked like models from a 1920's Vogue magazine. Ophelia had a rhinestone tiara, that distinguished her as royalty, although both Scarlett and Daisy objected. They each wanted a similar crown but settled for elaborate headbands with feathers.

Holly and Gabby wore sequined dresses and very fashionable small hats that looked more like the contemporary fascinators that are popular now in London.

Chloe, and Anna were dressed in very traditional flapper dresses with fringes that shook everywhere and anytime they moved. Chloe's accessory was a long cigarette holder, and Anna's was a feathered boa. Alex, also in costume , was dressed like a gang member from the movie *The Godfather.*

After all the pictures were taken, and we agreed to meet at *The Vault* bar, they all left, leaving me to finish dressing.

When Eric arrived he had a wrist corsage for me that was made from aromatic magnolias. I too, gave him a matching boutineer that I attached to his lapel. I could never deny that Eric was incredibly dubonair and handsome. Even with his formal tuxedo, top hat, and cane he could turn every head in a room when he entered. It was difficult for me to understand why he is still single. Even more confusing is why he has any interest in me?

I decided to think only how much fun this evening would be, and ignore any negative vibes that my brain might want to send.

When we were ready to leave, Eric escorted me to a black limousine, where the driver opened the door for me. I looked at Eric completely surprised.

"Is this ours for the evening?" I asked

"Yes it is, my lady. And, it won't even turn into a pumpkin at midnight. We have it for as long as we want," Eric answered, walking to the other side.

Once we were comfortable, I noticed, that there was a bottle of champagne on ice that Eric uncorked, and poured into my glass. He then made a toast that almost made everything I was now feeling relevant for the first time.

"Let tonight be the moment we stop the thoughts, and open the path to our kindred spirit."

I looked far past the depths of his inviting eyes and tasted the future in one small sip that cleared my way, and unleashed the past.

Chapter Forty Four

I found my flower, there she was, she caught my eye and captured my heart. I listened to her…she called out to me with her colors and warmth, held me with her softness and beauty, silently asking only that I let her grow, and let her be, and love her for what she was: my flower.

—Bodhi Smith

SABRIEL, ERICA and THE CHRACTERS

When Eric and I arrived at *The Vault,* there were so many people on the streets that you might think you were in New York at Times Square. It was clear now why Eric opted for a Limo. There was not any open parking anywhere in the city. The limo line was at least twenty cars backed up, and moving extremely slow.

"This is why we have our driver and chilled champagne. Just sit back and watch the street entertainment. This will take at least forty five minutes," Eric said, offering me more champagne.

"I had no idea it would be this crazy. Is it like this every year?"I asked.

"Pretty much. Although this year it does seem to be at full capacity. But, don't worry nothing really gets started until 10pm," Eric assured me.

"What exactly is happening here tonight? I know that we needed to RSVP but there really was no specific details," I said.

"There will be photographs taken as we enter. Tables are set up in the Grand Ballroom, where a variety of food served all night and early in the morning. Then later a costume competition, dancing, trivia challenge games , and even a room with black jack, craps, and roulette. There is no possible way you will get bored," Eric said, looking at the crowds lining the streets.

"I had no idea what a grand party this would be. It has been years since…" I stopped myself from finishing my thought.

Eric, took my hand.

"It's alright Sabriel, I do understand. We will only stay as long as you are comfortable. Just let me know when you want to leave," Eric said, reassuring me.

How could he know? Unless Ophelia told him about my New Year's Eve wedding, he could not understand. And, I was sure Ophelia would never do that without letting me know.

Finally our driver was able to move to the front of the line. There was a red carpet, and photographers taking our pictures as if we were celebrities. Once inside, we were able to find our way to the bar, where Alex , Chloe, and Anna were sipping some exotic cocktails.

"Hi guys! We reserved a table close to the MC VIP Table. It is also near the dance floor which will be important as the crowds start moving in," Anna said.

"Do you want to roam around a little before we settle down?" Eric asked me.

"Yes, I think once I get to the table I won't want to venture out," I said, smiling.

Eric was not exaggerating. There was so much to do in every connected ballroom that it would take us days to complete all the variety of games and other activities. At one point, there were so many people in the casino that Eric and I were separated for a few moments. When I heard my phone ringing I was glad it was him.

"Stay right where you are, Sabriel, I will work my way back to you," Eric said.

Once reunited, he insisted on taking my hand to avoid getting lost again.

"It really is possible to be searching for someone all night. If we don't stay together, who knows what flapper might hit on me?" Eric said, laughing.

He may have been joking, but there were many single ladies roaming around that could not take their eyes off of Eric. Once we started holding hands, most of them moved on to search elsewhere.

The evening went by very quickly, much faster than I expected. Soon the Master of Ceremonies was warning everyone that there was fifteen minutes away from the New Year. Until that announcement, this seemed like just another party. But, then it all started returning to me. Like a flashback video, movie clips of Bradley and I at the alter, waiting for the official announcement of the New Year and fireworks to complete our vows.

I was surrounded by so many people counting down, jumping up, and searching for anyone nearby to kiss once that sparkling ball started to fall in Time Square. When I looked up, Eric's arms were cradling me. I could feel his lips touch mine, so very gently, and yet with such dynamic force that I felt as if a volcano was erupting inside of me creating an intimacy that I never even knew existed. Eric's kiss was more sensual at this moment than any sexual encounter that I have ever experienced.

Feeling our mouths touching, and our eyes looking deep into one another can only be described as spiritual. Nothing has ever made me feel so connected to anyone ever before. But, then instead of wanting it to last, I pulled away frightened of what would come next.

Before Eric could say anything to stop me, I was running through the crowds of guests, who were still singing Auld Lang Syne, blowing on party horns, and throwing confetti in the air. It was a maze of strangers that I had to strategically find my way around, to somewhere outside where I could breath.

For this moment I was no longer Sabriel trying to escape some unknown demon, I was Alice falling through a rabbit hole, impulsively being drawn deeper, and deeper to some unknown world, maybe even into outer space.

Then, I finally stop falling, but, like Alice I was now approaching a corridor lined with doors. They all appeared intimidating. When I saw a curtain, I decided to explore. Perhaps, at the very least I would be able to hide here until it was safe to leave unnoticed.

I am pleasantly surprised to find that beyond the curtain is a lovely garden, with twinkling lights that create a relaxing mood, after all the neon flashing colored sparkles inside the ballroom. Sitting down alone, watching the waterfall naturally flowing, I begin to breathe normally once again.

Then, from nowhere, a familiar shadow appears , and takes a seat next to me on the marble bench.

"Correct me if I'm wrong, but this is a 1920's celebration not a production of Cinderella that we just walked into," Eric said, smiling.

"I mean, the moment that you took off like a bolt of lightning at the sound of midnight, I do believe you moved much faster than any person that I know," he added, more serious now.

For a few seconds I had no reply. What I did was just so instinctive that there is no explanation. How am I to explain to Eric that his kiss was so surreal that I did not know how to respond?

"Eric, I really have no idea why…"

With his finger slightly touching my lips Eric stopped me from completing my thought.

"I know, Sabriel. I understand. I was there with you, feeling the same heat and ice sensation traveling through my veins; our veins. This has nothing to do with you and Bradley's wedding , or his death. What just happened is about us," Eric stopped to see how I was reacting.

How could he possibly know anything about Bradley and me? Even I have been searching for those answers. But, what he is right about, is the two of us. Something is changing and we both need to decide what will come next.

"When you moved here in February from New Orleans and created the **CARCOSA,** and I met you for the very first time at the opening celebration, I knew immediately that you were sent here, or maybe even drawn here because I was searching for you. And, then when all the characters started to appear I understood the plan," Eric said.

"The plan? What plan? And, what do you know about the characters?" I asked, now anxious for some answers.

"I was the one who summoned the characters to St. Augustine. But, when Ophelia decided to have tea with you that first day at *The Corazon Theatre,* it was clear that she was going to organize her own plan in her own way,"Eric revealed.

I was shocked! Not even sure how to react. Eric just revealed to me, not only does he understand who the characters are, but that it was him who requested that they appear. My life was becoming more bizarre every moment.

"But, how were you able to do this, Eric? I mean is there some supernatural spell that you use to draw characters out of their novels? And, why do you even need
them?" I continued to ask.

"There is no supernatural, or spiritual methods. As Ophelia explained to you, characters have no spirits because they were never human. However, about ten years ago when I was in Dublin, Ireland writing an article about Bloomsday, I discovered that many of the characters representing those from James Joyce's famous novel, *Ulysses,* and even *The Dubliners,* were not actors, but actually the real characters that Joyce created. It sounded extremely eccentric; at the very least unbelievable. But, then after spending days with Old Cotter, Mahoney, and Araby they convinced me that they were definitely real. Each of them took me through the city. Wea shared ale, at the pubs, and listened to some authentic Irish music. At the end of the day, they literally stepped back into the novel on my desk," Eric once again stopped to see how I would react.

"Why didn't you ever write about this experience. My God, Eric if you could prove this really happened, you could win the *Pulitzer,"* I said, excited.

"Really, Sabriel? Who would ever believe me? I wasn't even sure that I believed myself until Ophelia appeared here. And, I really have no idea how I was able to get her here and the rest of the characters to visualize. All that I ever did was read through some of these novels, and of course *Hamlet,* to try and find something that we would have in common. I knew that it existed, but I wasn't sure what it was. Whenever I have any questions about my instincts I turn to the literary examples that I have always trusted. Maybe that is how the characters appeared," Eric said.

Well, it was definitely a possibility, since each of the literary works that Eric chose were also mine. Maybe I now should start referring to them as "our", characters who are living with me.

"What we haven't really discovered is what the character's plan is. For Christmas they gave me this very odd Book, titled **The Twin Flame Mirror** . What is strange is that all the pages are blank. But, then when I asked what Twin Flame means the pages begin to fill with answers," I said.

"Then you must understand now, why I asked you at the Regatta if you were sure about taking the next step with me. I have known about The Twin Flames my entire life. I was told about it first by the woman who saved my life and took me to the homeless shelter. Now I know what I have been waiting for. And, I will continue to wait until you realize the same," Eric said, very determined.

"I promise you, as soon as I am able to answer that question I will. But, I am no longer running away. Tonight, I do know that we share something that is impossible to ignore," I said, relieved.

We were both now completely exhausted. It was as if all the oxygen surrounding us had been sucked up by a vise and the only way for us to continue breathing was to stay close to one another. Once we felt normal again we both decided that it was time to leave *The Loft.* I suggested that we return to our table and let everyone know that we were leaving.

Anna, Chloe, and Paul were the only ones seated when we returned.

"Where is everyone else," I asked, surprised that the table was empty.

"I really don't know. All the girls were dancing with several nice gentlemen, but then at midnight, they all disappeared. Oh, but this was left on the table, for you, Sabriel," Anna said, handing me a white formal looking envelope. When I opened it, I noticed the gold foil, and Ophelia's very distinctive handwriting.

Happy New Year's Sabriel and Eric,
Please join us tomorrow, January 1, 2020 at noon at The Otttis Castle. We have included directions for you just in case you have never been there before. Please be on time, since the gates will open at exactly at noon, and close after you arrive, to assure complete privacy.
Ophelia
Holly Golightly
Scarlett O Hara
Gabriella Girard
Daisy Buchana

I handed the note to Eric, since he was also included, and I felt now that he was as vested as I was in this odd arrangement.
"This sounds quite intriguing. My journalist instinct is to take a film crew, as I am predicting that what we will soon be experiencing is to be quite spectacular. But, of course, this is a private premiere performance and we will respect their request," Eric said, handing me back the note.

"Do you know where this Otttis Castle is, Eric? I have heard of it but never visited it," I said.

"Yes, I do know exactly where it is located. The castle can be barely seen from the street but it is very private. Tours are by invitation only. I am impressed that Ophelia was able to reserve it on New Year's Day, but then again nothing should surprise me anymore," Eric said, smiling.

We decided that after all of this evening's revelations, and it being almost 2:00am, l that we would return to Eric's condominium, since it was closer to the Castle. It also allowed us at least an hour more to sleep.

I knew that sleep was all that either of us wanted, anticipating what was going to happen in a few hours. Thankfully, I did have several outfits left still in the closet, that I could change into later today.

Whatever was about to happen at noon , was not enough to keep either of us awake any longer. The moment, our heads hit the pillow we were both out immediately.

Chapter Forty Five

Now the wren has gone to roost, and the sky is turnin' gold, and like the sky my soul is also turnin',
Turnin' from the past, at last and all I've left behind.

—Ray Lamontagne

SABRIEL and ERIC

Castle Otttis was originally a garage that two men, Rusty Ickes, and Otttis Sadler were inspired to build between 1984-1988. Modeled after Irish castles built one thousand years earlier, it's design reflects the outdoor landscape sculpture, open to the natural surrounding elements, rising up fifty feet toward the sky.

The main objective of both these men was to create an object of art that invokes the spirit of Christian Abbeys , and even more so, as a tribute to Jesus Christ.

This was all that I had time to read about Otttis Castle before Eric was ushering me out the door.

"We might just have enough time to pick up some coffee, and a breakfast sandwich at *Odd Birds,* if we leave now," Eric said.

"It's New Year's Day, do you really think *Odd Birds* will be open?" I reminded Eric.

"This is the Marina. Life here is not like in the city. I am sure they have been open since 6:00am for the fishermen. Maybe not a complete meal, but at least coffee and a muffin," Eric said, pulling in front of the small coffee shop.

He was right about it being popular with the locals. Every time we stopped by for sandwiches or even breakfast they were hopping. But, today we were the only ones parked in front.

After about five minutes, Eric reappeared with two coffees and a white paper bag.

"Your favorite, darlin' the Cuban," Eric said handing me the bag.

He was right. Nobody made a better Cuban sandwich anywhere. I unwrapped Eric's and handed it to him to eat while driving. Not always the best way to enjoy this delicacy, but we were definitely on a strict time schedule.

Barely finishing our meal, we turned into the dirt road that leads to the front gate. Just, as Ophelia said, at exactly noon the gate opened, and closed behind us . Eric parked close to the entrance.

The moment we got out of the car, I felt as if we were entering a gothic fairytale land. The immaculate stone structure was immediately calming and reassuring. It was a place that resonated serenity; a peaceful atmosphere.

"It is hard to imagine that all of the masonry was completed by only two men. There was no additional laborers to help with the concrete block, or even the steel reinforcements. Just imagine, Sabriel, the weight of this building is estimated at 7 million pounds," Eric said, impressed at the finished accomplishment.

Before I could respond, the front door opened and Ophelia greeted us. I at once noticed that she was wearing a traditional sixteenth century lady in waiting gown. It was the first time that I recalled she resembled an Ophelia from any pictures that I have ever seen.

"Welcome to Otttis Castle. This is not only a remarkable example of faith, but it is also filled with so many interesting details that we could spend days here exploring. I will share with you that when anyone questions how all of this could be accomplished, the owner says that, 'the building seemed to exert its own insistent will.' A remark that I find pertinent to many questions that have no definitive answers to," Ophelia said, taking my hand and leading me in. Eric followed behind.

"The interior of the castle actually took an additional three years to be completed and did require the assistance of a woodworker, who chose to use cypress wood, and some southern heart pine for the additional eight staircases. Where we will be meeting. The remainder of our group, is upstairs in the sanctuary," Ophelia said, continuing to lead the way.

Just as Ophelia noted, there were so many questions that I had about what I was witnessing. But, I knew that we were not here for a history lesson on the castle. Whatever reason Ophelia had to bring Eric and I here, was spiritual in itself, and the irony of her returning to a castle with a medieval likeness did not go unnoticed.

Once we reached the main area Eric and I were seated on the wooden pews facing an altar, a pulpit, and even a Bishops chair. That was when I noticed Bradley's urn . I then looked up at the choir loft and there was Holly, dressed in her quite famous black sheath dress, with a string of pearls, and carrying a long cigarette holder.

Next to Holly was Scarlett, wearing her most well known green dress that she made from her mother's curtains. It is the one that she wore to seduce Rhett Butler. What is significant about her wearing this gown is that it represents how she will use whatever method necessary to keep her dignity.

Then I see Gabriella, in the most exquisite wedding gown that I could imagine. It not only includes similarities to Grace Kelley's wedding gown , she wore in Monte Carlo, when she married her Prince Charming, but Gabby also included some Irish lace, and symbols, remembering Caden Cassidy, who left her on New Year's Eve.

Why didn't I recall that both Caden and Jake left Gabby on New Year's Eve? That similarity to me is now finally obvious. We both shared that heart ache on New Year's Eve?

Our attention is now directed to Daisy Buchanan looking as spectacular as she did last night, but wearing a different outfit. Today she is wearing a dress with, "a three cornered lavender hat," as I recall Nick Carraway describes it. It is the one that she wears to the tea with Gatsby. The first time that they have been alone together since he left for the war.

"Now that I am sure you are both anxious to discover why we have asked you here, let me begin by saying that, speaking for us all, this time that we have spent together has been delightful. We hope that it has been the same for the two of you?" Ophelia said, more as a rhetorical question.

Eric took my hand, as if he was preparing me for some unknown, unexpected catastrophe.

"Are you okay," he whispered into my ear.

I responded with a nod, not wanting to miss anything that might happen next.

"Very well, then. By now, Sabriel you know that it is Eric who inadvertently asked us here. And, we agreed, because Twin Flames are so delicate that we knew it would be necessary to intervene. What I want to emphasize is that, Sabriel inside of you lives all of us. We are like mosaic pieces that when placed together in the correct order, illustrates who your really are. It is much easier to see this in the reflection of another person. This is why Eric is your Twin Flame. He is able to help you see how being an orphan as a child is not who you have become today," Ophelia stopped signaling for the others to join her.

"Having breakfast at Tiffany's on Fifth Avenue, in New York at 5:00am in the morning is only a small reflection of who I am. And, when I sent Paul away in the rain, it only made me stronger. Everything I did was a learning curve, and this is why at the end of my novel there is no resolution. I am still growing like you, Sabriel," Holly said, blowing me a kiss.

"I was also much more than a pawn in the political world of a royal family in Denmark. And, that is why others have created better, different versions of who I really am. Learn, what I have, my dearest," Ophelia said, walking toward me to kiss my forehead.

Scarlett moved downstairs from the upper choir loft, and stood next to Holly.

"I know that many modern ladies no longer see me as a role model. My life was much different in the south before, and after the Civil War. But, Sabriel, you are the new generation of southern belles. Take the best that I have to offer and build from that. There is sometimes strength in choosing tomorrow to face your problems. Much can happen in twenty four hours to change the course of your life," Scarlett said, with a curtsy.

I was beginning to see a pattern that made sense. All of these five characters came from different places but their stories were similar. They were all strong woman that survived more than they imagined they could.

Now Gabby walked directly toward me. Took both of my hands and started speaking in a soft, but very serious tone.

"I made so many wrong choices in my life. Some were made for me. Others were made because I never trusted my own survival instincts enough to move forward alone. You have that spirit. Sabriel you have achieved everything that I wanted, but you are not yet happy. It was not until I realized sitting on that rock at Tybee Beach, watching the ocean moving serenely around me, did I understand what my best friend Molly was saying. Beautiful Sabriel, let me be your Lighthouse. Follow the beacon of light to your safe harbor."

When she was done, Gabriella returned to the front with the other characters. It was Daisy Buchana that was given the last story to tell.

"Many people do not realize what I am about to say, but I know that you will, Sabriel. Even I, who have been manipulated by the greed of a wealthy society that restrains us from real happiness, could not prevent Jay Gatsby from reliving the past for a short time. He was also destroyed by a false American Dream that never existed. Jay was not in love with me, as he thought he was. He was in love with an image that never existed. Knowing this does not make me a better person, but it does make you a better person, Sabriel," Daisy concluded.

The last words were spoken by Ophelia, just as I noticed everyone beginning to fade away.

"We are the female characters, created by a variety of authors. We all returned to the twenty first century to prevent the breeding of hollow, shallow human beings, that resemble zombies with no respect or empathy for the values offered by invincible writers, poets, artists, dramatists, and musicians. We are all here to remind you that your time on this earth is limited. Take advantage of every lesson learned, and wrap your mind around every gift that we have given you, knowing that we will always be a part of who you are."

And, with those last words, they were all gone. Eric and I were left alone.

"I am speechless. What else can ever be as impressive as what we have just witnessed," I said, hoping that Eric had something profound to say.

But, instead, he walked over to the altar, picked up the urn, and kneeled in front of the cross. It was so silent that I could hear my heart beating.

After a few moments Eric stood up genuflected and returned to me

"Now, we will take this urn, with Bradley's ashes together, to *Cassadaga*. That will be his final resting place," Eric said, solemnly.

We held hands together we walked downstairs. Once outside of the castle walls, I asked him what moved him to say a prayer.

"What we just experienced in a castle that is located on the same latitude as the Great Pyramids of Egypt, built by only two men, who chose to spell Otttis with three t's to represent the three crosses on Calvary, is nothing less than a miracle. The characters have left us

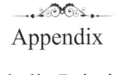

Appendix

Ophelia Painting

This painting is by James Waterhouse, 1894.
Ophelia is sitting over a brook on a willow branch.

Harry's Bar

Located at Avenida Menendez, St. Augustine

Otttis Castle

Entrance to castle

Otttis Castle is the final setting in the novel. It was built by two men, Rusty Ickes, and Ottis Sadler, devoted to Jesus Christ. It took four years for these two men, independently to complete their project in 1984.

Scarlett O'Hara

70 HYPOLITA STREET, ST. AUGUSTINE

St. Augustine Photo Journal

La Maracon French Pastry; Afternoon Tea delights; The Spice and Tea Tea Exchange, on Hypolita Ave.; Fountain of Youth; Eric's yacht, *Paper Chase; Raintree Restaurant,* San Marcos; *Blithe Spirit, Lincolnville Theatre; Lightner Museum,* inside; *Lightner Museum,* outside; TS Eliot, at E Shavers Booksellers; Pax on Lions Bridge; Nights of Lights; Regatta Eric's boat; Downtown St. Augustine, Nights of Lights;

Corazon Movie Theatre and Café

Corazon Movie Theatre and Café Take in a movie and enjoy a freshly-made Sandwich or salad in the friendly atmosphere of Corazon Cinema and Cafe. 36 Granada St. St. Augustine, FL 32084 (904) 679-5736

Work Cited

Here is Everything you need to know about the magic of a Twinflame relationship. Sylvia Sallow, November 7, 2018

AJC Atlanta, News Now, Museum pays tribute to *"Gatsby" author and wife Zelda.*

Chautauqua: Susan Marie Frontczak as Mary Shelley, www.greeleytribune.com, August 10, 2013

10 Fascinating Facts About Gone With the Wind, wwwmentalfloss.com, by Stacy Conradt, June 30, 2018.

Scarlett Ohara character analysis, Mary C M Philips, caffeineepiphanies.com

In Search of the Real Truman Capote, Jonathan Russell Clark, September 10, 2015.

Roots in the Sand, Ken Clarke, Sentinel Staff Writer, February 22, 2004

Holly Golightly and the Endless Pursuit of Self Actualization in Breakfast at Tiffany's, Zachary B Winrow,

Ophelia's Outspoken Emotion, John Kely, March 26, 1993, The Washington Post.

Drowning Ophelia, Rachel Luann Strayer, New Play Exchange.

The Most Beautiful Ophelia: The Duality of Femininity in Shakespeare's Hamlet, Emma McGrory, May 7, 2016.

History of Afternoon Tea, afternoontea.co.uk

Psychology: The Truth About the Paranormal, David Robson, October 30, 2014.

Our History E. Shaver, Bookseller, www.eshaverbooks.com

7 Ways to Chase New Orleans Literary Ghosts, Janis Turk

The Ghosts of the Court of Two Sisters, ghostcitytours.com

JD Salinger's Women, Paul Alexander, February 9, 1998.

Florida is Home to a Huge Gothic Castle and it is Absolutely Beautiful, Rachael Volpe, March 25, 2019.

Mad Ophelia moves to the Center of the Center of the Stage Theatre of the Deaf Performs Signed Play Howard County Diversions, Patrick Hickerson, February 12, 1993.

The True Spirit of Cassadaga, Robin Minma, February 27, 2017.

About the Author

Eleanor Tremayne is the author of four award winning novels, Destiny Revisited, Destiny Revealed, Seven Days in Lebanon, and The Mermaids Grandson. All have been recognized for innovative character development, striking settings, historical insight and elegant prose by Literary Titan Book Awards. In 2019 , at The Dayton Book Expo, Seven Days in Lebanon was awarded the Best Selling Historical Novel Award.

Moving to St. Augustine, Florida in July 2019, with her husband, Mark, inspired Eleanor to write High Tea with Ophelia. It allowed Eleanor to literally bring alive five of her own favorite characters. The original concept started as a creative group project that Eleanor assigned to her Advanced Placement English class over twelve years ago.

That concept surfaced once again when Eleanor and her husband, Mark attended a lecture at the Lightner Museum, at St. Augustine about Victorian art and literature. Sitting close by was a young girl dressed as if she might have stepped out of a Jane Austin novel. During the entire evening she remained in character. Nobody from the museum had any idea who she was. That event initiated the idea that developed into *High Tea With Ophelia*.

Eleanor continues to promote all of her novels through, speaking events, book festivals, book clubs, and creative workshops. Writing has allowed Eleanor to pursue her lifetime dream. Each of her novels express a variety of literary themes from Bildungsroman, to historical fiction, to historical fantasy.

Mrs. Tremayne has already started work on her next novel, *Journey of the Agape*. When a carpet maker from 6th century Siberia creates a rug for a noble family there is an unknown spiritual connection that follows that carpet through centuries of fascinating adventures. *Agape* will be available in the summer of 2021.

Made in the USA
Columbia, SC
13 November 2021